DISORDER ON
THE COURT

IRON VALLEY SERIES

TAMARA GIRARDI

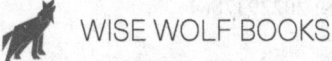 WISE WOLF BOOKS LAS VEGAS

WISE WOLF
BOOKS

DISORDER ON THE COURT. Copyright © 2022 by Tamara Girardi.
All rights reserved.
For information, address Wolfpack Publishing,
5130 S. Fort Apache Road, 215-380 Las Vegas, NV 89148

wisewolfbooks.com

Cover design by Wise Wolf Books

ISBN 978-1-953944-81-8 (paperback)
978-1-953944-82-5 (hardcover)
978-1-953944-80-1 (ebook)
LCCN: 2022937864

First Edition:June 2022

"*Gridiron Girl* lives and breathes football with the same intensity as its star athlete. A compelling book about drive and bravery and believing in yourself."

—Stephanie J. Scott, author of *All Last Summer*

"Julia's got as much grit as she has heart, both of which she'll need to navigate obstacles on and off the field. A well-written debut novel. Tamara Girardi is a literary talent to watch."

—Tina Ferraro, author of *Top Ten Uses for an Unworn Prom Dress, How to Hook a Hottie,* and *The ABC's of Kissing Boys*

"*Gridiron Girl* delivers on so many levels, and features a fierce, clear-eyed heroine who isn't afraid to fight for what she wants, both on the field and off. I loved it!"

—Kes Trester, author of *A Dangerous Year*

"Girardi has crafted an uplifting, powerful story about a girl who refuses to give up!"

—Simone Elkeles, NY Times bestselling author of *Perfect Chemistry*

DISORDER ON THE COURT

IRON VALLEY SERIES

To my Mom – the late ChrisAnne Simpson,
who didn't mind when I passed a volleyball against the
side of the house for hours.
And so much more.
All my love.

"ADVERSITY, IF YOU ALLOW IT TO, WILL FORTIFY YOU
AND MAKE YOU THE BEST YOU CAN BE."
—KERRI WALSH JENNINGS

CHAPTER ONE

THE DAY AFTER I TOLD MY MOTHER I'D BEEN INVITED to Julia Medina's surprise birthday party, she plowed into my bedroom with four bags of new outfits.

Skirts. Shorts. Dresses.

No athletic clothes to be seen.

"Mom, thanks, but..."

She made eye contact with the ceiling. "Melanie, you cannot wear a T-shirt and workout shorts to a party." After sucking in a deep breath, she ran her manicured fingernails through the straight brown hair of my ponytail. "You're fifteen now. And so beautiful. Give yourself the chance to experience what that feels like."

No way it could feel better than the soft cotton of a well-worn T-shirt. Besides, I didn't get the double standard. If guys didn't have to wear short skirts that revealed the world down under when they bent over, why did I?

My mother held up a flowing, light pink tank top in her right hand and a floral summer dress with a bold green-and-purple print in her left. The silly eagerness on her face had me reluctantly reaching for the clothes.

"I have two more bags in the car," she said. "In case you don't like these."

Two. More. Bags?

"Stop with that look, Melanie Corwin."

"I don't have a look," I said, but I'd bet my savings account I did.

Mom pressed her lips into a straight line. "Humor me and try something on."

"My pleasure." I swiped the multicolored pile of clothes from her arms, locked myself in my closet, and dropped everything onto the floor.

Part of me wanted to go—a small part, but I'd watched my older sister get ready for parties. The process was more complex than the science experiments my best friend and next-door neighbor, Harris, devised in his backyard.

Ally Malone, one of the seniors on our volleyball team, had messaged everyone that they'd better be at Julia's birthday party—or else. Julia would likely be the captain of the team. She'd lead us to a regional championship. Maybe a state title. When I watched her play, I saw everything I wanted my future self to be. Fast. Strong. Fierce.

The whole volleyball team would be there. Julia's brothers had played football, so most of the football team would likely come too. And then all the other friends she had at school. Maybe her family.

A lot of people. Too many people.

"You can time a set, pike your jump, and crush the ball against the floor on the other side of the net before the six girls there can do anything about it," I said to myself in the mirror. "You can do this."

I picked up a red strappy thing from the floor. Was it a shirt? A dress? How could it... What side was the front? Why were there six straps when I only had two shoulders? I tossed it back onto the ground. Wait. Was that a tube top? Seriously, Mom? Shorts small enough to fit my little sister. No. No. No!

The floral dress caught my eye. I held it up. Full coverage on my shoulders. No random straps anywhere. I could do without so many flowers, but I could wear a sports bra with it.

Done.

"The dress is perfect," I insisted, opening the door.

"Are you sure? You haven't even looked in the other bags."

"Positive. Thanks, Mom!"

"You know, when I ask you to try something on, I'd prefer to see it on you."

That would be hard since I hadn't removed it from the hanger. "I wanted to surprise you this weekend."

She smiled and hugged me. "I look forward to it."

I kissed her cheek and curled up in my bed. The pillow cooled my face, and I exhaled, letting the stress of the day slip away into the air. The book on my nightstand had a sticky note on page twenty-four. I always wrote the date I started reading a book on my sticky note bookmarks. If a week passed before I finished the book, that meant one of two things: 1) it wasn't very good, or 2) I wasn't trying hard enough.

The date on the sticky note was a day old. I leaned against my pillows and read the same sentence three times. I tossed the book aside and slid onto the floor. Maybe a few yoga poses would help. Child's pose. Downward dog. Plank pose.

Nope.

If reading and yoga couldn't force the stress of the day to fade, I only had one other option.

Volleyball.

The year before, our ninth-grade team had been undefeated. The rush of that perfection couldn't be matched. Not by the framed team picture in the school's trophy case or the commemorative banner hanging in the gym.

But that was last year. New year. New goals. Unfortunately, new team.

Now sophomores, my classmates would have to fight for playing time on a squad that was so solid room for newcomers hardly existed. Six seniors started varsity. The juniors filled the junior varsity slots. Nothing like playing every minute of every game one year ago and now having no hope of seeing varsity—or potentially even junior varsity—playing time. Expecting the worst, three of the girls in my grade had quit to play tennis instead. Not that I could blame them, but I knew my sport.

And I knew if I wanted to play it, I'd have to practice every chance I had.

I swapped my sweatshirt for short sleeves, noticing how lonely the dress for the party looked in my closet filled with hoodies, quarter zips, and athletic shoes. I turned off the light and closed the door, glad I had a few days before I'd have to wear it. A few days to stifle the flutters that plagued my chest every time I thought about walking into a party of people I didn't know. If I thought too hard, the flutters increased to a pace that threatened every breath I pulled into my body.

Wearing black spandex shorts and a baggy, purple school T-shirt that wrapped my body in sweet comfort, I grabbed my favorite, well-worn volleyball from the mudroom and headed for the back yard. Mister adorable, my sister's boyfriend Josh Brighton, with his backward hat and tight tee, sat on one of the swings, swiping his phone screen.

I threw the volleyball at his stomach. It landed with a thud.

"Hey!" he yelled, but there wasn't any anger in his voice.

"She have you waiting again?"

He stood and tucked his phone into the pocket of his cargo shorts. "Tell me you're surprised."

"Not in the least."

Josh dated my older sister, Elle. Mom never had to pick out clothes for Elle or encourage her to wear makeup. She did that all on her own. And in the process scored a pretty cute boyfriend, I had to admit. But Josh was more than looks. A wide receiver for the Iron Valley High School football team, he worked out hard all summer to prepare for the season, which had a major question mark hanging over it since the team lacked a quarterback to throw him the ball.

Oh, and he happened to like volleyball.

Months earlier, while he'd waited for date number four, I'd taught him how to pass with his forearms instead of palming the ball in a carry, which boys did, like, all the time. It might have been date number seven that we'd graduated to setting lessons. He'd had sufficient hitting skills from the beginning. All that to say, I'd taught him to pepper—pass, set, hit with a partner without stopping. It was our tradition to pepper in the back yard while he waited for Elle to perfect her perfection.

I'd also taught him the basics such as there are six players on the court—three in the front and three in the back. The outside hitter is on the left, and the middle and right-side hitters are fairly easy to follow. He'd picked up serving skills, too, although we didn't use those as much in the confines of my back yard.

I started with a toss. He passed it to me, soft like I'd taught him. I set it back to him and got low, ready for his hit. I picked it up with ease and passed to him, starting the cycle all over again.

"We're going to the festival tonight," he said.

"Sounds great," I lied.

"You know, you could come with us. You're always welcome."

"Thanks, but I'm good."

Elle swatted the ball out of the air. "Yes. She's good. And very... sweaty."

Josh kissed her on the cheek, and she leaned into him with a smile on her pink lips. I had no clue how she did it, but the bags of cosmetics I could only classify as squares, circles, and cylinders somehow managed to paint her heart-shaped face with a natural glow. If I were wearing her outfit, I'd have to stand completely still for fear of flashing any number of body parts. Not to mention wearing it on rides when everything was spinning and flying in the wind. And her hair. How could anyone ride the swings or the whip with hair like that?

Josh whispered something in her ear, and she sighed.

"Melanie?"

"Elle?"

"Come with us."

I tossed the volleyball back and forth in my hands. "No thanks."

"You sure?" Josh asked. "They have killer funnel cake."

"Yum," I said. "But I'll pass. Thanks."

"Wait for me in the car?" Elle asked, and Josh waved to me.

My sister raised herself to her full height, which didn't compare to mine, and embraced her authority. "Mel, listen. I'm all about working toward your dreams, but you play volleyball in this yard every day. You go nowhere. You see no one."

"I see my team," I said. "And my family."

"And me," my best friend yelled from the other side of the beaten and bruised wooden privacy fence that clearly failed at offering any actual privacy.

"And Harris."

"Harris doesn't count," Elle said, loud enough for him to hear from his back yard. "Mom says you're going to Julia Medina's birthday party this weekend."

I nodded. If it had been anyone else's party, I'd bail on that too. I wasn't really the *Who's going to be there?*, *What are you gonna wear?* kind of person.

"I'm glad. You need to get out more. Make some friends. Actually experience high school."

As if the high school experience was a singular thing defined by...whom? The Homecoming Queen? The captain of the football team? My sister?

Sparks erupted next door, and Elle jumped.

"I'm getting out of here," she said, and I mentally thanked Harris for his timing.

"You don't want to keep Schnookums waiting," Harris called, teasing my sister for the pet name she used for Josh. If Harris thought anything was stupid, it was starting an experiment without a hypothesis, and lovey-dovey nicknames.

Once my sister was gone, I hopped onto the small trampoline I kept next to the one sturdy panel of the fence to work on my vertical jump and bounced until I saw Harris with an alarmingly large open flame.

He nodded at me. I touched down on the trampoline and jumped again.

"She's right, you know?" he said.

"Said no one ever," I answered when I hit the apex of the jump.

"Will you get off that thing and come over here? It makes me nauseous."

I exaggerated a sigh. And a groan for good measure before hopping off the trampoline and slipping through two broken pickets of the fence, my private doorway to Harris's world. "I don't want to get blown up today."

He wore a fire-resistant protective jacket over his blue-and-green flannel shirt and handed me safety goggles and a fire extinguisher. Just another day in the life of Harris Fullerton. "You should take these then."

I knew enough to immediately position the goggles over my eyes. "And my sister thinks I lead a boring life."

"You do lead a boring life," Harris said.

"And you don't?"

He tilted his head to the side, a smirk on his boyish, round face as if that were a joke. And I suppose it kind of was. Harris had a thriving social media channel for his backyard experiments that he'd monetized to raise money for his more "serious" scientific research. He'd built the world's biggest sand volcano and erupted it—to the dismay of the grandmas who walked down the alley each evening and had ended up wearing "lava" on their joggers. Even worse—he'd nestled raw eggs into a cushioned device he'd launched into the air like a rocket with his hose. Those had come back to Earth in some interesting places, also to the dismay of the neighbors.

In fact, when it came to Harris and the neighbors, there was a lot of dismay.

With the camera set up a seemingly safe distance from the open flame—although with Harris, nothing was ever certain—he handed me a foam sword.

"Are we playing princess-knight?"

"Cute. No. We are transforming that," he flopped his too-long light brown hair out of his eyes and pointed to the toy, "into a flaming sword."

I tossed it to the ground. "I'm out."

"It's not as bad as it sounds," he pleaded.

With Harris, it was always as bad as it sounded. "Your stepmom is going to lose it."

As if on cue, she yelled from the back porch, "What in the world is on fire? Harris! You know the rules. No open flames."

"Tell Melanie that. It's her open flame."

"Oh no you don't," I said.

Mrs. Fullerton fired back, "I'm so sure. Clean it up."

He looked up at the darkening sky. "Nobody appreciates my brilliance."

I nudged him the slightest bit, and he tripped over a tree root. "Come on. I'll help you."

I scooped up the more benign pieces of the experiment and returned them to their designated spaces in Harris's shed. He might mess up his yard and sometimes the entire neighborhood with his explosions, but he organized his shed with the attention to detail of a surgeon.

"You really going to Julia Medina's end-of-summer party?" he asked. "Is this because you're on the volleyball team with her now?"

"Ouch. Are you trying to say I wouldn't be invited otherwise?"

He raised an eyebrow, an effective weapon.

"Fine. You're right. And it's technically her surprise birthday party."

"Team event or no, it's not like you to go to a party, let alone *the* party. The Medinas are high school royalty," Harris said.

I'd prefer he didn't remind me. We let the conversation drop while we cleaned up, moving in the kind of silence that worked between two people who'd known each other since birth, reaching around, above, and below each other. Once everything was back in its place, we slipped through the fence to my yard and sat on the swings.

"You're giving off that lab-experiment-gone-bad vibe like a chemical reaction ready to explode," he said. "What's going on?"

I stopped swinging and let my head hang over my knees. What *was* going on? It felt like everything all at once yet nothing at the same time. That made no sense to me, so how could I explain it to anyone else?

"This school year feels different already," I managed—a stupid explanation, but at least a start.

"We still have two weeks left of summer."

"Speak for yourself," I said. "Volleyball camp starts next week. My mom and sister are on my case about being more social."

"Do you think you need to be more social?"

Yes.

"No."

Harris stopped swinging and watched me with the same depth of inquiry in his dark brown eyes he had in the midst of science experiments. I gazed at the stars sparkling in the twilight sky, refusing to make eye contact.

"You know I've collected enough empirical data to state with certainty—you're lying."

I hopped off the swing and paced the yard, wanting to make sense of the thoughts swirling in my mind, if not for Harris, for myself. "I want to play varsity this year. At least a little. I don't see how spending the evening eating funnel cake at the festival is going to help me with that."

"Does everything have to be about productivity? About reaching some goal?" he asked.

"So says the guy who turned his backyard into a laboratory."

"I might be a bad example. Follow Elle's lead. She crushes her archery competitions and manages a social life at the same time."

But I wasn't Elle. I'd never be. I'd managed to accept that and wished everyone around me could too.

CHAPTER TWO

AFTER A FEW DAYS OF READING IN THE HAMMOCK AND hitting my volleyball against the side of the house, the day of the party arrived. I'd challenged Harris to build a time machine that would allow me to skip over the day altogether, but he'd failed. Some scientist he was. I'd hoped the dress had somehow disappeared from my closet and I'd be forced to wear an athletic tank top and shorts. No luck there either.

I slipped the unyielding material over my head and wiggled until it fell into place. With my back to the mirror, I bent forward and cringed at the prime view of my underwear. Yet another reason to own lots of spandex. I pulled my newest pair of black volleyball shorts from my drawer and tugged them into place. Nobody would know I was wearing them—unless I bent over—but *I* knew they were there. That was what mattered.

With ribbons and medals from years of volleyball tournaments hanging on the wall behind me, I studied my reflection and debated what else I should do. A dress was one thing, but what about my hair? Watching Elle over the years had told me the situation called for more sophistication than a ponytail. Problem: I didn't do anything more sophisticated than a ponytail.

I twisted my hair into a couple loops, pushing for that messy-bun look that worked for models and celebrities. On me, it looked plain messy. I tried loops again, this time on the side of my head, and...

no. Just no. I sighed. I could braid but not French braid. A side braid would age me down at least two years.

A ponytail would have to do.

Shoes? Black flip-flops. Check.

Don't even get me started on accessories. Unless knee pads counted, I had absolutely no idea how to accessorize the dress to achieve any sort of fashionista justice.

A pile of clean T-shirts and shorts tempted me from my bed.

Elle peeked into the room. "That dress looks great on you. Love the bright colors."

"Thanks." In my heart, I knew she was trying to be nice, but her critical gaze put me on display, like a spinning platform had manifested beneath my feet to give her a 360-degree view.

She tapped her cheek in a semi-scowl. "I have the perfect bracelet and purple shoes to match."

I looked down at the dress and back at my sister. She was able to memorize her wardrobe enough to put an outfit together for me in five seconds?

"I mean, if you want them...?"

If I was going to do this party thing, might as well do it right. "Sure. Definitely."

She ran to her room, leaving me to lament the many reasons why I didn't go to parties. As if high school hadn't made enough of an exhibit of every person to grace the halls, why not intensify the uncontrollable emotions of irrational teens with sex, drugs, and alcohol? And compare who arrives with whom, in what car, wearing what label.

"I can't believe you're going to a party!" Elle pulled me to the bed, so I could sit and try on the shoes—wedges with purple straps—she'd fetched from her room. Indeed, a perfect match.

"Neither can I."

She slipped the bracelet around my wrist. "And at the Medinas'. That place is like the palace of Iron Valley."

The whole team had scored a blanket invite. Not exactly exclusive, but my sister oozed excitement. I didn't want to disappoint her with a little thing like the truth.

"You've been there?" Shoes in place, I stood. My feet slid forward thanks to gravity and smashed my toes into the straps. They weren't shoes. They were torture devices.

"Lots of times. Jake Medina used to throw the best parties—like clean fun parties. His family doesn't go for any drinking or anything."

At least that was something.

"Why aren't you going tonight?" I asked.

"Josh is taking me somewhere special. Since I have a competition tomorrow and he has football practice starting this week, tonight's the last night of summer for us."

They were so cute I could puke.

Elle ran her hands through my hair, wrapped it into some shape I couldn't make out in the reflection, and clipped it. "Their house is awesome. A pool. A football field."

"A football field?"

With concentration in her eyes, she pulled a few pieces out of the clip, and they fell around my face. "Oh, and a sand volleyball court you will love. Obviously."

If I got the chance, I'd need to impress Julia and all the other seniors. On the court. Off it, I endeavored not to embarrass myself too badly. I adjusted the spandex under my dress.

"You look petrified," Elle said. "You know, people are inherently nice if you give them a chance."

"Nice to you." One look from those princess-sized eyes, and Elle dug her arrow in deep.

"Just have fun, okay?"

Having fun. An insurmountable goal. Something more manageable might be surviving the night without tearing my dress into a T-shirt. Not embarrassing myself so badly I couldn't show face at school that year. Making a friend.

That might be insurmountable too.

***

MY MOM DROPPED ME OFF IN FRONT OF THE MEDINAS' house. I know. So cool.

She leaned out the window, not ready to let me go. "Have so much fun, Melanie."

"Thanks."

"Wait. Do you have your cell phone?"

"Yes, Mom."

"Do you need money?"

"I don't think they're charging for cupcakes."

She shook her head, but even my dig couldn't dull her mood. Her daughter was going to a party. Be still her social heart. She drove away, leaving me on the sidewalk in front of the Medinas' brick, two-story house. Wait. It was the Medinas', right? I checked the address on my phone. The house number was right, but what if we were on the wrong street? The flutters started swirling in my chest. If a party was happening here, where were the cars?

I was about to walk to the end of the block and check the street sign, but three of my teammates waved from down the sidewalk. I looked behind me, but nobody was there.

"We're waving to you, dork," said the junior middle hitter, Ashley Fiori. We'd partnered up on middle-hitting exercises at some of the summer workouts, so I knew her well enough to know she'd meant the jab playfully. She wore a low-cut black tank with lace edges, black shorts, and lots of black eyeliner. Her short brown hair was straight and, along with her sparkly gold purse, stood out against the sea of black she wore.

I waved back.

Ashley was with our junior setter, Chandra Jackson, who also managed an impressive contrast with her outfit—white shorts and a light pink crop top over her gorgeous brown skin. Her dark brown, tight curls were wild and free, softened with blonde highlights. Rounding out the trio was one of our senior middle hitters, Rachel Baxter, a friendly girl with loose curls in her long, red hair and blocking abilities I only wished I had some day. She wore a pastel, floral dress. At least I wasn't the only one wearing flowers. Or a dress. The three of them looked like an advertisement you'd see in the mall. Without my mom and sister, I would have worn my best—meaning not stained or torn—school T-shirt and spandex shorts.

Chandra called for me to join them. "Nellie, right?"

"Melanie," I said, falling in line behind them, grateful not to walk into the party alone.

"Right. Sorry. Terrible with names. Love the dress. You're a cutie in real clothes."

"Um, thanks." I could feel my cheeks reddening.

"You are actually blushing," Chandra said. "I love it. I missed a few summer workouts, so sorry—I should know this. You're a sophomore, right?"

I nodded.

"Perfect. From this point on, you're Soph."

I couldn't decide if I should be excited to have a nickname or angry she refused to learn my real name. "What will you call the other sophomores?"

"Hmm," she said. "Good question. I guess I call them nothing, and you get all my attention."

Lucky me.

I had imagined an entrance that involved me tripping up the stairs or knocking on the door and nobody answering. Even if it was the right house, my head kept telling me something would go wrong.

My teammates walked through the front door like they belonged. When we got inside, I realized why. Coach Medina greeted each of them with hugs. Julia's grandmother, who everyone called Abuelita, high-fived us, and Julia's brothers chatted with them. They did belong.

I pretended I did too.

Pictures of the Medina kids competing in every sport you could imagine covered the mantel, the built-in bookshelves, and every table in the living room. Standing with the rest of the volleyball team behind Julia's family, excitement sputtered in my gut. I urged myself to stay cool, but every time I thought of the height on Julia's jumps, how she killed sets from the outside position, and her jump serve that I did not look forward to being on the receiving end of, fangirling over her was the only choice I had.

I thought I might have yelled, "Surprise!" a little too loudly when Julia opened the door with Ally at her side, but no one noticed.

Julia greeted the team after her family, hugging us all one by one. "Thank you for coming."

"Were you surprised?" asked Sam Strutters, one of our senior starting middle hitters.

"Completely. I had no idea."

I tried to maintain a smile without revealing that when I grew up, I wanted to be like Julia. I squeezed my hands together behind my back to hide their shakiness and hoped I'd grow up some time soon. She slipped away to greet her boyfriend Owen Malone, who was also Ally's twin brother, and the crowd filtered outside to the back yard.

My adrenaline-inspired shaking didn't stop when I hit the food tables. Everyone smiled and joked like they all knew each other.

Like they were thrilled to get together. Like they had no intention of talking to the girl who kept her mouth shut and tried not to draw any real attention while also trying not to be completely invisible.

I achieved the goal of not being invisible when I stumbled in Elle's stupid shoes and dumped the contents of my overflowing plastic plate into the grass. Quesadillas, pasta, and a slice of ham from a pig Julia's dad had literally roasted over a spit fell. All that deliciousness lost.

"Party foul!" someone yelled. People laughed. I wanted to hide until everyone there forgot who I was—say, maybe seven years.

Cheeks burning, I knelt to scoop the remnants from the grass, infinitely grateful for the spandex beneath my dress.

"Let me help you."

A big guy wearing an Iron Valley Football T-shirt crouched next to me and retrieved the pieces of quesadilla that were out of my reach.

"Lucky," I mumbled.

The smooth brown skin of his face and closely-shaved head was like a perfect canvas for his bright smile to send shock waves in my direction.

"Not lucky," he said with a playful smirk. "The only reason I didn't drop my plate is because I devoured the food on the way to my table."

"No. Sorry." I focused on standing without doing anything stupid. He helped by pulling me gently upward by my elbow. The softness of his fingertips tickled my skin. *Focus on not falling, focus on not falling.*

I didn't fall.

And I managed to regain my train of thought. "I meant you were lucky because you get to come to a party wearing a T-shirt. My mom made me wear a dress."

My mom made me? Was I ten? I should have thanked him and left it at that. As I debated whether I could get any worse at this party thing, he scanned my body from head to toe and smiled. But not in a creepy way. Thank the sports gods for that.

"Personally, I say wear whatever makes you comfortable, but if you don't mind me admitting," he leaned forward and whispered in a smooth, confident voice, "your mom has good taste."

I mentally digested his words, and my face warmed with each new depth of understanding.

"I'm Square Weaver." He extended his hand, which was covered in sauce from the pasta he'd cleaned up from the grass but pulled it away. "Sorry."

"Don't apologize. You were literally cleaning up my mess. I'm Melanie Corwin."

"I know that name. You have a sister, right?"

I nodded. "Two actually. Elle's a senior."

"Yeah. I know Elle." He nodded through an awkward silence that left me studying the shape of his eyes. "You play volleyball with the birthday girl?"

"Yes." I nodded too, as if nodding and answering in the affirmative were both necessary. *Say something else. Say something intelligent.*

I said nothing.

He gestured to the pile of food mixed with torn blades of grass on my plate. "Can I get you something else?"

"No. Thank you. Um, thank you for the help."

"You sure?"

"Absolutely. It was nice to meet you." What was I doing? The last thing I wanted was to walk away from Square, but I had essentially bid him goodbye with my rambling.

"Nice to meet you, Melanie. Good luck this season. Maybe I'll see you at a game."

"Yeah. That would be great. Definitely." *Just. Stop. Talking.*

He walked toward the pavilion, but before he got too far, he looked over his shoulder at me. For the first time in my life—that I could recall—my sister was right: people were inherently nice if you gave them a chance.

Square Weaver was inherently nice.

And nice to look at.

CHAPTER THREE

THE PARTY ROLLED ON AROUND ME AS I WALKED WICK-
ed carefully with my second plate of food to the table where my
volleyball teammates sat. I didn't spill it, thank you very much. Ally
Malone, our varsity team setter and the player who had insisted everyone attend the party, leaned across the table before I even sat down.
"Did I see you talking to Square?"

I slipped off my shoes under the table and wiggled my toes to
enjoy the freedom. "Yeah."

She shook her head in a way that reminded me of my third-grade
teacher who liked to tsk about everything. "You do know that Sam
totally has a thing for Square."

"No. I didn't."

"She has since sophomore year. Besides, he's a senior. You realize
that, right?"

In other words, Sam was higher on the volleyball hierarchy, so
she had dibs. What was I thinking possibly "stealing" a senior guy
from a senior girl?

And parties were suddenly as frustrating and annoying as I'd
always imagined them to be. An image of Harris in the backyard
tinkering with some experiment flashed in my mind. My chest twisted
with the wish I could be there. Or in my hammock. Or on the rooftop

balcony of my house, curled up with a book. Those places were safe. Easy. Comfortable.

Parties were none of those three things.

"We were talking," I said. "That's it."

"Just trying to give you some advice. Your team should come before guys is all I'm saying."

I did not think for a second that would be all Ally ever said. She didn't seem like a "one message" kind of girl.

I took a bite of a quesadilla piled high with the most delicious spicy guacamole and wondered when life had gotten so political. I didn't come to the party for a guy. I wanted to play volleyball.

No. More than *playing*, I wanted to kill it. Every game. Every play.

Every time.

If keeping my distance from Square would buy me the team's respect and the opportunity to learn from the older girls to get better, decision made.

By the time my dinner settled enough for me to hit the sand volleyball court, the seniors had already challenged our coach and anyone else who wanted to join her to a game. I cheered from the sideline, hoping for an opportunity to jump in.

"Five all," Ally called before rocking a jump serve over the net.

Coach passed it with ease, and a well-placed set and hit followed. The volley continued in a series of slapping arms and words only those familiar with the game would probably understand: "mine," "outside," "back," "middle," "free." As I watched, itching to get on the court, it didn't take long to realize the birthday girl was missing.

I found her sitting on a swing with her older brother. One of them anyway. Jake had graduated a few months earlier. Everyone at Iron Valley High School knew Jake Medina, high school quarterback extraordinaire. I'd never actually met him.

"He's used to girls staring, but you could try to hide it a little," whispered Chandra.

"I wasn't..."

Chandra ignored my protest. "I heard Ally giving you a hard time about Square. Don't let her get to you."

I could feel my cheeks warming again. "I wasn't. I mean, she didn't."

"Yeah, yeah." She turned to me. "Listen, Soph. You're a great player, but you need to get to know people. I'm actually surprised you showed."

I *get to know people,* I thought. But I didn't say it. Mostly because it wasn't true.

"This team is all about the bonding—supposed to make us play better. The idea is we avoid factions and cliques that tend to crop up on teams. Not sure I believe it works since there is also a real possibility we will all get sick of each other, but it is what it is. And how many summer bonding sessions did you join, Soph?"

None.

"None," Chandra answered.

"Kind of you to keep track," I muttered.

"You know Ally will keep track. Only reason you got this far is because she was gone most of the summer."

I groaned.

She nudged her hip against mine. "It might be good for you. At practices, you keep to yourself and barely speak to anyone else. And then you kill it on most plays. That's a bad combination. Girls could think you think you're better than them."

I had to replay her words a few times to make sense of them. "But you don't?"

She shrugged. "I have a high opinion of myself."

I laughed at her candor.

"Trying to help you out, Soph."

"Corwin," Ally shouted. "Jump in over there to hit outside."

"I hit middle," I said automatically.

An awkward silence gripped the court kind of like those prison movies when a newcomer stupidly challenged the leader without realizing it. Chandra raised an eyebrow at me.

"But I've always wanted to try outside," I said with a smile.

Not.

"Good girl," Chandra whispered.

Ally forced a smile of her own. "Great. Let's do this then."

I dried my sweaty palms on the dress and ran onto the sand court. The view from the outside-hitter position on the far left made me feel like I was sitting at the end of a table live with conversation. In the middle position, the action surrounded you constantly, but outside, I watched and waited for the action to find me.

Coach and the other grown-ups bowed out of the game to give more players the chance to jump in. To extend the volleys and intensify the competition, the teams divided sophomores, juniors, and seniors. But the starters and some of the other older players were easy to spot when they racked up points with their jump serves. They didn't simply pop the ball over the net and use the jump as an intimidation tactic. No. Their serves were carefully executed, so they could crush the ball at the height of their jumps. Being on the receiving end of them left your arms stinging for the next few plays.

If you could return the serve at all.

The first set to come my way was off Chandra's fingertips. High and outside. Perfect for a well-trained outside hitter, not a middle accustomed to coming in quick. Ahead of the set, I connected when I came down from my jump and, trying to correct, hit the ball high and out of bounds on the other side.

Chandra crossed the court and slapped my hand. "You got this, Soph."

Not entirely convinced she was right, I nodded and hustled back to serve receive. On the next play, I stayed at the net to block the other team's outside hit—which was what a middle hitter did.

The ball dropped exactly where I should have been standing, playing defense.

Major mistake.

"Melanie—" Sam started, but I held up my hands.

"I know. I'm sorry."

She fist-bumped me. "Don't worry about it. Have fun."

Have fun? When I was totally messing up and my team was losing? When Julia was watching? Not happening. I'd spent years training as a middle hitter. I came off sets quickly. I blocked on every play. I didn't fall back to get low and play defense. Chandra must have shared my lack of confidence since she set middle and back row without sending another ball my way. I could have sat on the sand and watched the football game across the yard. Or swiped seconds from the food table.

Once I rotated to the back row, I settled into the rhythm I knew well. My first pass fell into Chandra's waiting fingertips. I dug three straight hits, my forearms burning from the contact. After a few plays, the world beyond the white tape of the court's boundaries didn't exist, and I finally felt at home.

***

CHANDRA DROPPED ME OFF AROUND NINE, AFTER I'D made a pathetic excuse about chores my mom insisted get done that weekend. Lucky thing none of the other sophomores were with us. They knew my mom pushed me to socialize any chance she got. The rest of the team was on the way to Sam's house for more bonding.

"You know we have craft night to make our scrimmage shirts," Ashley had said. "Ally will not be happy about you missing."

I painted a smile onto my face. More time? I'd eaten with the girls. Played a volleyball game with them—from a position I didn't usually play. I'd even laughed a couple of times. After hours of pushing my energy out into the world, my soul wanted—no, needed—solitude.

"Another time," I'd promised.

I waved goodbye and climbed the porch steps to find my mother leaning forward in the glider. "Mom, I can't believe you. What if a boy had dropped me off, and he wanted to chivalrously walk me to the door and kiss me good night?"

She clapped her hands together. "Did you meet a boy?"

I'd meant my question as a joke, but Mom's response sent an image of Square's smiling face into my head. If I'd been holding another plate of food—or anything, for that matter—I might have dropped it all over again.

"You did meet a boy!"

"Mom, please." A tingling sensation crept up my arms at the thought of Square Weaver's smile. *So* not telling my mom that. "There were lots of boys there. I met lots of boys." That didn't sound good.

But my mom didn't seem to mind. "Were any of them cute?"

"Mom..."

She stood and crossed her arms. "Fine. At least tell me how you liked the dress."

I'd worn it in by dripping chocolate icing on it, sweating through it during our game, and tearing the hem when I dove for a well-placed hit. "Well..."

"Is that a tear? Already?"

"We played volleyball."

Mom's eyes widened to cartoonish ovals. "In a dress!"

I lifted it and flashed her my spandex, and she shook her head.

"Go shower and bring me the dress. I'll mend it and have it in your closet by tomorrow."

I considered objecting. Telling her no need as I never intended on wearing it again. But she was happy for me. So hopeful. So *Mom*.

I agreed and headed for the shower.

"Oh wait, honey," she called. "It was your first party at the volleyball star's house. Did you learn anything new?"

Always the existentialist. "Sure did," I said on my way up the stairs.

I learned I'd suck as an outside hitter, and the adorable Square Weaver was definitely out of bounds.

***

THE HOT SHOWER WATER MELTED AND WASHED AWAY the tension of the evening. So what if I'd met a cute boy. Or if Ally hadn't approved. Or if I was better sticking to hitting middle. I'd actually made a friend in Chandra. Maybe even Ashley too.

Maybe even Square.

That was a thought.

Clean and in my favorite pajamas with my favorite snack under my arms, I grabbed the book from my nightstand—now on page forty-three—and headed for the rooftop balcony. It wasn't much of a balcony. Outside of an attic window, the roof sloped in a way that was relatively flat. On an unusual weekend when my defense lawyer father had actually had time to do something other than work or drive Elle to a shooting competition, he'd installed a railing that gave the space a balcony look and made sure I wouldn't roll anywhere when I fell asleep reading or watching the stars.

After the day I'd had, I was tired enough to do exactly that.

A flash of light blossomed in the backyard next door, and a tree branch caught fire.

"Harris!" Mrs. Fullerton yelled.

A puff from the fire extinguisher Harris always kept nearby huffed the flames.

"Everything's fine," Harris called back, and I covered my mouth to stifle the laugh hovering on my lips.

"Harris, you come in this house right now."

The boards of the fence clattered, and the trellis climbing the side of my house shook.

"Harris!" his stepmom yelled again.

I reached my hand over the edge of the roof, and within seconds, Harris found it and welcomed the extra help to pull him over the edge and onto the balcony.

"How's that *no open flame* rule going?" I asked.

"Shut it," he said.

Mrs. Fullerton huffed once more and slammed the back door.

"Is she gonna lock you out?"

"It's possible," Harris said. "More than likely, she'll calm down when the rest of the tree doesn't burn down."

"Glad to hear it."

"I was surprised to see the light come on up here. Aren't you home from the big party early?"

"I needed some time alone," I admitted.

He stood. "I'm sorry. I'll go."

I threw a piece of popcorn at him. He caught it and ate it. Good thing. Wasting popcorn was an equivalent sin to missing a serve in my book.

"You don't count," I said.

He squeezed himself into the corner of the small balcony. "Thanks. I think."

"It's not an insult. You're Harris. Being with you is like—I don't know..." I searched my tired brain for an analogy that made sense, but I came up empty both in my language of volleyball and Harris's language of science. "It's like being around an extension of myself."

Did that even make sense? A fog of exhaustion settled over me, leaving behind no energy to analyze myself.

No more heels. No more boys. No more political games with teammates. No more compliments to give. No more perfect poses. No more jokes to pretend to find funny.

Me, my best friend, and a sky full of stars.

"If it's okay," I said, scooting closer to him, "can we not talk?"

He lifted his arm, allowing me to snuggle against his side. I sighed, letting the weight of all the things fade with the comfort and safety of him.

"Thanks," I whispered.

"Always."

"You're the best."

"I know it."

I pressed my chin into his ribs. "What happened to not talking?"

He chuckled, and a real smile crept across my lips. I couldn't think of a better way to end the day.

CHAPTER FOUR

OTHER THAN THE BALCONY WITH HARRIS, THE PLACE I felt most at home was the volleyball court. Monday morning couldn't come soon enough. The first day of camp. Of legitimate high school volleyball. We'd spend the entire day working out. Lifting, running, diving, passing, setting, hitting, blocking, serving, scrimmaging. The gym floors shined with fresh wax. The volleyballs smacked against the hardwood and the walls, the sound echoing and multiplying in the cool morning air.

Beautiful.

We ran bleachers and lifted for conditioning. In the afternoon, I pushed myself even harder. When I passed to Chandra on a hit-and-dig drill, I wanted to deliver the ball so accurately she didn't need to take a step. On free balls, I was nearly flawless, but with hitters like Julia Medina and Sam Strutters on the other side of the net, more often than not, an explosion of power forced the ball downward on hits. If I was lucky to dive fast enough to get under it, the majority of the time, it soared into the net or the bleachers.

Not anywhere near Chandra.

After each play, one of my teammates picked me up, slapped my hand, and offered a consolation.

"Good hustle."

"Next time."

"You got it."

I tried to believe them. Back at the service line, I evaluated my tosses, letting any bad ones fall to the ground to avoid a missed serve. And I attempted my float serve, which I'd been working on all summer. Elle had lost her patience with my serving goal the first week of June—since I'd been using the side of the house to achieve it. After a couple weeks of annoying my sister—bonus!—I could pop the ball the perfect distance and pull my hand back at the exact moment to make it float over the net.

The thought of trying it out in a real game had me bouncing on my toes.

"Get a drink," Coach called.

We piled into the corner of the gym, all chugging our marginally cool water. In the morning, we'd all had ice. By lunch, it had melted. In the late afternoon, sipping a refreshment below room temperature was a luxury.

The seniors, including Julia, joked a few feet away. I stretched my arms and legs, wondering what I would say to her if I had the chance. *Hey, Julia. You are crushing that ball. You're really awesome and clearly work super hard at this sport. Can you teach me everything you know?*

Most of the girls chatted or sat in comfortable silence. I watched them, wondering if I should talk to someone or let them rest for the few-minute break without being bothered. If I did talk, would I annoy them? If I didn't, would they think I thought I was too good for them, like Chandra had said?

Was socializing as complicated and confusing for everyone else as it was for me? That question led to a whole new circuit of *Should I talk to someone about that? Or would it be annoying?*

The mental stimulation of the water break exhausted me more than the physical challenge of the workout.

"Varsity! Line up over here." Coach pointed to the side of the court on her right.

The starters cheered and hustled onto their stage, clapping hands all around: Julia and Molly Mattola playing outside, Sam and Rachel at middle with Abby Turner playing libero for them when they rotated to the back row. Ela Gupta lined up as the right-side hitter—her power position as a lefty—opposite of Ally, our setter. Six positions. Solid. Tight. No room for newcomers.

I jogged with the rest of the team to the other side of the net and stood next to coach on the sideline. The only remaining senior, Vanessa Holt, lined up to hit outside on the JV court. Then there were juniors—Nikki Knight at outside, Ashley Fiori and Taylor Domain at middle, Olivia Andre hitting right side, and Chandra setting. Even the JV side of the court felt tight, but I measured myself against them, sure I could find a way to work in somehow. I had the height and the hitting skills. I played defense well enough. My serve was pretty solid.

On a team like ours, I couldn't say whether it would be enough.

Seven players were left without a spot. Two of us hit middle. Yet another reminder of how far I was from where I wanted to be. Even if I earned some time on the JV court, which was not my end goal, I'd have to claw my way past four other middles to buy time on varsity.

I took a deep breath and vowed to make the best of it by studying the movements of the seniors on the varsity court. They talked constantly, never missing an opportunity to claim the pass, to call for a set, and to yell for help. They moved as beautifully in sync as dolphins in the ocean. Looping around each other for complex sets and shooting upward to block or crush the ball any chance they got. Their serves crushed opponents' spirits, exemplified by their current streak of aces against the JV team.

"Melanie!"

I turned to find Coach looking at me. "Me?"

"Unless you'd rather watch."

"No! I'm ready."

I'd had my eyes on the varsity so intensely that I almost ran onto that court instead of the JV one. That would have been embarrassing!

Coach put me in the back row, serve receiving against Ally Malone. "Who wants this? Someone has to pick up the serve. I'm going to keep replacing players until someone stops the server. Who's it going to be?"

The whistle blew, and Ally nailed her jump serve to Nikki Knight, the junior outside hitter to my right. Nikki didn't move her feet quick enough to get into position, and the ball ricocheted off her arms into the bleachers.

"Next," Coach called.

Nikki left the court to be replaced by an eager face from the sidelines.

Ally lined up again, straight across from me. I watched through the checkered lines of the net, wondering if her serve would come to me. Hoping it would. Hoping it wouldn't.

It didn't. It smacked into the chest of Vanessa Holt and thunked to the floor.

"Next!"

We started the dance over again. Vanessa off. New victim on. This time, I swore Ally smiled at me. I remembered her arrogance when she'd discouraged me from talking to Square and when she'd called on me to play outside hitter at Julia's party, knowing that wasn't my position. Flutters came alive in my gut, and I tried to release them by wiggling my fingertips and bouncing on my toes.

The toss went up. Ally jumped, and the ball spun through the air in my direction. I moved into position and stopped my momentum. When the ball contacted my arms, I pulled them toward my body, taking some of the power away from the serve. With my platform aimed directly at the setter position, I passed the ball, a little high but still, right to Chandra.

She quick set it, and our middle, Ashley Fiori, crushed a kill around Sam's block.

Side-out.

Everyone in the gym except the seven seniors on the other side of the net erupted into raucous applause.

After a few seconds, Coach raised her hands to quiet us. "Good job, girls. You should celebrate that. But never, never, let one server beat you. You can't let someone serve point after point on you." She nodded to me. "Get it in your head that you're going to make the perfect pass."

"Yes, Coach!"

"Melanie?" Coach's grin further fueled the high I felt from nailing that pass, especially given my suspicion Ally wanted nothing more than to make me look bad.

"Yes, Coach?"

She gave me a high five. "Nice pass."

I didn't want to be obnoxious, but no way was my smile going anywhere.

After that, I stayed in the rotation. And what would a brilliant high be without a dangerous low? Tough serves kept coming my way. As much as I admired Julia Medina, being on the receiving end of her crushing hits had me reconsidering. At one point, I had to duck so the ball didn't devour the side of my face. I remembered what Coach had said. We couldn't let one player beat us. So I dove. I sprawled. I left more of my skin on that freshly waxed floor than a forensics unit would need to declare a serious crime had occurred.

Still, the varsity reminded us that a few well-placed passes and the occasional float serve were not enough to earn the twenty-five points necessary to win a match. We needed to do more. *I* needed to do more.

At some point, Coach took pity on us and called practice. She led us to the bleachers for our daily review, or as I saw it, her opportunity to praise the varsity for being amazing. As if they needed it. Even the newspaper was gushing about the "Sizzling Six". They'd go to the state championship for sure, and it was our job on the JV side of the court to push them every practice, so that when they got there, they'd win. After praising two other starters with a symbolic game ball—nobody actually kept the balls—Coach threw the last metaphorical trophy to Julia.

"Coach," Julia called. "Someone else deserves this more than me."

I studied the faces of the veteran players. Their confused expressions told me whatever Julia was about to do was not the norm. Coach went with it, and commanding everyone's attention, Julia stood.

"As hard as I swung and as many times as I returned the ball over the net, there was one girl there to pick it up. Melanie?"

I stilled. Was Julia Medina recognizing me in front of the whole team? With her own game ball? Was my brain really exploding inside my skull?

Julia smiled and hit the ball to me. "This is for you."

I caught it with the same shaking hands I'd dropped my dinner with at her house. She knew my name. She recognized my efforts.

She gave me her game ball!

I might have mumbled, "Thank you." I might have collapsed in confused happiness on the bleachers. Coach said something. Girls moved. I held the game ball in my hands and debated how I could smuggle it out of the gym to the trophy shelf in my room.

***

"SOPH! NEED A RIDE HOME?" CHANDRA ASKED AFTER the team had elected Julia Medina our captain, and Coach finally dismissed us.

"That'd be great," I said. "Thanks."

Look at me. I was bonding!

The team filed out of the gym and toward the parking lot, but before we made it to Chandra's car, a dark SUV stopped nearby and beeped. The driver window rolled down, and a bright smile had me forgetting the pain in my bones.

Until Ally said so loud it was clear she had no concern about who might hear her, "You've got to be kidding me."

"Is that Melanie Corwin, volleyball player extraordinaire?"

Square Weaver.

He put the SUV in Park and hopped out, leaving it there haphazardly taking up five parking spaces in the lot. "How was the first day of camp?"

"Good," I said, glancing back at the rest of the team. Including Sam, who was watching from a sideways position like she didn't want people to know she was watching. The look on her face revealed she was still crushing on Square, a revelation that exploded a pang of guilt in my side.

"Ladies!" Square called, waving to them.

We stood awkwardly for a few quiet seconds, and despite Ally's demands, I couldn't bring myself to be rude to Square. He didn't deserve it.

"Are you on the way to practice?" I said in a feeble effort at politeness.

"Heat acclimatization." He stumbled over the pronunciation of the second word, which made me feel slightly better at not knowing what he was talking about.

"Which means...?"

"We run around in the heat for a few hours to get acclimated to it—despite the fact it's the end of the summer, not the beginning, and we're basically already acclimated to it."

"That makes no sense."

"Exactly." Square smiled, and it was like the sun had burst out from behind a bank of clouds. But there wasn't a cloud in the sky.

"Melanie!" Chandra called from across the lot. "You want a ride, or is that beautiful football player taking you home?"

My face flamed redder than the stripes on the American flag waving above the parking lot.

Square pointed to his car, which was still running. "I would. Definitely, but..."

"No. I get it. You have practice." I was not attempting to pronounce that *heat accli* word and look even more like an idiot than I already did.

He'd gotten out of his car to talk to me instead of hanging out the window like every other teenage boy on the planet. He'd felt bad he couldn't take me home.

Was Square Weaver for real?

He waved at the girls. Then winked at me. "Good to see you, Melanie."

"You, too."

Ally's glare when she climbed into the driver seat of her car told me I was on dangerous ground.

After Square drove away, Chandra and Ashley teased me relentlessly. I couldn't bring myself to make eye contact with Sam. I didn't want to hurt her feelings, but on the other hand, I didn't want her reaction to make me feel bad enough to not like Square.

I wasn't sure anything could stop that storm from brewing.

CHAPTER FIVE

AFTER DINNER, I TOOK TO THE DRIVEWAY TO HIT THE
ball against the side of the house. Nothing calmed me more than the
power I felt smacking the ball at the exact moment to send it flying
on a perfect trajectory back at the wall.

When my arm screamed for a break, I switched to passing.

Using the light from the spots on the garage, I chose a brick to
target and with controlled passes, I counted to twenty-seven touches
before the ball hit the ground. Not bad for the first round. On my
second attempt, I kept the ball in the air for fifty-two touches. My
goal was one hundred. I achieved it on the seventh try and shifted
back to hitting.

"Mel, is that you?" Harris called from over the fence.

I hit the ball at the house again. "It isn't Elle or Lily." Harris
knew Elle's sport of choice was archery. My little sister Lily's was
the Math Bowl.

"The question was more of a conversation starter than a legitimate
inquiry."

The bathroom window on the second floor whipped open. "Melanie, for heaven's sake," Elle shouted. "Please stop taking out your
frustration on the house. It's like trying to shower in the middle of a
ping-pong table." The window slammed shut, and she disappeared.

"Listen to your sister," Harris called. "Come over here. I have something to show you."

Reluctantly, I dropped the ball and pushed through the rickety pickets. I couldn't say the view on the other side of the fence surprised me. Harris stood tall and lanky with a wobbly grin on his face. His brown hair was shaggier than usual.

"You need a haircut."

"Thanks for noticing."

In front of him was a contraption with a dozen or so PVC pipes all pointing upward.

"What are you blowing up now?" I asked.

"I resent that. Can nobody appreciate the scientific genius that occurs in this yard?"

Although Harris's stepmother carried serious embarrassment over the number of times she'd had to apologize to our neighbors, I found Harris's experiments endearing.

"So what's the experiment tonight?"

His eyes brightened. "On Saturday—when my stepmom was at church—I tested a carbide cannon."

"Oh no," I mumbled.

"It's harmless!"

"Said the guy who lit the tree branches on fire days ago."

"That—was due to an unfortunate miscalculation in my hypothesis."

"Uh-huh."

"If you had been here for the initial experiment, you would know the risks are minimal." He adjusted the cannons in some minute way I assumed could only be deciphered by someone who possessed an equally incomparable attention to scientific detail. Someone like my little sister.

"How was your first day of camp?"

I rubbed the bruises forming on my hips from diving—and sticking—onto the newly-waxed floor.

"You don't want to talk about it. Got it. Back to my experiment. While you were at the star quidditch player's birthday party—"

Leave it to Harris to make me smile after a long day. "You're an idiot."

"Thank you—the carbide cannon shot Puddles's stuffed mouse onto the roof."

"You stole your cat's toy for an experiment."

"Yes," he said.

"And shot it onto the roof?"

"Yes. Keep up. So I got to thinking: What if I had my own fireworks show of sorts?"

The burning tree flashed in my mind. "So you're setting off fireworks?"

"Just take this." He gave me a bottle of little black crystals and a scale. "Pour a gram into each one of these caps."

I filled the caps, and he screwed them onto the bottoms of the PVC pipes. "You might want to stand back. And maybe cover your ears."

The magic words that always made me want to run. I scooted toward the fence while Harris poured water into a tube that wrapped around the contraption. "If my design is accurate, the water should drip into each of the cannons at the exact same moment, and I apply a little heat—"

He lit a flame, and the cannons erupted, shooting a display of glow-in-the-dark socks into the air with a boom. Against the backdrop of the black, night sky, the soaring socks created a stunning effect.

"It's beautiful, Harris."

He pumped his fist in the air. "Right!"

A few of the socks caught in the branches that had survived the recent fire. Others hit their peak and fell to the ground in a beautiful array.

A few met the same fate as Puddles the cat's toy mouse.

Porch lights throughout the neighborhood lit up.

"That's not good," Harris said.

"*Harris!*"

His name was bellowed, not by one person but by a chorus of angry voices. Elle. Mrs. Morski from across the alley. Someone down the block I couldn't identify, and, of course, his stepmom.

"I should go." I backpedaled toward the fence.

Harris's stepmom came onto the porch with her hair in those spongey night-time curlers I didn't think anyone under the age of seventy-five used. "Harris, we talked about this!"

"Nothing's on fire."

"Is that our standard around here?"

I had to cover my mouth to keep from laughing.

"Take it up with your father when he gets home. Clean this mess and get inside."

"It's a scientific work of art," Harris mumbled.

With a sugary tone miles from the one she'd used with Harris, Mrs. Fullerton said to me, "Hi, Melanie, dear. Say hello to your parents for us, and please apologize for the noise."

"Hi, Mrs. Fullerton. I will."

She disappeared into the house.

"Don't apologize," Harris said. "Your parents appreciate my genius more than mine do."

They also appreciated their house not going up in flames.

Harris collected the socks from the grass. "So seriously, tell me about today."

I climbed the dilapidated tree to retrieve the socks that, even at his height, he couldn't reach. "Let me break it down for you mathematically. There are two middle hitters on the court at one time. Two teams: varsity and JV. So four possible spots. On the team, there are two seniors who hit middle, two juniors, and two sophomores. Or... six middles."

"For four spots?"

I stretched as far as I could and grabbed the last of the stray socks. "Exactly."

"And what position do you play again?"

I threw the socks at his face.

"Kidding."

I hopped down from one of the lower branches and stood hands on hips as we both let those numbers sink in.

"Mel, can I be honest?"

"You're going to light my dreams of starting varsity on fire—metaphorically, of course."

"On the contrary. I don't care how many middle hitters on that team are older than you. Or have more experience than you. I see you training—well, I can't see through the fence, but I hear you. Every day. For the last five years."

"Six."

He grinned. "Exactly. Being the brilliant scientist that I am, I have a hypothesis."

"Go on," I said, refusing to take the bait of arguing the point of his brilliance.

"I worked with Lily all summer." He looked at the sky and rested his hand on his chest. "I like to think of myself as her mentor. And have you seen her improve?"

I had actually.

"Not sure," I lied.

He scowled at me. "Ask the star quidditch player to mentor you."

Hmm. I had wanted to learn from Julia, but asking her directly? That felt...weird.

"Go for what you want, and good things will happen. I promise."

Harris couldn't possibly promise something like that, but the vote of confidence fueled me to want to try.

CHAPTER SIX

AFTER A SOLID NIGHT'S SLEEP, I WOKE FOR THE SECOND
day of volleyball camp thinking about Harris's suggestion. I'd turned
over a million questions in my mind the night before. Would Julia
want to help? As an outside hitter, could she? Would I be better off
to ask a middle hitter for help? Or was the better plan to ask Chandra
to set with Julia and me, so we could run the offense side by side?
Would playing next to her elevate my play?

First to practice that morning—secretly hoping to chat with Julia
before everyone else arrived—I helped Coach Steve carry the poles
across the gym to set up the net. He cranked the handle until he
measured the correct height while I warmed my arm up against the
wall where the players would arrive.

My teammates strolled in one by one, carting gym bags, water bottles filled with ice, and lunches. Nine o'clock ticked closer. I
grabbed a quick drink of my icy water before Coach yelled to start
laps.

"They're the toughest team we'll play all season," Sam said.

Chandra plopped onto the floor next to us and stretched her ham-
strings. "Who?"

"Pacific," Sam and Ally said in unison.

They'd been the toughest team the ninth graders had faced the year before, too. They built their program from elementary school up, like Iron Valley.

"They have a strong right-side hitter," Sam said. "Our blocking has to be on point. It's a good thing Julia can cover that side."

At the mention of Julia, I scanned the gym but realized she still hadn't arrived yet. Odd.

Ally stretched her neck. "She'll shut her down for sure."

Ally and Sam spoke without doubt. Julia could do it. She would do it. Their voices dripped with admiration. I hoped someday my teammates would talk about me like that.

"Her back-row attack is impressive, too," Sam said.

"You and Julia will be in the back to pick that up," Ally said with a grin. "We got this. I know we do. Beating them will practically guarantee us a regional title and a bid to States."

Ally's unwavering confidence in her best friend also softened any feelings I'd had from her pushing in on my interactions with Square and my private time. Maybe Ally was like an M&M, a tough outer shell but a soft-and-sweet middle.

Sam sighed. "I hope, but don't count your chickens. You never know what can happen."

Ally rolled her eyes.

"Seriously, Al. Don't jinx us!"

"Let's go, girls!" Coach Steve called, and we hopped up for warm-up laps. The team kept relatively close for the laps, jumbled together. All except for—

"Where's Julia?" Sam asked at the same moment I thought it.

"She must be sick," Chandra said. "If something was really wrong, her mom wouldn't be here."

"She's fine," said Ela Gupta. "We saw her outside video chatting with Jake on our way in."

My teammates went starry-eyed. When Jake had graduated earlier that summer, he'd left a legion of admirers behind.

Molly Mattola pressed her hand against her chest and sighed. "Jake Medina."

"If I had the chance to video chat with him, I'd be late for practice too," Kate said.

"Mm hmm." Molly gave a low whistle. "One look at that boy,

and you know there's a God."

When we finished laps and stretches, Julia still hadn't arrived. Huddled around the coaches, awaiting instructions, we turned our heads to the door when it finally opened. Julia walked toward us without making eye contact with anyone. Normally, she held her shoulders back and head high, the epitome of strength. In that moment, she slumped forward, a faded version of herself.

"You're late, Captain," Coach Steve called. "Get your knee pads on and warm up."

"Coach?" Julia's voice had a serious tone that had the girls around me stepping away from the group or standing on their tip toes to get a better view.

"I have something to say to the team," she said.

Coach Steve raised his arm in a gesture that invited her to say whatever she needed to. A crushing weight in my chest warned me something big was about to happen. My teammates glanced sideways at each other with creases in their brows and pursed lips.

"You girls have been like sisters to me. We grew up together playing this sport."

Several of the girls nodded.

"That's why it's so hard for me to say this, but I can't be your captain. I've thought about it, and I'm not playing volleyball this year."

Not. Playing. Volleyball?

The words trickled through my ears into my mind as if arriving on the slowest means of transportation in existence.

It wasn't possible. Not with her hitting ability. Her vertical jump. She could block the right-side hitters we faced. She could dig and pass. Her serves...they cut through the air, ruthless and on target.

Julia Medina couldn't quit volleyball. She *was* volleyball.

"You're joking," Ally said.

The girls' stares intensified. I studied Julia's face for any hint of a smile. There wasn't one.

"Volleyball has been my life forever," Julia continued. "You all voting me your captain meant so much to me, but I can't lead you if my heart's not in it."

Looking at Coach Medina sent a ball of nausea bouncing around my stomach. Her face creased in pain, and she took a deep breath as if trying to hold back a waterfall of tears threatening her every second. Ally's anger radiated through her wide eyes. A suspicion crept into my mind—she hadn't known this was coming. If she had, she wouldn't have bragged about Julia shutting down the right-side hitter from Pacific before practice.

A huge decision like this, and Julia hadn't even told her best friend.

After the kind of silence that lasted so long people squirmed, Sam pushed through the group and wrapped her arms around Julia, saying something I couldn't hear. One by one, my teammates hugged Julia.

To say goodbye.

I didn't move. I'd been about to ask this girl to mentor me. I wanted to learn from her. She had offers to play college ball. She was the best hitter on this team, and she was quitting? Her present was the future I wanted for myself, and she chose to walk away from it.

If for no other reason than it was my turn, we hugged, but I didn't say anything.

On her way out of the gym, Julia said, "I'll root from the stands this year. You'll do amazing."

The door crept closed and clicked into place, loud in the silent gym.

My mom always said that sometimes in life you strived. Other times, you survived. There was no striving that day at practice. Considering the heart of the team had been ripped away, the fact we survived had to be enough.

***

HAMMOCKS HAD THE KIND OF VERSATILITY IN LIFE I wanted to have on the volleyball court. They could be romantic—not for me ever, but for some people, I guess. They could be peaceful or exciting, calm or fun. That night, I collapsed into the hammock in our back yard, letting the woven ropes support my numb body.

I opened the book I'd been reading. The date on the sticky note bookmark was close to a week earlier. I wasn't reading. I wasn't resting. I wasn't focused.

How had everything gone so wrong?

I figured Julia's decision to quit meant three things. First, the team was about to be shaken up. Majorly. Part of me selfishly wished she'd been a middle hitter, and then at least her absence would've created an opportunity for me. Second, we'd have to find a way to compete in one of the toughest sections in the region without her blocking the strong right-side hitters we'd face, like the one at Pacific.

Third, asking her for guidance was no longer an option.

The night sky was much clearer than my thoughts. My ninth-grade year, I'd taken astronomy. I loved the tale of the vain Queen Cassiopeia who angered Poseidon and attempted to sacrifice her daughter Andromeda—how Perseus saved her, and their story was preserved in the stars above. Knowing what I was actually looking at in the night sky made the galaxy and beyond feel more real somehow. When I'd had that revelation in freshman astronomy, I realized that was how Harris felt about his wacky experiments. They made the world relevant to him. I envied his conviction in science. Now, the expanse reminded me how insignificant I was, both in the universe and on my team.

"Do I smell the vanilla-sugar scent from that cutesy store in the mall?" Harris said from the other side of the fence.

Speak of the scientist.

"I do. That must mean my friend Melanie is on the other side of this fence stargazing."

"Your empirical skills have no bounds, scientist Harris."

"Why, thank you," he said, and I could practically hear the smile on his lips. "Why don't you get out of that hammock and get over here?"

I pushed my toe into the grass, so the hammock would swing. "Because it's too comfortable."

"I have the telescope out...," he said in a singsong voice.

I couldn't resist the telescope, and he knew it. I pushed the pickets aside and slipped through the fence to find Harris hunched over the telescope with one eye hovering above the lens and both of his hands turning the knobs to align his target.

"Good night for stargazing," I said.

"Perfect."

The PVC-pipe contraption was gone. "I'm a little surprised by the benign nature of your scientific endeavors tonight. No cannons? No explosions?"

"My stepmom pleaded that I take a break from the heavy stuff for a while."

I gave him twenty-four hours until the "heavy stuff" was back in action.

Still looking into the lens, he lifted his arm and waved me toward him. "Take a look at this."

I hurried to his side and looked through the lens to see a glowing ball surrounded by an elliptical ring. "Saturn!"

"The rings look brilliant right now."

They did. Saturn—through the telescope—reminded me of those glow-in-the-dark bouncy balls you got at the grocery store machines. The planet appeared so tiny you could reach out and grab it. But of course, it wasn't tiny. It wasn't close enough to grab, and it absolutely would not fit in my hand. If humans could create a device that magnified a planet from 750 million miles away, couldn't anything be possible?

Like finding a way to win without Julia Medina on the team?

The planet moved from the left to the right of the area Harris had magnified.

"Is it disappearing?"

"Yep." I stepped back and bumped into Harris. He leaned forward to readjust the knobs and wedged me between him and the telescope.

"Awkward," I said.

"Sorry." He held his right arm back, so I could step away. I'd made the comment out of silliness, but I had a strange feeling I'd somehow insulted him.

"It's ready. Go ahead."

I leaned forward and, once again, watched Saturn and its rings move from one side of my view to the other. Too magnificent to be contained.

"How was day two?" Harris asked.

I groaned. "Awful."

"Can't have been that bad."

"Julia Medina quit the team."

"Wow. Okay. That's bad."

"Yep."

"So what does this mean?"

Nobody knew. The Sizzling Six had become the Sizzling Five that day. Even in the name, anyone could see the appeal was lost. The perfect motion on the varsity side of the net developed over years of playing side by side—destroyed. When someone, presumably another senior outside hitter, maybe Vanessa Holt, took Julia's place, the team's intuition would suffer.

Not to mention Vanessa on her best day wasn't half the hitter Julia was on her worst.

Julia might have left a single hole to fill on the court, but it felt much bigger than that.

"All I want," I said, "is to play volleyball. That's it."

"And go to parties with important volleyball superstars."

"Stop. You know how impossible my mother can be about my need to get out of the house and be social. Like I'm not social at practice."

"You're social over here."

"Exactly!" And why should I change my world? I liked to be at home. I liked to play volleyball in the yard. I liked my life drama-free. "And now that Julia quit, the team dynamic will be total drama."

"I hate to be cold, but will her quitting improve your chances of playing?"

I squirmed because I'd wondered that same thing. "Nope. She hit outside."

"And you hit middle. Right?"

"Shut up." I couldn't take Harris's teasing. He'd memorized the periodic table and knew the name of every constellation above us. He could remember what position I played.

He pretended to zip his mouth and lock it with a key, a silly gesture that had clearly survived our childhood.

"I honestly don't know if I can explain why this feels so monumental. I guess everyone on the team saw Julia as our anchor. Her competitiveness raised the bar for everyone, but it was also like, I don't know, we could do anything because she was in our corner."

"And now she's not in your corner."

"Exactly. It wrecks my whole vision."

"What vision?"

"I'd watch the seniors, learn from them, let their hits and serves push me to get better. I'd sit the bench this year while they went to States and learn from the experience, so I could help take the team back in the next two years."

"Sounds like a lot of pressure."

To me, it sounded like a plan.

"So what's changed?" Harris asked.

"The entire team. Everything."

Harris rolled his eyes. "C'mon, Mel. She's only one person."

"Take one chemical out of a reaction in your experiment. Will the experiment be the same?"

"Okay. I see your point." He snapped his fingers and pointed at me. "But what if you had another chemical that you could substitute to save the experiment? That could work."

Maybe in science, but not in sports. Or, at least, not in *this* sport on *this* team. Not when the seniors had played so well together.

Not when the missing chemical was Julia Medina.

CHAPTER SEVEN

THE TEAM DIDN'T APPROACH WEDNESDAY-MORNING
drills with the same fervor we had on Monday, but I couldn't blame
Julia's absence entirely. Day three had my quads screaming from
squatting in a defensive position for hours on end. I felt it that morning walking down the stairs in the same awkward side-to-side style
as the green army men in *Toy Story*, which Lily had made me watch
with her every day when she was four.

The smell of Icy Hot permeating the gym told me I wasn't the
only one in pain.

"We're going to try some new things today," Coach announced
after lunch. Not that the news constituted much of an announcement.
With Julia gone, our only choice was something new. "Vanessa, start
on this side of the court today."

Vanessa smiled and hustled to the varsity court. Ally greeted her
with a huge hug.

"What's that about?" I asked Chandra.

"Ally and Vanessa are cousins. Ally's been secretly, or not-so-se-
cretly hoping Vanessa got Julia's spot. We all sort of assumed it with
her being the only other senior on the team, but..." Chandra shrugged.

"What?"

"Vanessa's great, but she's no Julia Medina."

Coach moved Vanessa to the back row and instead put Molly Mattola into Julia's former starting position in the front row. Both the sophomore outside hitters bounced on their toes at the chance coming their way. Someone would need to replace Vanessa on the JV court.

"Melanie!" Coach called. "Serving position, please."

My breath caught and fluttered down a spiral slide to my chest.

The outside hitters gaped at me as I jogged onto the court, and I remembered what Chandra had said about making friends. My best shot at that was playing hard to earn the respect of the girls on the court who wanted to win as much as I did. In the back row opposite Nikki Knight, the JV outside hitter, the painful reality hit me—Coach was prepping me to play defensive specialist for JV. Yes, I'd wanted playing time. Yes, playing back row would make me a better player for when I finally got my shot at varsity.

But I wanted to hit.

S*tay positive and work hard,* I thought. Chandra high-fived me and pulled me in for a half hug. "Don't let anyone give you shit."

I felt everyone's eyes on me. Vanessa had been the expected replacement. I was the wild card.

Coach rolled the game ball to me. "Let's go!"

I dribbled back to the line. Coach blew the whistle. I took a deep breath and tossed the ball into the air. A little left, but I swung anyway and popped my arm back at the perfect moment. The serve floated over the net toward Vanessa.

"Mine!" she called and launched the ball across the varsity court, sending Ally into the bleachers after it.

The JV pounded our feet and clapped our hands, shouting, "Ace!"

As we did every time a serve ended in an immediate point.

"Do it again," Coach called.

So I did. This time, in the middle back position of the varsity court, Rachel popped up an erratic pass to Ally. She set on the run and pushed the ball high and behind her to the outside position. Molly hit it with respectable power, but she didn't crush it. Next to me, Taylor picked it up on a nice pass to Chandra, who pushed a quick set to Ashley in the middle.

And so the volley went.

By the time the ball hit the hardwood on our side, my teammates on the JV court breathed heavily through big smiles. We rushed to each other in the middle of the court, clapping our hands and stomping our feet.

For every impressive volley we celebrated, the varsity crumbled. And criticized each other. The perfect fluidity of the Sizzling Six seemed too far to recover. Taylor dominated the net in the middle on our side and crushed an overpassed ball right back at the varsity. Coach closed her eyes and sighed.

When I got to the front row, Coach took me out and sent in a sophomore outside hitter, Amelia. On the next rotation, she gave the other sophomore outside, Sophia, a shot. Both did okay, but neither stood out significantly above the other. At least not to me.

On the varsity side of the court, Vanessa struggled. The whole team did, especially with Molly switching from back row to Julia's former spot in the front. A couple times, they lost a point for being out of rotation.

"We've had that same rotation for two years," Ally said during a water break.

In her usual optimistic way, Sam said, "It'll take some time, but we'll adjust."

Ally dropped her bottle against the hardwood, and it rolled to a stop in the corner. Chandra raised an eyebrow at me, but neither of us dared to speak and attract Ally's wrath.

In the end, the varsity beat us 25–18, 25–21, and 25–20. They'd crushed us earlier in the week, so that felt as good as a win to me.

"We're finishing shirts tonight at Sam's house," Ally said while everyone took off their knee pads and slipped their toes into slides and flip-flops.

"Oh. My. Gosh." Chandra swiped her phone furiously.

"What?" Ashley asked.

"I don't believe this!" she answered. "Julia tried out for quarterback."

"Of the football team?" Ashley said. "Good for her."

"Yes," Chandra insisted, and her drama-loving eyes widened more than I'd ever seen them. "And against her boyfriend."

"That's not possible," Sam said.

"It's true." Ally threw her backpack over her shoulder. "Don't be late tonight."

She left the gym without another word. Silence lingered. What could any of us say? Julia Medina had been our captain. Our leader. I'd started the season embarrassed by the fangirl inside of me. After Julia quit, I'd realized we'd been a team of fangirls.

Chandra broke the silence. "Soph, need a ride to team bonding tonight?"

I didn't answer right away. Instead, my brain churned for a possible excuse. On the one hand, with the rush of playing beside them every day, I'd connected with the girls. On the other, after exhausting my body at practice and pushing myself to be present and pleasant and social all day, I needed sleep and silence.

But I'd also promised myself I'd make an effort. Sleep and silence would have to wait.

"Sure," I told Chandra. "That'd be great."

Maybe I could wear my noise-canceling headphones.

"Melanie," Coach called from the doorway to the locker room, "can I see you for a minute?"

The girls teased with a chorus of oooohs. I said my goodbyes and headed for Coach's office. Maybe she wanted to tell me I'd had a good practice. But wouldn't she have said that with a game ball? Chandra was the only player on the JV court to get one, besides when Julia had given hers to me.

I tapped at her door.

"C'mon in." She pushed a chair towards me. "How's everything going?"

"Good."

She nodded and waited for me to say something else, but I wasn't sure what that might be.

"Okay...well, I wanted to ask you about your goals for the year."

That was easy enough. "I want to earn playing time. Perfect my serve. And learn everything I can to succeed on varsity."

She smiled. Did she think I was being presumptuous?

"Not that I think I'm playing varsity this year. I mean, there are some really great middle hitters on this team."

"You're right about that. What we really need is some strength at the outside-hitting position."

Since her daughter had quit on us.

Thankfully, I didn't say that aloud. Coach studied me in that way adults did when they expected you to get something they were trying to say but you totally didn't get it.

"Melanie?"

"Yes?"

Coach folded her hands in her lap. "I've decided to move you to outside."

"Move to outside?"

She nodded.

"But I've played middle my whole life."

"And you're good at it," Coach said. "But more importantly, you're an excellent server and passer. You're tall enough to block well, and your hitting is strong. But I can't use you at middle. I need someone outside. With your height next to Sam, we'd have incredible blocking potential, which we'll need to be competitive."

Sam had said blocking the right-side hitter from Pacific would mean everything. Wait. Coach continued talking, but I got stuck on the word "Sam". Sam was our captain now that Julia had left. She was the starting middle hitter. On varsity.

Varsity!

"You want me to play varsity?"

I might have interrupted her, but she smiled politely just the same. "I can't make any promises, but I'd like to give you a try."

Giddiness bubbled from my core until I was in a cloud of teeth-bearing happiness that prevented me from feeling the ground beneath my feet or seeing the world around me for anything less than rainbows and starlight.

I think I told Coach that I would try outside. And maybe I said goodbye. Hopefully I threw in a thank you too.

On my walk home, the rainbows and starlight faded, replaced by memories of the dreadful few minutes when I'd lined up in the out-side-hitter position at Julia's birthday party. How awful I had been. How my body had been trained to move on the court like a middle hitter: be at the net, block every play.

Could I retrain my actions to play outside? Would I be any good at it?

If I was good at it, how would the team feel about my hopscotching two seniors, a junior, and two other sophomores to claim the starting spot? Suddenly team bonding seemed more important than ever. I'd need to make an extra effort.

I groaned at the thought.

By the time I got home, the rainbows had dissipated completely, and I wasn't sure they would ever return.

CHAPTER EIGHT

I STOOD IN FRONT OF THE HOODIES AND T-SHIRTS IN MY closet and died a little inside. Athletic gear did not scream *making an effort*. I snuck into Elle's closet. Not snuck. I mean, if she were there, she would've shared her clothes with me. She already had, so that meant I was allowed.

Sort of.

Whatever. I pushed the clothes along the rod the less than an inch they could actually move to get a look at them. How did she know where anything was? Clothes in totes up on the shelves. Clothes in crates on the floor. She even had clothes under her bed.

I needed something that showed Melanie Corwin was friendly and trying the appropriate amount. Not too hard. Not too little.

I settled on jean shorts and two ribbed tank tops—one pink, one yellow. I added a belt with a heart-shaped buckle, some blush and lip gloss, and a necklace with a heart. Then I took off the necklace. Too many hearts.

Fifteen minutes early, Chandra beeped her horn in front of my house. Good thing I'd settled on a ponytail. Ashley and Chandra shouted from the car windows for me to run. I jumped in next to three overflowing trash bags of clothes.

"What's with all this?"

"Donations for the domestic violence shelter," Ashley said proudly. "Chandra is amazing like that."

"Don't make me blush," Chandra said. "It's a little thing I do. That's all."

I had no idea. In the spirit of volleyball team bonding, I asked questions. "Are the clothes secondhand?"

"Mostly," she said. "But I do random collections of new items throughout the year. Socks in the fall. Lip balms in winter. Kids' books for summer reading in spring and summer."

Wow. I didn't do anything like that. "Does it count toward your community service graduation requirement?"

Chandra laughed. "And then some. It takes a lot of time,"

"If you ever need help...," I said.

"Thanks, Soph." She took a turn way too fast, and I slid sideways into the bags. Good thing they were cushy.

"Whoa," I said. "We're early, not late."

I gripped the handle above the door when she whipped around another turn.

"We're not going to Sam's," Ashley said.

"Ally will kill us," I said.

"Don't worry, Soph. We're going. Just have a pit stop first."

Being with my teammates in such a small space made my tiny secret expand ten sizes. It was a small thing. Coach had asked me to try a new position. No guarantees. No promises. An opportunity. But would the girls see it that way? Would they be angry I didn't say anything? Or if I did say something, would that suggest I pompously believed the starting position was mine for the taking?

When I stayed home in the evening, practicing in the back yard or hanging with Harris, life was uncomplicated. Easy. Comfortable. Besides the soft bags of clothes, nothing about flying around town in the back seat of Chandra's car while keeping a secret from my new friends could be defined as comfortable.

Chandra pulled into the high school lot and parked in a spot near the stadium. "Let's go."

I followed the girls up the bleachers we usually ran for conditioning. From the top row, we had the perfect view of the football practice field. In seconds, I found Julia with her brunette braid hanging down her back. On the field. Wearing a helmet. And shoulder pads.

Not that I expected something else. Seeing it though...wow.

"Ain't that some shit," Chandra said.

Julia stepped up to the center, called for the snap, dropped back, and placed the ball right in the receiver's hands. I felt the urge to cheer but kept quiet for fear of getting thrown out.

I hated that Julia had quit on the team, but when you saw a girl delivering passes on a football field, it was hard to feel anything but respect.

Not to mention, I had a shot to not only play but to play varsity. No way to predict how my season would have played out had she stayed, but her leaving had been the catalyst for this opportunity. I couldn't deny that.

"She's amazing," Ashley said. "She reminds me of my sister."

"Your sister plays football?" I asked.

"She's a wrestler," Chandra said.

"A good one," Ashley added with pride.

Chandra rubbed her hands together. "I hope Julia kicks their asses."

"She will," I mumbled.

Julia Medina was a tough competitor. Strong. Fierce. Determined. She'd gotten that way playing volleyball on *our* team. With the girls I lined up beside every day. She might have left the team behind, but we were still a team. Every player wanted to compete and win the same as before. I couldn't believe Harris might be right about anything other than science, especially human nature, but maybe we could substitute another "chemical" and end up with an equal outcome.

What if that chemical was me?

Football practice ended, and we made our way down the bleachers. When we hit the bottom, the players came around the corner all sweat and smudged dirt. At the head of the pack was Square, looking more square than ever in his shoulder pads. He'd pulled his shirt up, about to tug it over his head, but stopped when he saw us. The result was a sneak peek of his abs and me choking on my saliva.

"I can't believe you're stalking me," he said.

Chandra might have swooned. I wasn't far behind, but I'd managed to build a slight tolerance to his powers.

"Thought I'd watch your practice," I said, clearing my throat. "Make sure you're not slacking." My stomach flopped. Was I flirting? More importantly, was I terrible at it?

Square laughed, so I couldn't have been that bad. "And what did you decide?"

I shrugged. "You're still getting acclimated."

"I see." He tilted his head and squinted the slightest bit in a smoldering look that had never—and I mean never—been directed my way. When he spoke, his voice did that soft, confident thing that melted my insides. "I guess I'll have to show you how hard I work when I want something."

"Oh my damn," Chandra said from behind me. I turned to see her fanning herself.

"Maybe you want to wait in the car," I told her.

"Not a chance, Soph."

Square took my phone, swiped, and tapped at the screen. I held my breath and refused to make eye contact with Chandra. "Hit me up, *Soph*."

Standing still with a cool smile on my face tested me like the toughest jump serve or the most perfectly placed hit. Inside, I jumped and danced and did an impressive amount of squeeing.

He rejoined the cluster of sweaty, smelly football players on their way to the locker room, and Chandra squeezed my hand so hard, I thought the bones might break.

"Did he give you his number?"

He'd programmed in his name with an actual phone number. Not a social media handle. A phone number.

"Yep."

"That's next level," Chandra said. "He's not playing around."

I couldn't stop the smile tugging its way onto my face. Until I thought of Sam's reaction when I'd talked to Square in the parking lot the day before.

My squeeing transformed to groaning.

The Sizzling Six had been dismantled. Someone would take Julia's place. If I had any chance of it being me, I had to put the team first. Before a boy. Even one as fine as Square. Being around him was a lesson in the laws of attraction. I'd never felt that pull with anyone before. I wanted to be close to him. I wanted to make him smile. I wanted him to make me smile. His number burned in my hand. I might as well have let it burn to ash and blow away in the breeze because I'd never get to use it.

***

ALLY TOOK THE LIBERTY, AS SHE DID, TO POINT OUT WE arrived fifteen minutes late. I considered offering some advice on appropriate bonding, such as *don't hound the people you're trying to bond with.*

But Chandra ushered us to a folding table in Sam's back yard.

"Here's your shirt, Soph." Chandra threw it to me. She and Ashley laughed in a way that told me something was going on. Something I wouldn't like.

I held up the shirt. Chandra had been kind enough to paint the back for me on Saturday when I'd skipped. Instead of *Corwin*, the name across the top was *Soph.*

"Are you for real, Chandra?"

"Gotta learn to show up," she said.

My paintbrush rolled off the table. I knelt to pick it up and yelped at the soreness in my quads.

"Camp's brutal," Chandra said. "But you played well today."

I tugged on the side of the table to alleviate some of the work my muscles had to do. "Congrats on getting a game ball."

"Yeah, that was a surprise." She squirted purple paint onto a paper plate. "I honestly don't remember Coach giving game balls to anyone but varsity until Julia gave you hers."

"I'm glad it's changed. You deserved it."

"You're all right, Soph." She hugged me, and her brush swiped paint across my cheek and hair. "Oops!"

"You did that on purpose!"

"You're right but look at us bonding."

Before I had a chance to paint her back and send the whole evening into an out-of-control paint sling-fest, Ally called, "How's everyone doing?"

Chandra and I rolled our eyes and got to work. We painted the fronts of our shirts with Iron Valley Viking logos. Or in other words, blobs of purple-and-black paint.

"These look awful," I said.

"Basically," Chandra agreed.

Ashley rested her head on my shoulder, a gesture that surprised me into stillness. "You know who doesn't look awful?"

"I know where she's going with this." Chandra grinned and pressed her fingers into both of her cheeks to create an impossibly huge smile.

I swatted her hands and shook my head, apparently too subtle because she continued in a low voice she must have thought sounded like his, "Square Weaver."

Sam tensed.

"What about Square Weaver?" Ally asked.

Maybe there was a hole under the table I could crawl into.

"He was all over Melanie at football practice," Ashley boasted.

"He was not," I objected as Ally said, "You went to football prac-tice?" and Chandra smacked Ashley's arm.

At least the revelation didn't have me in trouble alone. Ally stomped off, and the team put their heads down to finish their shirts.

"Hey, Melanie," Sam whispered, "Ally has this fierce friend thing going on, which don't get me wrong, I appreciate about her usually, but I'm totally over Square. It was a stupid crush from ages ago. If you like him, you guys should go out. He's a great guy."

I studied her expression. She seemed sincere, but growing up with two sisters had taught me that sometimes a girl might say something but subtle cues revealed a different story entirely. Was the offer some sort of test? If I went out with Square, would I fail it?

"Thanks," I finally said. "But...I'm not sure what... Maybe. I mean, I might."

Melanie Corwin. Articulate as ever.

Sam's smile revealed nothing but sincerity. "He's really cute, right?"

My laughter ushered the tension in my muscles away. "Definite-ly."

"That smile," Chandra whispered over my shoulder.

We all appropriately swooned for a few seconds before finding our way back to the task at hand—purple-and-black blobs. My shirt was shameful. Some of the girls embraced their mess by finger painting purple-and-black swirls across the front of their shirts. Fearing the wrath of Ally, I didn't go abstract, but I might as well have.

While our masterpieces dried, the team roasted marshmallows around Sam's firepit. Every time Sam spoke or smiled, I admired her a bit more. A few days around her and I wondered why I'd placed Julia on a pedestal and not Sam. Maybe it was her humility. Even in her position as captain, she deferred a lot of the decisions to Ally, sometimes to the team's dismay. Until we piled around the fire that night, I hadn't realized Sam lived with her grandparents. Her grandfather carried out trays of chocolate, marshmallows, and graham crackers and playfully said he had his eye on us.

"Chandra, we have some clothes on the front porch for you," he said. "Can I load them into your car?"

"Thank you," she said. "But I'll grab them later."

Ally lowered a marshmallow into the fire and toasted it to perfection. She passed it to Vanessa. "For my cousin, the new varsity outside hitter." Ally curtsied, and the rest of the team clapped. Vanessa took the marshmallow with a humble smile.

"Thanks everyone."

"I'm proud of you," Ally said. "You've worked toward this for years. It's your time."

My stomach dropped. My conversation with Coach after practice had shown me that wasn't entirely true. Ally might think the position is easily her cousin's, but tomorrow, I'd line up to hit outside and fuel this fire that was building between me and Ally.

Vanessa embraced questions and praise about her new opportunity yet humbly noted her mistakes.

"I have a lot of work to do," she said. "My serve receiving for one. And I have to get the rhythm of the rotation."

"It's the beginning of the season. You'll adjust. Keep playing hard," Ally told her, and the team nodded in agreement.

The good ghost stories and s'mores we enjoyed around the fire couldn't trump the fact that we were competitors. I imagined how the team might react the next day at practice when I lined up to hit outside. None of my imaginings led to bonding or laughter. If I agreed to Coach's change of my position—not sure I really had a choice in the matter—but if I really went for it with everything I had, that meant shaking things up on the team even more when we were working so hard to get settled.

I studied the faces of the girls quickly becoming my friends. A sadness crawled into my soul. I already knew what I was going to do.

Like I said—we were all competitors.

CHAPTER NINE

IN MY WHOLE LIFE, I'D NEVER SUBMITTED A SCIENCE project or assignment without talking to Harris first. Over time, his advice had expanded from scientific matters to other topics. And when he'd needed to successfully shoot a basket or serve a volley-ball to pass gym, I'd helped him for two straight weeks, so he could conquer both. He had refused to risk his GPA by only learning one.

Maybe the fact we'd been turning to each other for years was the reason that when Chandra dropped me off, I left my bag on the porch and pushed through the broken pickets of our fence. I found him in the corner of his yard under a spotlight with a plethora of power tools and glassware in front of him.

"Harris! So glad you're here. I have a question. A couple questions actually."

"I'm a scientist, so I have lots of answers." He held a Dremel in one hand and noise-canceling headphones in the other. He wore his heavy-duty mask and goggles.

In other words, as expected, he was back to the heavy stuff.

"You're a wonderful scientist," I said, hoping flattery worked with geniuses, "but I'm asking because you're a boy."

He lifted his goggles. "You're asking me about a boy?"

I nodded. "You are a boy, right?"

He turned away from me and organized his tools. Twice.

"Is that okay...? I thought since we're friends."

He faced me with a forced smile on his face. "No. Yes. Of course, we're friends. Ask whatever."

Maybe his experiment had gone wrong. Maybe his stepmom was on his case. Maybe his odd behavior had nothing to do with me. Maybe...the hypotheses might never end.

"You're sure?" I asked.

"I'm sure."

I told him about Square. And Sam. And how she'd said I should go for it, that she was fine with me dating him, but my instincts totally said the opposite. After I pleaded my case and revealed the sordid tale, Harris simply said, "Square Weaver? Seriously?"

"You are no help whatsoever."

Maybe I shouldn't have talked to Harris about boys. What experience did he have with girls anyway?

"What are you talking about?" a voice said from behind me.

I spun to see my little sister Lily, pen and notebook in hand, hovering in the shadows. "That's a little creepy."

"Don't worry," Harris whispered. "She just came through the fence. Your secret boyfriend is still secret."

"He's not my—"

"I'm assisting Harris on his latest experiment." Lily smiled, her braces reflecting the spotlights on Harris's garage. "It's absolutely brilliant—and something Mom and Dad would never let me try at home."

I scowled at Harris.

"She'll be completely safe."

Lily giggled. "We're making fire tornados!"

"Harris!"

He had the decency to look slightly embarrassed. "It sounds more exciting than it is."

"The first step is cutting the vases," Lily said.

"You're cutting glass?"

He repositioned his goggles. "The key is to keep water on the glass at all times."

"You're mixing water and power tools?"

He shrugged as if that was a perfectly logical thing to do.

"And to buy cheap glass at the dollar stores," Lily said.

"Because I will break at least half of these." Harris pointed to the table of vases next to him.

The duo alternated sentences explaining the experiment. With each detail they revealed and each smile they shared, I turned greener and greener until I feared I might resemble Oscar the Grouch inside and out. What was wrong with me? Lily collaborated with Harris all the time, but I guess I never witnessed it before. How naturally they worked together. How much fun they had. How my little sister belonged more than I did.

"Maybe I should go."

"No!" Harris said. "Stay. We're almost ready."

Part of me wanted to, but Harris already had an assistant.

"Mel, are you okay?" Harris asked.

"Tired. That's all. Good luck with your experiment."

"You really don't have to go. I can set up the hammock over here for you. You have to see these fire tornadoes. They're gorgeous."

"Harris, let her go already!" Lily pleaded. "Science is waiting."

I waved to them and slipped through the fence. Back on our property, I leaned against the wooden boards and listened to the two of them. Discussing calculations and chemicals. Linked in a space that I didn't belong. I belonged on the court where I could compete and push myself to my physical limits.

Or I could if I made varsity.

Or maybe the older outside hitters would despise me, and I'd never belong.

***

THE NEXT MORNING AT PRACTICE, I EXPECTED—OR maybe feared—Coach would announce I'd be hitting outside. Maybe with music. And purple-and-black confetti shooting into the air. And backup dancers.

She said nothing.

And no music, streamers, or dancers. Before lunch, we ran the bleachers overlooking the empty football field. We treaded water in the swimming pool. We sprinted, dove, and sprawled. I considered standing in the middle of the team with their lunch-meat sandwiches and potato chips, shouting, "I'm going to hit outside!"

I didn't.

I nibbled my orange slices and grapes and tried to ignore the insecurities inching closer with every tick of the clock. The first afternoon drill would be hitting.

We lined up in three rows—one outside, one middle, and one back—on either side of the net. The coaches threw underhand balls to Ally on one side and Chandra on the other. They set them, and the hitters worked on their approaches, jumps, swings, and timing.

Julia hit high sets, quick sets, short sets. If I had any hope of filling the hole she'd left behind, I'd need to perfect my timing on them all.

I started in the middle line on Chandra's side of the net and crushed a quick set to the right side. I jogged to the back of the middle line and watched Molly Mattola in the outside position. She waited for the set a few feet out of bounds, roughly behind the ten-foot line. In the middle, I usually approached the net and was already in the air before Chandra released the ball on quick sets. But outside, Molly waited until Chandra released the set. She eyed the ball, approached, and jumped.

Waiting on the set would be the toughest part.

Or maybe not. After a few more observations, I realized as a middle, my job was to jump and be ready to swing. It was the setter's job to put the ball in my hand. Outside hitters had to adjust their approach and jump, especially if the set was off. Maybe adjusting to the set would be more challenging than training myself to actually wait for it.

"Melanie," Coach called after I hit four more sets at middle. She tilted her head toward the outside line. A mix of anxiety and excitement bubbled up my throat like a hiccup. The drill continued. The girls paid me no attention. Until I lined up behind Nikki Knight outside. Then the heads turned. Chandra—always up for some good intrigue—raised her eyebrows at me.

I did my best at giving her a pleading look and hoped she interpreted it as *Give me a good set, like the best set you've ever pushed into the air. Please.*

Coach threw the ball to Chandra. I checked my position. A few feet off the court. Roughly at the ten-foot line. Chandra stepped into the set and pushed it high and outside. A good set. I rounded my approach toward the net and exploded into my jump. I swung at the ball and connected with a loud slap. My arm came down fast and hard. I wanted to crush the ball. And I did. Right into the net.

I might have heard a snicker.

Pretending it didn't get to me, I fetched the ball and ran it back to Coach. I got in line again to hit outside. On the next set, I didn't wait as long. I rushed toward the net quicker, jumped, and landed before I touched the ball. That time, I crushed it out of bounds.

Too slow.

I'd get it. Eventually. I recovered the ball, delivered it to Coach, and got back in line.

Next hit: cross court, out of bounds by inches. I was getting closer.

I theorized and adjusted on each approach. Some of the hits landed in play, but they weren't well placed or strong enough to be guaranteed kills.

Coach called for a water break when I finally felt a rhythm to the process.

"Chandra," I whispered. "Can you stay out with me?"

Her shoulders slumped. "Like, give up my break?"

I nodded.

She held the ball between her forearm and hip and sighed. "Ashley! Toss me some balls."

I lined up outside. Ashley tossed. Chandra set, and I exploded into my approach. The ball landed hard cross court.

It could have been harder.

I lined up again. Deep middle.

And again. Cross court. I'd love to hit down the line, but that would take more practice. For now, I decided to work on my cross court hits. We went on like that for minutes. So long that I didn't realize a few of my teammates ran around the gym, fetching the balls, so Ashley could keep tossing, and I could keep hitting.

My confidence grew with each well-placed hit. I swung harder. And harder. And began to feel the beauty of the outside-hitting position, the power position on the court. Crushing a set as hard as you could felt—wow!

Coach blew the whistle. I smacked Chandra's and Ashley's hands to thank them.

"Next time, you do the tossing, and I get to hit," Ashley said.

I smiled at her. "Deal."

We rounded up the stray balls and hustled to the huddle. I might have imagined it, but I swore Coach nodded at me ever so slightly, the corner of her mouth curved into a barely-there smile. I felt a tug in my chest at the prospect of making her proud.

We moved into team scrimmage, and Coach called for Vanessa to line up outside on the varsity court. To avoid the confusion in the rotation, she moved Molly back to the serving position, and Vanessa claimed Julia's former left-front position.

My growing pride and confidence sank to the hardwood like a mistimed dive, one that left you on the ground to wallow in shame.

"Don't sweat it," Chandra whispered to me. "No way Vanessa can fill Julia's shoes."

Even if she couldn't, that didn't mean I could.

Or that I'd get the chance to try.

CHAPTER TEN

ALLY CORNERED ME IN THE LOCKER ROOM AFTER practice. "What was that?"

I closed my locker. "What?"

She pointed toward the gym. "Out there. Do you honestly think that you're going to change your position and suddenly be God's gift to this team?"

Was there a right answer to that question? None of my teammates were in the same row of lockers as us, but the silence in the room told me they had all stilled in their respective spots to listen.

"Good. Because there are seniors and juniors ahead of you for this position."

I wanted to say that playing varsity wasn't like waiting at Disney World. The position wasn't given to the next in line. If the juniors and seniors wanted it, they needed to work for it. Like I was. By the time I fought my burning anger and had any hope of formulating my thoughts into cohesive sentences, Sam appeared and stepped between us.

"Ally, cool it." She turned her back to her co-captain and smiled at me. "Nice job today, Melanie."

Ally looked like she'd shoved a fistful of Sour Patch Kids into her mouth.

"Thanks." *I think.*

"There's this party tonight," Sam said.

"Sam, she doesn't want to—" Ally started, but Sam interrupted her.

"The team goes together for bonding."

I nearly dropped my gym bag at the exhausting possibility of more bonding, especially if that bonding meant spending time with Ally, who so clearly adored me. "No offense, but didn't we do that yesterday making the shirts?"

Ally crossed her arms. "You wanna be on varsity, yet this is the effort we get?"

So now she wanted me to go? Maybe if I smacked a locker as hard as I could against the side of my face, I could excuse myself from any more bonding.

Sam held up her hand to silence Ally and turned to me. "Mel, we're not like most teams. We rise to the top because we work our asses off all year long, and when we get on that court during season, we play like sisters."

"You have sisters, right?" Ally said, arms crossed.

"Yeah." Although I wasn't sure the team would appreciate the sibling dynamic between Elle, Lily, and me being modeled on the court.

"Then you should know what we mean," she said.

Theoretically.

"Chandra will pick you up." Sam ushered Ally away. "See you tonight."

***

AFTER A MUCH-NEEDED AFTER-PRACTICE NAP, I LAID in bed brainstorming ways to get out of going to the party. The fact I knocked on Elle's door at seven o'clock for style advice clearly indicated the failure of said brainstorming. She was watching virtual tours for a few colleges she still hoped to see before making her decision. Sometimes I forgot she'd be gone in a year. Sometimes I liked the idea.

Sometimes I didn't.

"We mustn't lurk in doorways," she said in her best Ursula the

Sea Witch voice. "It's rude..."

"One might question your upbringing," I said.

We'd watched *The Little Mermaid* daily for five months solid when we were four and six, respectively. Ever since, we'd pull lines from the film—and other favorites—to entertain ourselves. Her quoting the movie now and the fact I needed her help to get through the night—and probably through high school overall—had me on the side of not liking the fact she was going away soon.

I sat on the edge of her bed. "I need help."

"And all I need...is your voice."

"Elle, seriously."

"It's a small price to pay." She waited for me to respond. I didn't. "Fine. What do you need?"

"There's this party tonight."

She nodded. "At Ben Jones's house."

"How'd you know?"

She rolled her eyes. "Don't insult me. You need clothes without athletic labels on them."

"Apparently." Maybe I should have kept more from the bags my mom had brought home. Instead, I'd told her to return everything other than the dress I'd worn to Julia's party.

"Accessories? And shoes?"

"Gotta wear shoes."

"And makeup?"

"Let's not get carried away."

Elle pulled dresses, skirts, shorts, frilly things, sequined things, and flowing things from her closet and mixed and matched them on the bed. The moment I thought something might not be half bad, she shook her head at that very outfit and shuffled the pieces again. It was like a game board, and I had no chance of winning.

She settled on a deep purple mini dress. That was tight. Like, way tight.

"I can't wear that."

She slumped forward. "Why spend every day working out in the gym if you're not going to show it off?"

"To get better at volleyball."

She threw the dress back onto the bed. "Fine. What about this one?" She held up a jean skirt and a white tank with a navy-and-tur-quoise geometric-shape pattern.

"That shirt looks kinda tiny. You sure it will fit me?"

Elle threw me the clothes. "Try it on, and we'll see."

It. Did. Not. Fit.

"Look at those abs!" She pushed me in front of her full-length mirror and pulled my hands back. They'd been covering all the bare skin at my waist.

"Where's the rest of this shirt?"

"Material shortage last year. That's why crop tops became a thing."

That didn't sound remotely believable.

"You look good, Mel. Embrace it!"

I rested my hands on my hips and studied myself in the mirror. My abs did look incredible. A flat stomach with lines of definition down either side. And the flowing crop top made my waist look tiny.

"It's not bad," I said. But could I actually wear it in front of other human beings?

"Think it over. And sit." Elle pushed me to the bench seat of her vanity and rounded up a collection of thin and thick brushes, circles and squares of shimmering powders, and liquids.

"Close your eyes."

I obeyed, debating whether I should have knocked on my sister's door. Not that I distrusted her skills. She stunned. Always. But that didn't exactly mean I wanted to look the same.

"So I hear that Square Weaver was flirting with you after football practice yesterday."

My eyes shot open, and Elle nearly poked me with a pencil.

"Close!"

I obeyed. "Where did you hear that?"

"Is it true?"

I thought about it. The day before, I'd been so concerned my flirting was meek that I overlooked the fact *he* was flirting with *me*. "I guess he was."

"What do you mean you guess? Did he or did he not take your phone and put his number in it?"

I caught myself before I nodded my way to a zigzag charcoal line across my face. "Yes."

"Respect, Mel. Square's hot."

I envisioned his smile. "Yes. He is."

Harris hadn't been any help, but maybe Elle would know whether Sam's encouragement to go out with Square had been genuine.

"Open."

I did, and Elle tilted her head to the side. At first, I thought she was studying her handiwork, but she said, "Be careful, okay. He's a good guy, but he has a past."

"Don't we all."

"First of all, no. You don't."

She wasn't lying.

"His," she continued, "is with an unsettling ex-girlfriend. I know enough about the situation to say with certainty that he's not a virgin, and she's extra with jealousy."

Oh. The sentence was too jam-packed to process.

"You're still young," Elle said. "And new at all this. I want you to be prepared for what you're facing dating a senior like Square."

I closed my eyes and hid behind the guise of wanting to let my sister finish my makeup. "Consider me prepared," I said, although I felt anything but.

Maybe going to the party wasn't such a good idea.

My phone buzzed on top of the dresser. Elle tilted it, so she could see the screen. "Chandra says she'll be here in ten minutes."

Maybe I didn't have a choice. "Are you done?"

"Take a look."

I stood in front of the mirror and studied the reflection. I looked like...Elle. Except for my hair, which was twisted up into a clip.

"You like your makeup?"

I shrugged. The eyeliner was a little bold for my tastes. So was the purple shadow.

"Nothing like a glowing endorsement," Elle said with her straightener in hand. "Sit back down."

She alternated spraying my hair and running it through the straightener. The result was shining silk.

"You need some layers," she said.

"I'll get right on that. Between workouts and mandatory bonding sessions."

She combed my hair one last time and tossed me a pair of flip-flops from the closet. At least her choice in shoes had been merciful.

"Hey, sis," I called from the doorway. "Thanks."

She nodded. "Mel?"

"Yeah?"

She turned her back to me, ran one hand through her hair, and popped the other onto her hip. "Don't underestimate the importance of...body language."

I couldn't deny the smile that crept onto my lips as I hustled down the stairs. My sister the sea witch. Totally bonkers, but you had to love her.

CHAPTER ELEVEN

THE PARTY WAS AT A FOOTBALL PLAYER'S CABIN IN the middle of the woods. Seriously, the roads we drove on the way there could have been lined with cardboard cutouts of horror movie serial killers, and they'd have been completely at home. With the windows open as we crept down the dirt road, we heard a mix of crickets and music. The large, rustic log cabin hid behind a row of trees along the street.

The team met in the front yard, which had been turned into a makeshift parking lot. No way was anyone getting out of there without the place turning into a monster-truck rally.

Maybe working a little too hard to make me feel at home with the team—not that it wasn't appreciated—Sam looped her arm in mine and led me through the open front door to a party jumping with dancing, shouting, and drinking. People sat on every piece of furniture. Cups and plates littered flat surfaces. The blur of faces moved too quickly and loudly for me to focus on one.

"Volleyball's in the house!" someone yelled, and the declaration was met with hoots and hollers. Guys appeared from the crowd to greet us, while some of the girls smiled, pretending to accept our rush of attention, and others outright glared. Now I knew why the team had insisted on crossing the threshold together.

Square appeared, sending a shiver of giddiness through me. As much as I reminded myself I shouldn't like him, something about Square refused logic. I swore Sam's arm tightened around mine. But only for a second. She leaned toward me and whispered, "Go say hi."

She released me, and I teetered on the edge before Ally grabbed my other arm and called for the team to follow her to the back yard. I waved to Square and followed the current my school of fish created through the crowd.

"We're here to bond with each other," Ally said once she successfully dragged us to the corner of the back yard. "Not to separate and hook up with guys."

"Unless you're planning to stick your tongue down my throat, that's not gonna work for me," Chandra said, and I totally loved her for it.

Ally, however, crossed her arms and glared.

"Seriously," Ashley asked, "why bring us to a party if we can't talk to other people?"

"You can talk to other people," Sam said at the same time Ally answered, "Because we have to be seen occasionally to keep up our community support."

How romantic.

A couple of football boys waved at Chandra before peeling off their shirts and shorts and running toward the creek in their underwear. She dropped her purse and peeled away her outer layers too, revealing a swimsuit underneath. "If this is all about volleyball, I'm about to go tread water."

A few of the other girls nodded.

"Get in some extra conditioning," Ashley added.

"Let them have fun," Sam said. "They deserve it."

"But we play a pickup game at this party every year."

"Play one in the creek," I suggested with a shrug. Ally's darkening eyes communicated my opinion was neither required nor desired.

After the girls disbursed, I felt a tap on my shoulder. Square wore camo cargo shorts and a faded red T-shirt. The shirt clung to his shoulders and biceps in a way that had excess saliva threatening to spill from my mouth.

"Soph," he said, "I haven't heard from you."

He said the nickname jokingly, but I preferred to hear him call me Melanie, not the moniker Chandra had assigned me. A name that pointed out I was younger than just about everyone I'd spent any time with lately, including him.

"I've only had your number for two days." And calling—even texting—him was a dangerous complication I tried my best to avoid.

He rubbed his shaved head from back to front. "You think I'm coming on too strong?"

Before I could answer, two girls I didn't recognize bumped me from behind. Square steadied me, but his strong hands couldn't protect me from the girl's beer cup pouring onto Elle's skirt.

I wiped away the excess liquid. "Watch it!"

Before I could blink, a blonde with angry eyes was in my face. "I know you aren't talking to me."

I wanted to tell her I was talking to her if she was the one who spilled beer on me, but my heart raced in a way that it never had before. With the exception of my sisters, nobody had ever gotten in my face like that. With such malice. My brain couldn't process a response, and my body stiffened as if ready to protect itself.

Square stepped between us. "Lacey, leave her alone."

"Aw. Does she need a big football player to fight her battles?"

"This isn't her battle. It's not even mine. It's yours. You should give it up."

Their exchange reminded me of Elle's warning. Best guess? Lacey equaled Square's jealous ex.

She glared at me one last time, and I wished for a brilliant one liner. A verbal slap in the face. Maybe it would come to me a day later. Clever me.

When she finally walked away, Square sighed deeply and looked up at the sky, a move he could have borrowed directly from my mother. He stared at the stars, which were totally brilliant away from the city's light pollution. I wondered if he was asking himself the same question I was: *Is it really worth it?*

"She's going to kill me," I said, trying to defuse the tension.

Finally, Square faced me. And lit that familiar spark. "Nah. She won't come near you again."

"I was talking about my sister. This is her skirt."

I gazed across the yard where Lacey watched with her friends. At least they appeared to be talking her down instead of riling her up. The fire and moonlight shone off the smooth, flawless skin of her athletic body.

I thought she might be a cross-country runner I'd seen around school. "She's gorgeous," I blurted. And felt immediately self-conscious for thinking it, let alone saying it aloud.

"Are we still talking about your sister?" Square asked.

"Yes!" Definitely.

"You're a terrible liar." Again, he ran his hand over his shaved head. "Wait here." He walked toward Lacey, spoke a few words, and turned back to me. Anyone with a fraction of intellect could read the anger on her face, but she did walk away.

"Sorry about that."

"No problem," I lied again, looking around the field for my teammates. I hoped they would back me up if things escalated. Maybe having intense Ally around wasn't so bad after all.

What was I saying? I could be stargazing from the hammock in my back yard, but instead I was at a party I didn't want to be at, wondering if a backyard brawl was in my future?

"You are so not calling me now, are you?" His lips curved into a frown, and I couldn't help but roll my eyes and laugh.

He tucked his hands into his pockets. "Can I get you a drink?"

The red cups everyone held taunted me: *Drink. Drink. Drink!*

Why was being social so hard?

"I don't really drink."

"No problem." He raised one finger telling me to wait there and slipped into a side door to the cabin. A few seconds later, he returned with options. A bottled water. A Capri Sun. Or Kool-Aid.

I took the water.

"Good choice. I'm not sure I was ready to share the Capri Sun."

"You're not going to drink that," I teased. They'd been Lily's incomparable favorite—at the age of seven.

"Don't peer pressure me, Melanie Corwin." He grinned that beautiful grin, peeled open the straw, and poked it into the foil pouch. With an obnoxious slurp, he chugged the juice. By the time he drained and flattened the pouch, I couldn't stop giggling.

"You surprise me, Square."

"Let's hope that doesn't change." He tossed his trash and rubbed his hands together. "Now that I've had my refreshment, I need you to teach me how to play volleyball."

"You're serious?"

"I always wanted to learn. It's like when you're a kid and you keep tapping a balloon in the air to keep it from touching the ground."

"Exactly like that. In the same way American football is actually soccer."

"Hey! Balloon volleyball was my game back in the day."

"Sorry," I teased. "I left all my balloons at home."

He grabbed a volleyball from a plastic storage box nearby. "Let's do this, Soph."

"Don't."

His expression turned serious.

"Don't call me Soph."

"I'm sorry."

"Don't be." Warmth poured into my cheeks like an overflowing volcano that was just getting started. Lacey's angry face flashed in my mind—a warning not to speak another word. "I like when you say my name."

Warning officially ignored.

Square's smile spread across his fine face so slowly that it could have been a series of pictures. Gorgeous, social media–worthy pictures.

"You like when I say your name? *Melanie?*"

I covered my face as the volcano of my embarrassment erupted so massively everyone on the continent should have taken cover.

He pulled my hands away. "Okay. I quit. I'm just playing." He held the ball out to me. "So lessons, or what?"

I took it from him and turned it over in my hands. "Let me guess? You want to know how to hit?"

"Don't go imposing your stereotypes on me, Melanie. Because I'm a big, Black dude I want to hit things and be all aggressive."

I might have been mortified at offending him, if he hadn't been smiling. That smile spoke of flirtatious brilliance. "Aren't you a linebacker whose primary purpose is to crush anyone with the ball?"

"You want me to teach you how to tackle?"

That grin. Oh my gosh. Nothing on the planet could have been redder than my face.

"I thought I was the one teaching the lesson?" I managed.

He shrugged. "Maybe another time."

I actually fanned myself. And of course, he laughed.

"What do I need to know about volleyball?"

"For starters, it's not like hitting a balloon in the air." Which was how the guys at school played in gym. They used their palms to hit the ball—both hands at the same time, which any ref would call as a double hit. The guys got away with it because they didn't know better. Not that gym class was meant as a place of learning or anything. "The only time you can touch the ball with your palm is when you're hitting or serving. And you can never hit the ball with both palms at once."

"I see Ally Malone doing that all the time."

"If she hears you say that she will kill you."

He raised his hands in surrender. "Enlighten me."

I selected a panel on the ball and framed it. The index finger and thumb on my left hand formed an L, and the fingers on my right mirrored it. With that starting point, I showed Square how the rest of my fingertips formed around the ball. "Now look at my palms." I lifted the ball, so he could see. "Are they touching the ball?"

His eyes widened. "No way! Let me try."

After several times repositioning his fingers, while I tried to ignore the tingles of his touch, Square managed to shape the ball—the most basic lesson I'd learned as a kid going to summer camp at the YMCA.

"Hell yeah!"

His enthusiasm was adorable.

"You want the next step?"

"Let's do this."

I stood next to him. "Legs shoulder width apart. Bring the ball to your hairline."

He raised an eyebrow at me...toward his razor-shaved head.

"Okay, where your hairline would be if you had hair."

"You're lucky I don't have a frail ego." He lifted the ball toward his forehead.

"Looking good, Square!" someone shouted from across the field.

"If you're not learning, you're not living!" Square yelled back to a chorus of chuckles. "Next?"

I showed him how to step and push the ball upward. Once he got the motion down, I had him throw the ball to me a few times.

"How you feeling?"

"I'm a natural."

"Okay, Natural. Let's step up our game." I set the ball to him, and he immediately slapped it back to me with the palms of his hands.

"No! That's a carry."

"I can do better."

"Let's hope so," I said. From that moment on, the laughter didn't stop. I tossed to him, set to him, practically dropped the ball into his waiting hands, and each time, his palms made a loud smacking sound against the ball. Sometime along the way, the thought struck me that I was there to bond with my teammates, but I had no idea where they were.

Part of me didn't care.

A bubble made of equal parts the sport I loved and a guy who made me laugh enveloped me, and the last thing I wanted was to leave it for complete strangers in a packed party.

"Soph! Let's go!" Chandra called.

The bubble popped.

"It's okay," Square said. "We'll pick up this lesson another time."

"Between now and then you need to practice. Like, lots of practice."

He grinned. "I might need some tutoring."

"You might need to skip football practice and really invest in shaping the ball for hours on end."

"I'll talk to Coach about it."

We laughed again. So. Much. Laughing.

"Soph!"

I sighed. "Sorry."

"Don't apologize. I had a great time."

My heart resembled the sound of the whole team slamming their volleyballs against the gym walls to warm up their arms. Loud. Incessant. "Me too." I raised my now empty bottle. "Thanks for the drink."

"Any time."

I turned to go, but Square grabbed my wrist and pulled me to him. My chest smacked against his with a *humph*. Those dark brown eyes dug into me as a smile pulled at his lips. Our mouths were inches apart. Square pressed his warm cheek against mine and lingered there. "Use my number. *Melanie*." He brushed his full lips against my cheek. Slow. With perfect pressure. Which had me tempted to turn my head and press my mouth against his.

"Soph!"

"Good night." Square stepped backward, and I stumbled forward as if I might fall face first into the grass without his support. I righted myself and waved. He backpedaled, that smoldering gaze of his following me as I joined Chandra with an immovable smile on my face.

CHAPTER TWELVE

MY FIRST SERVE CRASHED INTO THE NET. SO DID MY
second. Chandra's tire had gone flat on the drive home the night
before, and by the time her older brother had helped us change it,
an hour had passed. She'd dropped me off last, and despite being
exhausted, I'd laid awake staring at my ceiling as if the curves in the
plaster had been Square's face.

Square Weaver.

Gorgeous and adorable at the same time. So much fun. Incredibly
cool. Attractive enough to crush my better judgment where his ex was
concerned and completely distract me from the goal I'd been working
toward for months—earning playing time on this team.

If the late night had affected anyone else, I couldn't see it. Ally especially practiced like a pro. And managed to point out when I didn't.

"Everyone on varsity has a jump serve. You're not even hitting
your topspin. You should probably work on that."

We were never gonna get along.

I collapsed onto the hardwood during water break.

"You okay out there, Soph?" Chandra asked. "Looks like you're
struggling."

"Probably stayed up all night thinking about that fine football
player," Ashley teased, but she was partially right.

"Guess that was a bad idea then," Ally said.

Chandra shook her head. "Ignore her," she whispered.

"I'm tired," I said. "Too much practicing and team bonding."

She sipped her water. "I'm used to the late nights."

I wasn't. And I didn't think I ever wanted to be. I stretched my legs and took a few deep breaths. Only one more hour of practice for the week. I could get through it. The problem? That hour was scrimmaging, when I needed to put together all my skills and perform at my best to impress in game situations.

Ugh.

Coach called us onto the court. I started back right in the serving position.

"JV serves first," Coach called.

She threw me the ball. At the serving line, I made the mistake of looking at Ally. She issued a challenge with her eyes. It could have meant *You should leave Square alone.* Or *You're a measly sophomore, not good enough to compete with us.* Or *I dare you to serve to me.*

Or any number of things.

I bounced the ball twice.

"You got it, Soph," Chandra called.

I wasn't so sure but serving required confidence. "You got this," I whispered to myself.

I tossed. Swung. And crack! The ball soared over the net. Phew. I hustled into my position on the court, but Coach blew the whistle.

"Foot fault," she yelled.

What? I studied the end line as if it were going to move. I had never foot faulted. Never.

Chandra slapped my hand. "Shake it off. Give me a good pass."

I didn't.

I shanked Ally's serve into the bleachers. Chandra picked up the second serve and called for help on the set. Olivia set the ball to Nikki outside, and the volley began. Muscle memory took over, but my moves weren't quite on no matter how much I wanted them to be. My feet dragged on my approaches, and I crushed as many hits into the net as serves. Or I hit them out of bounds. Or so tentatively that the varsity easily picked them up. With each disappointing swing, I feared Coach Medina regretted moving me to outside.

I feared I regretted it even more.

After practice, I packed my things and bailed before my teammates shed their knee pads. Ally jogged out of the gym behind me, causing the words *That can't be good* to flutter through my head.

"What are you doing?" she said like I was skipping out mid-practice.

"Going home to rest. What are *you* doing?"

"Don't be cute. Who do you think you are? You take away Sam's crush even though I told you she liked him. What kind of person does that?"

I opened my mouth to answer that she needed to mind her own business, but she cut me off.

"And now you want the chance Vanessa has worked toward for years."

"Maybe I've worked toward it for years, too."

She crossed her arms. "By the looks of today, you have more work to do."

"Or maybe you shouldn't make everyone on the team go to parties when they should be resting."

"Sounds like an excuse to me."

"What is your problem with me?" I said.

"I'm the one with the problem? Is that what Elle told you?"

"What does Elle have to do with this?"

"Please. I know you're a Corwin, but you don't get whatever you want, princess. Life doesn't work that way." She stomped away. Elle had warned me about Square and his ex-girlfriend, but she'd never said anything about Ally being a potential enemy.

I needed solitude and sleep, but I had to talk to Elle first. The second I got home, I knocked on her bedroom door.

"Come in?"

I poked my head inside. She was sorting through the clothes in her dresser.

"Oh, Melanie. Good. I have some stuff for Chandra." She pointed to a trash bag on her bed. "And since you're branching out from Adidas and Nike, this bag is for you. Also, thought it might keep you from rifling through my clothes when I'm not home." She tossed me a massive trash bag.

I cringed. "Sorry."

"Don't be. I'm glad to see you trying new things."

Hmm. My sister. The gracious one? Maybe I wasn't the only sister feeling nostalgic about Elle going away to college soon. I set the bag in the hall. "Thanks. This should get me through my twenties."

She laughed. "That's what you think. Just wait. You going out tonight?"

"No! I am not going out ever again."

"Did you drink too much?"

"Are you kidding? Me? Not to mention I'm in the middle of volleyball season!"

She shrugged. "That's usually what people say after they had a rough night."

I sat on the edge of her bed. "Can I talk to you about something?"

She joined me. "Is everything okay?"

"Ally Malone has been on my case a lot lately."

"Ugh. That girl."

"Yeah. So she mentioned that I'm not a princess, and I don't get everything I want just because I'm a Corwin. And your name came up. Anything I should know?"

She rubbed her face in her hands and took a deep breath. "I really hoped this wasn't going to be a problem. She used to date Josh. Forever."

"What do you mean forever? Did he cheat on her with..."

"Melanie! Have some respect for your older sister!"

My body flushed with guilt. "Sorry."

"They dated two years in middle school and ninth and tenth grade."

"Four years?"

"Yep."

"Wow. That's intense."

"They broke up months before we started dating. She acts like she's over it, but sometimes she does stupid things. Like, one time at a party, she totally came on to him."

"Seriously?"

Elle sighed. "It got ugly."

"Did you hit her?"

"Close."

"Sheesh."

"I really didn't think that she would take all of that out on you. She's dated other people since, but I guess Josh will always be her first love or whatever."

"But he's yours too," I said.

She smiled in that adorable, swoony way she always did when Josh was involved. "Yeah. He is."

I headed to my bed thinking about high school relationships. Lacey clearly didn't want to let Square go. Ally still had feelings for Josh. For two people to like each other at the same time and continue liking each other through all the drama of life sounded more like a miracle than anything natural. I couldn't decide if Square and I could be that kind of miracle or not.

Talking to Elle put the Ally situation in perspective. Ally wouldn't particularly like me because of my last name, but when she saw me talking to Square, it was like Elle talking to Josh all over again. Like I was taking something that didn't belong to me. Not that I agreed with her. She and Josh had broken up before Elle started dating him, and Sam had told me I should give Square a shot. I wasn't doing anything wrong.

But at least Ally made a little more sense to me. I'd figure out a way to deal with her after I got some rest.

CHAPTER THIRTEEN

SATURDAY AFTERNOON UNDER THE GUISE OF YET AN-
other team-bonding experience, the volleyball team poured into the
gym for a mandatory weekend workout. The original plan had apparently been to meet at Julia's for some conditioning in the pool and a
pickup game on the sand court, but since Julia was no longer on the
team, that was not happening.

Sam assigned us thirty minutes of cardio. "I don't care what machine you do. Just go hard."

I headed for the elliptical nestled in the corner, but when I reached
for the handle, Ally set her water bottle on the tray on the opposite
side of the machine.

"You know what," I said. "Take this. I'll grab another one."

She eyed me suspiciously. "Thanks."

I picked the elliptical as far from Ally as possible, between Chandra and Ashley.

"You better be ready to work," Ashley said. "I have a few ice
cream sandwiches to burn off."

"A few?" Chandra said.

"Don't judge," Ashley argued. "They're making the ones with
pumpkin custard now."

"With the snickerdoodle cookies?" Chandra asked.

"Yes!"

"We're going there after the workout."

Ashley covered her face with her hands. "No!"

"Sounds good to me," I said with a shrug.

We hopped onto our ellipticals and took turns challenging each other. Ashley made us sprint. Chandra pushed us to the edge, maxing out the machines' resistance. I rotated sprints and climbs. By the time we hit thirty minutes, the three of us collapsed onto the floor.

"We earned an ice cream sandwich," Chandra said.

Ashley and I grunted agreement.

I rolled onto my stomach and pushed my shoulders up to stretch my back. Across the room, a shaggy-haired boy in the free-weight section caught my eye. He looked like Harris. Like, exactly.

Harris worked out science problems, not his muscles—or lack thereof. But the more I watched, I became certain. Harris Fullerton was working out. At the gym. With free weights.

I forced my muscles to support my weight, stood, and wobbled over to see the lanky scientist amid muscled athletes for myself. Lying on his back, he boosted some impressive skull crushers.

I waited for him to finish his reps and called his name. He jumped as if the bar were about to fall onto his face, although his spotter had already cleared it for him.

"Sorry. Didn't mean to startle you. I had no idea you worked out here."

"I don't. I mean I do today, but for an experiment." Standing taller than me, he looked around as if for someone in particular.

He'd trained me well over the years. The empirical data my brain had collected in the last few minutes had me questioning his actions.

"What kind of experiment involves lifting weights?"

"Analyzing the effectiveness of various protein shake powders." He pointed to the collective of girls wearing Iron Valley volleyball shirts and black spandex. "I think your people are waiting for you."

He crossed his arms. For the first time in—maybe forever—I looked at them. They were more muscular than I'd remembered. I always saw Harris as a lanky scientist. Somewhere along the way, he might have grown up. Still, muscles didn't appear overnight, no matter what protein shakes he downed.

"Melanie, let's go," Ally called, probably because Sam was too kind to interfere with a friendly conversation on what was actually my own time—a Saturday afternoon.

"I have to go. Maybe I'll see you tonight?"

His eyebrows raised in interest. "No date with the big football player?"

"Actually, he left for camp today. He'll be gone a week, so if we do go out, it will have to wait."

Harris smiled. "I have an epic experiment planned."

"I bet you do."

We said our goodbyes, and I rejoined the girls.

"Was that the weird science freak with the YouTube channel, Henry something?" Ally asked, raising my heart rate more quickly than the elliptical ever could.

"No. His name is Harris, and he's not a freak. He's a genius."

Ally rolled her eyes. "Whoever he is, he needs a haircut." She walked ahead, leading the group to the ab circuit, but I wasn't letting the opportunity go. I caught up to her and tapped her on the shoulder.

"Ally, I need to talk to you."

She spun with a dramatic sigh.

"Listen, I know you have history with Josh and my sister, but that's history. And it has nothing to do with me."

She squinted at me like I was much farther away than the two feet I stood in front of her.

"I'm here to work hard and compete, and it would mean a lot to me if you let go of the other stuff and acknowledged that."

"Would it?"

"Yes."

She spun on the heels of her pristine white Nikes and ordered the team to get into position for our ab workout.

"That was a good effort," Chandra whispered from her spot next to me.

"You think it will help?"

"Can't hurt," Ashley said. "She's always been difficult, but since Julia bailed, she's in rare form. I wondered if Julia had dulled her edges. Guess now we know."

If I had to make a guess about anything, it would be about how much more of Ally I could take. Not much.

"Do you think if I stopped talking to Square—"

"No," Chandra said immediately. "No. Square is hot. He likes you. You like him. Sam said she's cool with it. Ally has nothing to say about it."

I wasn't sure. My skills navigating the social scene of high school sucked.

"She's right," Ashley said.

"Thanks," I managed.

My teammates lined up on the floor. We leg lifted, scissor kicked, crunched, and bridged until my back and abs cried. Literally. Cried.

"Hitters," Sam called, and we hustled around her. Or pretended to hustle with the little energy we had left. Ally headed in a different direction with Chandra.

"Help me," Chandra mouthed. Ashley waved to her, and we both laughed.

On yoga mats, Ally and Chandra started a repertoire of fingertip pushups.

"Ouch," Ashley wrapped her arm around my shoulders. "You know, Melanie. You surprised me."

I was afraid to ask, but I did. "How exactly?"

"I always thought you were kind of full of yourself. Chandra said you were cool, but..." Her voice trailed off, but a few seconds later, she added. "Sorry. That sounded better in my head."

"I know that feeling well."

"I meant it as a compliment."

"Thanks," I said, feeling like I'd managed to make three friends on the team—Chandra, Sam, and now Ashley. At least that was something.

Our group worked with the trainer, who happened to be a friend of Sam's, on exercises designed to improve our vertical jumps. Jumping with resistance bands. Calf raises. Squats super set into standing jumps. Box jumps on the plyometric pad, which I was pretty sure served as a torture device in at least a few countries.

After that workout, we wanted rest more than ice cream.

"Next time," Chandra said, and Ashley and I agreed.

I headed home, turned off my cell phone, and shut it in my top dresser drawer for good measure. No more drama. No more messages. No more workouts.

Just. Sleep.

***

THE REST OF THE WEEKEND PASSED WITH LITTLE EX-
citement, which suited me fine. Monday morning, I hustled to practice, ready for a good week. That dream shattered pretty quickly. I got no varsity playing time during Monday's team scrimmage. Or Tuesday. Or Wednesday. Ally ignored me. She worked with Vanessa during water breaks the same way I'd worked with Chandra the week before. I didn't dare join them and ask for sets too. I'd asked Ally to drop her vendetta against Elle. Was this her giving up causing me trouble? Or should I keep my guard up because this was some weird plot?

So. Much. Drama!

It twisted me in knots—the kind highly trained military officers tied. I hit the ball into the net, lost focus on defense, and even missed serves. Harris had suggested I try to be like Elle—working hard at her sport but managing a social life at the same time.

I'd failed.

Chandra and Ashley headed to the ice cream shop after practice Wednesday, but I passed. I couldn't bring myself to take off my knee pads and rise from the wooden bench in the locker room. Clearly, the shift—if you could call it that—to outside hitter hadn't been worth it. Coach wasn't going to play me, and I didn't blame her. If my hits fell inbounds, they floated to the ground like gentle taps, not the vicious kills varsity needed to be competitive.

"Melanie?"

I looked up to find Coach, car keys in hand and bag flung over her shoulder.

"Hey, Coach. I lost track of time. I'll get out of here, so you can lock up."

My knee pads slapped against the floor when I pulled them off. I shoved them into my locker and slipped into a pair of flip-flops. Coach lowered her bag to the floor and sat on the bench across from me.

"Anything you want to talk about?"

I couldn't bring my eyes to hers. How could I ask about playing time without showing my impatience? But should I lie when there was obviously something bothering me, and it was probably pretty obvious to her what it was?

I sighed. "I'm not sure how this whole switching-to-outside thing is going."

"It's still new."

I'd never remembered Coach being so short on words. It made me wonder if there was more she wasn't telling me. "Is there anything you want to talk about?" I asked with a weak smile.

She laughed. It reminded me of Julia's laugh. "I think you can do better."

My insides sank to the dusty locker room floor. Not that her words had been a surprise. I'd hoped that my insecurities were just that— mine. Knowing my coach felt that way too, well, it sucked.

"I suggested the switch to outside because I really thought you could be an asset to the team there, but in practices, I get the sense you haven't fully committed to it. Like you still see yourself as a middle. Your passing is strong, but I don't see that edge in your hitting or your serving, the one that made you really stand out those first few days of camp."

Her words were like truth daggers to the most sensitive parts of me.

"Do you think you can do better?"

I didn't trust my voice to demonstrate any kind of confidence, but my response had to be more than a noncommittal gesture. "I know I can."

Coach smiled. "Me too."

"So what do I do?"

She stood and waited for me to join her. "Find that edge that you had those first few days. Don't worry about my expectations or compare yourself to anyone else on the team. Got it?"

"Yes, Coach."

Theoretically.

Practically, I wasn't so sure.

CHAPTER FOURTEEN

COACH BELIEVED I COULD DO BETTER.

I believed it too. At least I wanted to.

Rising to Coach's challenge, I vowed to spend the evening refocusing on volleyball. I wouldn't wonder how Square was doing at football camp or whether Ally held some old grudge against me. I'd practice the timing of my approaches. Coach wanted more aggressive hitting. I'd find a way to give it to her.

Chandra had insisted her arms and fingers needed rest. I couldn't blame her, but that meant I needed to figure out how to set myself. To time my approach and ensure I connected with the ball at the height of my jump, the ball had to be high. By the time I would toss it and approach, the ball would hit the ground before I caught air. That left me with the slanted roof of our house. The system was simple. Launch the ball onto the roof. Begin my approach as it bounced down the slope. Jump and catch.

It took a few minutes, but I eventually got into a good rhythm.

"What would it take for you to stop throwing that ball onto the roof?" Elle asked from her reclined position on the back porch. To be fair, the ball had rolled toward her once and launched her glass of iced tea through the air.

"I need to practice."

"You practice all day, Mel."

I tossed the ball onto the roof again and got into position. "You can borrow my noise-canceling headphones." The ball bounced down the slope. I took my three-step approach and exploded into the air, catching the ball at the peak of my jump. I didn't want to swing. Without a net, I couldn't gauge the height of my arm, and the last thing I needed was to develop more bad habits.

My phone beeped. I grabbed a sip of water and read the screen. A text from Square! He must have gotten my number since I hadn't texted or called him. Points for dedication.

I need a Capri Sun right now, it read.

I smiled, but my thumbs hovered above the screen. Chandra and Ashley had insisted I wasn't in the wrong for talking to Square. On the one hand, if I ignored him, maybe I could focus on volleyball more. On the other, talking to him gave me a similar burst as killing a volleyball into the hardwood.

Me: Ice breaker?

Square: Basically.

Me: How's camp?

Square: Interesting.

Me: Your phone plan limit you to one-word responses?

Square: Look who's getting cute.

Me: I'm offended. I wasn't cute before?

Square: Getting cuter by the minute.

Oh my gosh. I was all out phone flirting with Square Weaver. And with a ridiculous grin on my face. So much for refocusing.

"I'd know that expression anywhere," Elle teased from across our back porch. I'd forgotten she was there. "You're texting a boy."

Her expertise was a double-edged sword. "You're right. I should be practicing."

"Melanie! Not everything in life is about practicing! Besides, I'd rather you text sexy Square Weaver than throw that ball onto the roof every ten seconds."

My phone beeped again.

Square: Gotta get the phones back to Coach. You free Saturday?

Why did I have to give Elle a hard time? She would know how to answer that text. I mean, there had to be a right answer! A nonchalant *sure*? Or was that too peppy? Maybe... *maybe*? No. Not *no*, but no on the *maybe*. Oh gosh. I was going to give myself a mental hernia.

Square: No rush, but I have two more minutes until I have to turn in my phone or run gassers. You literally have me sweating here.

Me: What's Saturday?

Square: I'm out of time. Have to tell you tomorrow. ;)

The big, bad linebacker used an emoticon? He was getting cuter by the minute too.

***

AFTER A FEW MORE TOSSES ONTO THE ROOF—AND ONE erratic ball that bounced over Elle's head—she lost her cool in a loud way.

Seconds later, Harris peeked through the fence. "Is it safe?"

"I'm not sure." I explained my need to practice, which contradicted with Elle's need to relax on the porch without a ball potentially smashing her face in at any moment.

"I can help," he said. Memories of teaching him basic athletic skills to pass gym class surfaced, and I wondered if Elle would be in more danger if Harris was the one releasing the ball. But he insisted.

So did Elle. "Leave, Melanie! Or so help me, I will puncture every volleyball in this house."

"She sounds like she means it," Harris said.

"I'll cut holes in all your skirts," I said.

"What will you wear when that fine football player takes you out?"

I glared in her direction.

"I thought he was away at football camp," Harris said.

"He is."

We squeezed through the broken pickets, and he cleared some space in his yard. I instructed him on how to throw and where to aim, and after a few thousand tries, he developed enough consistency to help. Sort of.

"I'm no expert—obviously." Harris bent his knees and threw the ball underhand. "But catching isn't a thing in volleyball, is it?"

I approached and caught the ball with two hands at the height of my jump. "I need a net that's an exact height of seven feet, four and one-eighths inches to ensure accuracy."

"I respect numerical accuracy."

"Exactly. So how's your latest experiment coming?"

Harris released the ball erratically. I had to hustle after it.

I realized I'd never texted him to apologize for missing it the other night after I completely forgot about it—essentially a double foul for a best friend. "I fell asleep Saturday. Sorry I missed it."

"Oh, that. No problem."

"What did you think I was talking about?"

"Nothing." He was the worst liar.

I held the ball between my arm and hip and watched him through squinted eyes as if looking closely would reveal his innermost thoughts. "Harris...are you hiding something from me?"

"What would I be hiding?" Again, Harris launched the ball poorly—even for him.

I didn't believe him, but Harris was a good friend. I did my best to ignore my niggling curiosity (and bruised ego) and respect that he would talk when he was ready.

He threw about a hundred more slightly helpful sets, and when the stars replaced the orangish-purple hue of the sunset sky, we said good night, and I headed for the shower knowing at least I'd tried.

***

THE NEXT MORNING, HARRIS KNOCKED ON MY BED-room door at 7:00 a.m.

"Go away." I pulled my pillow over my head. The one morning we didn't have practice because we had a scrimmage later in the day, and he woke me up early.

"No," he said. "I have a surprise for you."

"Does it involve blowing something up?"

"Not today. Let's go."

"Fine," I said. "Wait downstairs."

I changed out of my oversized T-shirt and brushed my teeth. Grinning like a clown working a children's party rather than the super serious scientist he was, Harris waited at the bottom of the stairs, bouncing on his toes. He dragged me to the back yard and through the fence.

He'd transformed his yard. No more science contraptions, power tools, random materials for a plethora of experiments. He'd cleaned and cleared everything. In place of the mess was a volleyball net.

"Harris!"

He lifted his hand to the tape. "It's exactly seven feet, four and one-eighths inches."

My stomach swelled with pride at his attention to detail and also maybe a little love for the coolest best friend/next-door neighbor/lab partner on the planet.

"Oh and look at this!" He pointed to the white lines he'd spray painted on the grass. "I measured the exact dimensions of the court. I didn't have room for both sides of the net, but I figured you could practice hitting on that side and see if the ball is in or out. I measured the diameter of the ball and painted accordingly."

"Which means...?"

"If you hear the thud of the ball hitting the grass, the ball was in, but if the ball smacks the fence before a thud, it was out."

"Very scientific."

He raised his arms like *What did you expect?* I ran and jumped into them. Fortunately, he caught me. I squeezed him so tightly that he might have needed oxygen. Not pulling away from the hug, I rested my head on his shoulder and absorbed his energy as if I might collapse without it. I'd gone into the season ready to work in the middle-hitting position. Ready to learn from Julia and the seniors. Now, not only did some of them not like me, but I'd abandoned my hitting strengths and my flawless motion on the court to try an entirely new position.

With only the possibility it could pay off.

"Thank you," I whispered.

He squeezed me. "Of course."

I wanted to say more. That it'd been tough. That his support meant a lot. But he didn't need me crying all over him. He'd redesigned his back yard to help me train when he'd needed the space for his experiments. And the details! Measuring the court and the net. Developing a system to help me determine if the ball was in or out. Not to mention obligating himself to throw the ball to me—unless...

I stepped backward and smiled. "Did you invent a machine that will throw balls to me?"

"Never satisfied."

"I didn't mean that."

He crossed his arms. "Good because I was planning to throw to you. Unless you have big dates with football players or too much other stuff to do besides hanging out with your best friend."

I looped my arm in his and headed for the pile of volleyballs he had under the net. "I've got nothing but time."

I coached Harris on where to stand, how to toss the ball, how high it should go, where it should land, and so on. He practiced the tosses until he mastered them, which didn't take surprisingly long.

"I have some experience with this sort of thing," he joked.

Much like I had experience measuring his experiment ingredients. Without Harris living next door, I would have failed science. Without me, gym class would have destroyed his perfect grade point average.

We worked together in silence. He tossed. I approached and hit. We listened for the thud of the ball hitting the grass or the smack of it crashing against the fence. Gradually, there was more thudding than smacking.

When my body told me it was time for a rest, we piled onto the hammock in my back yard and watched the clouds skate across the sky.

"You feeling better about your timing?"

"A little," I said. "We have a scrimmage today against Pacific, so I'll get to test it out for sure."

"The big rival?"

I groaned. "I'm so nervous."

"What time?"

"Three."

"I'll be there."

"Really?"

He wrapped an arm around me and kicked the ground, so the hammock swung.

"Wouldn't miss it, Mel."

CHAPTER FIFTEEN

THE TEAM FROM PACIFIC HIGH FILED INTO THE GYM IN
brown, long-sleeved tees. Their short black spandex accentuated the
too long legs most of them had. I could see why they had a right-side
hitter with talent. Half of their girls were as tall as our middle hitters.

As tall as me, I realized.

"You look terrified," Chandra said, tossing me a ball to warm up.
"We can play with them."

I nodded, not totally convinced.

"Besides," Ashley added. "It's a scrimmage. No pressure."

"Let's get to know them now, so we can beat them when it matters," Chandra said.

"You two have it all figured out," I said.

"We have your back, Soph."

I'd need it. The afternoon marked my big debut at the outside-hitting position and my homemade shirt. Damn Chandra for painting
Soph on the back. There was absolutely no fixing it. Unless I wanted
a blob of paint to match the one on my front. Only the front of Ally's
shirt resembled the mascot. Everyone else's chest looked like a finger
painting of black and purple.

Surprisingly, Ally didn't seem to mind. Her intensity was showing.

She pulled me aside before the JV game. "You want me to give you a chance?"

The answer was so obvious I thought it might be a trick question. I decided to roll with it. "Yes."

"Fine. Here's your chance."

If I didn't play well, did that mean she would go back to being in my face all the time? The scrimmage was everyone's chance. Pre-season literally served that purpose.

"Don't let her get in your head," Chandra said. "Are you focused?"

Behind Ally, Harris walked into the gym.

"That's a no. Soph!"

"Yeah?"

"Focus. Shake off the nerves. You've played this game a million times."

"Never at the outside position."

"True," Chandra said. "But everything else is the same. I'm going to set the hell out of you, so be ready."

I nodded to her, trying my best to believe I was ready. Something was off. I couldn't explain it. Some days, things clicked. The sun felt brighter. My body moved in this fluid space. Other days, I felt like an old clunky car, with gears not quite matching up.

That afternoon, the gears clunked.

"Let's go, JV!" Ally clapped her hands and narrowed her eyes. Her words were more commanding than encouraging. "Get low on that pass, Taylor! Chandra, step into that set and really push it. That's it! Nikki, crush that!"

Who needed a coach when you had Ally Malone?

As warm-ups ended, the gym was stuffy and quiet—both indicators that it was still summer, and the season hadn't gripped the weather or the fan base. Pacific had brought a modest crowd decked in brown and scattered around the visitor bleachers. On the home bleachers, my mom and Harris stood side by side, both clapping wildly as we headed to the huddle for the start of the match.

Elle had a shooting competition that evening, so, as usual, Dad was with her. Lily had probably decided to ride along. Next to conducting science experiments, her favorite pastime was reading books in the back seat of the car when one of her older sisters dragged her to a sporting event.

My mom supported me enough to make up for the rest of them. Or at least she tried with her *Iron Valley Volleyball Mom* T-shirt, all blinged out from some party she'd gone to last year. The closest Harris got to athletic gear was a short-sleeved polo and cargo shorts. For a scientist, that was dressing down. Fair enough in that the polo had a big purple stripe across the front.

Coach Steve drew the JV lineup on his dry-erase clipboard. I was in the right front, which meant after the first rotation, I would serve. Chandra reached behind my back and squeezed my hand.

"They'll serve first. Get ready. Move your feet. It all starts with a good pass." He extended his hand, and we all piled ours on. "*Go Vikes!* on three. Ready? One. Two. Three."

"Go Vikes!"

I walked onto the court and inhaled the experience as if breathing in the scent of the first wildflowers in spring. That moment when the teams lined up in their starting positions, sizing up each other, and the refs checked the numbers to make sure the lineup was accurate. Those quiet seconds of preparation before every game—I relished them.

The anticipation. The possibility. The beauty of a 0–0 score.

Chandra slapped my hand and half-hugged me.

I stole a glance at the stands. Harris gave me a nod and an adorably dorky thumbs-up. He'd tossed balls to me for hours that morning. I wanted to crush Chandra's sets for my team, but I wanted to kill the ball for Harris too. As a mark of gratitude.

The whistle blew, and I dangled my hands in front of me, staying low and ready. The serve came to Taylor in the back row, and she passed it with ease to Chandra. A quick set to Ashley, a kill, and a side-out.

The purple crowd stomped the bleachers.

A Pacific player rolled the ball under the net to me. *My first serve of the year,* I thought as I stepped behind the end line and dribbled the ball. After a summer of practicing my float serve. And the need to prove my serve to Coach and maybe even Ally. If I wanted to play varsity, my serve had to be consistent. Impressive. Reliable.

The ref blew the whistle, and a vision of me hitting successive serves into the net from fatigue plagued my mind.

N*o. I can do this,* I told myself. I tossed the ball into the air and decided I didn't like the angle. Too far to my left. Had I hit it, there was a good chance it would've sailed over the net and out of bounds. I let the ball drop to the floor and got back into position for my second toss, knowing I had to hit this one even if it was awful.

I'd tossed the ball a million times. I could toss a volleyball in my sleep.

So maybe I should have tried with my eyes closed.

The toss was bad. Again, far to the left. Without a choice since it was my second toss, I swung across my body, and despite my best efforts of leaning to the right as if I were bowling and wanted to avoid the gutter, the other team rushed to the sideline and screamed, "Out!"

Unfortunately for me, they were right. I leaned forward, resting my hands on my knees, and looked at the ground. Nothing else I wanted to see. Not Ally's satisfied expression. Or Coach's disappointment. Or Harris's confusion over what had gone wrong when I was statistically more likely to have a heart attack at age fifteen than miss a serve.

My teammates tapped my back in consolation, and I got into position to serve receive. *Let it go. Shake it off,* I told myself. That was the danger in making mistakes. If you let them, they'd eat away your competitive spirit until another mistake followed. And another. It was like a plague of mistakes determined to spread and control every point of the game. I couldn't let that happen. I wouldn't.

I moved my feet and passed the ball to Chandra. I picked up a free ball with a good pass. I dug a few hits—none of them near Julia Medina or Sam Strutter's strength, but still. We rotated. We scored. I moved around the court much better than I had in practices. And while my play was solid—save the bad serve—it wasn't stellar. And stellar was what I needed to convince the coaches I deserved a shot at the varsity more than a senior who had been playing the position as part of this team for the last two years.

Nikki rotated back to the service line, and I stepped forward into the front row. If my back row play was only okay, I'd need to really step up my game in the front. Vowing to stand out, I raised my arms in a blocking position and faced the net. I'd be ready from the first play. Not a single ball would get by me.

The ref blew the whistle. Nikki's serve hit me in the back of the head. There wasn't an ounce of luck on the planet with my name on it.

"Melanie, you okay?" Coach called.

I nodded.

Nikki rushed toward me. "Soph! I'm so sorry."

"I'm fine. Let's play."

Play. Right. My elbow caught the net on a block. I stepped over the center line trying to scoop a bad pass out of the net. And I played a ball that was clearly—at least to the rest of the gym—out of bounds, essentially handing Pacific another point. Given my bad serve, that was four points I gave them on a volleyball-engraved platter. If I did that on varsity, it would almost certainly cost us the game.

Coach called a time-out and tried to pep us up.

"Dang, Soph," Chandra said when we were back on the court. "What's wrong with you?"

I shrugged.

"Keep shrugging. Until you shrug it all the way off. Got me?"

She was right. I couldn't give up. Every touch of the ball was an opportunity to earn my way. I had to get my head in the game and make plays happen.

Starting with a big kill.

"I'm not giving up anything," I said. "Set me, and I'll show you."

"There you go. I see you."

On the next point, I got my head back in the game. Literally. I jumped to block, and the Pacific hitter mistimed her approach and slammed the ball into the net.

And my face.

My eyes blurred. Someone led me to the bench. Someone pressed a paper towel against my nose to stop the blood. Someone cried inside.

Wait. That was me.

CHAPTER SIXTEEN

LATER THAT EVENING, ON THE COUCH IN OUR FAMILY
room, my mother propped my feet up on pillows—which I didn't
understand because my ankles were fine—and gave me an ice pack
for my nose. Despite the sensation that the extremity had exploded
into my skull when I'd gotten hit, it wasn't broken.

For good measure, Mom diffused lavender essential oil in the
room to calm and relax me.

I hated lavender.

My phone buzzed.

Square: How was the scrimmage?

If his coach hadn't limited the team's electronics usage, he'd sure-
ly have heard how it went.

Me: Close, but if I'm being honest, they got the better of us.

Square: Sorry. How did you play?

Me: Awful.

The admission lightened the weight over me, a little anyway.

Square: I'm sorry. Wanna talk about it?

Me: No.

The little conversation bubbles appeared on the screen. Then they
disappeared. Then returned. Apparently, he couldn't figure out what
to say either. After a few minutes of me dreading the message that

was about to come, my phone buzzed again.

Square: Who's all about the one-word answers now ;)

I smiled. Reluctantly. And soreness crept from my nose across my cheeks and forehead.

Me: If you could see me right now, you'd realize how big of a risk that was.

Square: I hoped you knew it was coming from a good place. And that I wanted to make you smile.

Me: It hurts when I smile.

Square: Must have been really bad. Sorry.

Me: No. It literally hurts. A girl on the other team hit the ball into my face.

Conversation bubbles. A bandage emoji appeared.

"Is that your football player?" Lily asked from the doorway. "The one you've been dressing up like Elle's Barbie doll for and going to parties with?"

I set down the phone. "Are you a private investigator now?"

She crossed her arms and looked much older than her eleven years. "Look, Melanie. I never got your whole volleyball thing."

"That much has been clear. Thanks."

"I get it's important to you."

My phone buzzed again, but I refrained from reading it right away. "Is this conversation going somewhere?"

"You have this shot at playing varsity, which is what you've always said you wanted, and suddenly, you're all distracted."

"I'm not distracted."

"Yes. You are. Even Harris said—"

Warmth radiated from my core. "You and Harris have been talking about me?"

"We just said—"

"Don't," I cut her off again. Was that why Harris had transformed his back yard into a training facility?

"Don't what? Tell you the truth?"

My head was starting to hurt again.

"You care too much what other people think," she said.

"Lily, please."

"And don't even get me started on Harris."

Her interference pushed me so far, I couldn't stop the edge in my voice. Not that I wanted to. "You mean the same Harris who's been discussing my life with my nosy little sister?"

"What's going on in here?" Mom asked, poking her head through the doorway.

"Lily telling me how to live my life while simultaneously complaining that I'm letting people tell me how to live my life."

Lily perked an eyebrow. "I see the irony there."

"Lily, honey? Why don't you go see if your father needs help in the garden?"

A scientific task. My mother knew how to play the instruments that were her family. I stifled a groan. Her skills would be directed at me next. My phone buzzed in my hand again. Square would have to turn his phone in to the coaches soon.

Lily left us alone, and Mom sat on the coffee table across from me, pretending to examine my face. "You want to talk about it?"

"I played terribly. What's there to talk about?"

"Tomorrow is a new day."

A new day of dealing with Ally and playing a position that I was proving to be very bad at.

Mom ran her fingers through my hair, caressing my head in long, peaceful strokes. I closed my eyes and let my weight and the weight of everything else settle into the couch cushions.

"This is all new, Melanie. Take the time to find your place in it, but you be the one to decide that. Nobody else. Okay?"

A muddle of faces flashed in my mind, essentially proving Lily's point that other people were dictating what my life should be. Elle. Ally. Coach. Sam. Even Harris and Square.

My goals hadn't changed. I wanted to excel at volleyball. Last year, that meant practicing harder and longer than everyone else. This year, playing varsity included making friends.

I didn't excel in that department.

"I hear you, Mom." I'd rest. Regroup. Focus my efforts and settle into my place before school started.

Lily knocked on the wooden door frame. "Melanie, look who I found in the back yard." Harris walked into the room with this hands in his pockets.

My mom greeted him and offered snacks. He politely declined, and she left us alone after saying, "Think about what I said, Melanie."

"I will, Mom."

Harris looked at me and back at the empty doorway before whispering, "That seemed intense. Sorry for interrupting."

"No. It's fine. Sit." I slid over to make space on the couch. He sat close and put his arm around my shoulders.

"You okay?"

He might have talked to Lily about me, but my anger fizzled at the look of concern on his face. I settled into him. "No."

"What can I do?"

"Be here," I whispered.

He squeezed my shoulders. "Always."

"I thought you were working on an experiment for your channel tonight."

"I was, but today looked pretty rough. I wanted to check on you."

I sighed. "*Rough* is one word for it. I don't know that I'm cut out for varsity. I can barely stay upright on JV."

He nudged me with his shoulder. "Come on, Mel."

"I mean it," I insisted.

"No. You've seen me in that back yard. How many experiments have I had go wrong?"

"A lot."

"I've burned down trees. Exploded more things than I can count. You remember that time I made a mini cannon that shot across the street and blew a hole in Mrs. Monteleone's garage roof?"

"How could I forget? She fed everyone eggplant parmesan while they put out the fire."

"Yeah. That was a silver lining." He lowered his voice. "Not sure if you know this, but the reason the pickets on the fence are broken is because of me."

I rolled my eyes at him. "Everyone knows that, Harris."

"Your parents never said anything."

"They like you."

"That's nice to hear."

"Is this whole trip down memory lane going somewhere?" I asked.

"Yes. I had a point."

"And that would be?"

"Some days, everything goes according to your hypothesis, and other days, you destroy the neighbors' property. Just because you have a rough day doesn't mean the experiment won't work the next time."

"What you're saying is today I destroyed property?"

"In the analogy, yes, that is the equivalent."

I rarely had days like that, but it seemed lately, I had more property-destroying days than according-to-hypothesis days.

"Vanessa had a good game today," I thought aloud. "Maybe she didn't contribute as much as Julia would have, but she also wasn't the disaster that I was."

"My biggest disasters have usually led to my best discoveries," Harris said with a shrug.

"Meaning I can rise up from this stronger?"

"Sure," he said. "Why not?"

Good question. "I'll think about it."

"Good." He grabbed the remote. "What do you want to watch?"

Harris's decision to change the subject managed to boost my mood at the same time. As my best friend, he had that effect on me.

"Harris Fullerton is going to watch television? You do mean something other than the Discovery Channel, right?"

"It's your disaster of a day, so you get to pick, but only if you come watch the Discovery Channel with me on my next disaster of a day."

"Deal," I said, grabbing the remote.

"Don't pick one of those romance movies."

"Hush. My choice, remember. Besides, it's the romances that always put me in the best mood."

He huffed and grabbed the blanket from the arm of the couch. He tossed it in the air, so it opened, and let it fall over our legs. I chose one of my favorite romantic comedies and shifted on the couch until we both landed in comfortable positions.

Just so happened those positions included his arm around me and my head on his chest.

He smiled down at me. "You good?"

"Yep. Thanks for being here."

"Of course," he said. "Always."

As my best friend, he'd help me get my mind off volleyball tonight but refocus on it tomorrow. He'd probably have a grand scientific plan for how to do it. But for now, we'd relax and let the disaster of the day fade with the setting sun.

CHAPTER SEVENTEEN

ALLY SET THE BALL BETTER THAN SHE'D EVER DONE
before. *Go,* a voice whispered in my head. I rounded my approach.
Right foot. Left. Feet together. Exploded into the air. My arm found
the perfect height and connected with the ball. The peak of the set.
The peak of my jump. I smacked the ball with wide fingers and a
strong wrist.

Down. Down. Down.

So hard, a collective gasp sounded in the gym.

"Melanie Rose Corwin!"

Huh? Mom?

I opened my eyes to sunshine bursting through the windows and
my mom standing over me in the family room, hands on hips.

"You wanna explain what's going on here?" She pointed next to
me, and that was when I realized my pillow wasn't a pillow. It was
Harris. His hair swooped across his closed eyes. He cradled me in
his arms, and we were still sharing the blanket from the night before.

Oh. My. Gosh.

I shot upright, leaving a smudge of drool on Harris's shirt. "Mom,
it's not what it looks like."

"Oh, so Harris didn't sleep over? On the same couch as you? With
you in his arms?"

Okay. It was exactly what it looked like.

"Melanie, you can't have boys sleeping over."

"It's not a boy. It's Harris."

Mom looked at the ceiling and mouthed a few words I couldn't make out.

"We were watching a movie and fell asleep. We're friends, Mom. That's all."

"That's not what your sister says."

"Lily or Elle?"

"Lily. She's the one who found you two. I don't have to tell you what kind of example that sets for your eleven-year-old sister. Do I?"

Harris stirred awake. "Good morning, Mrs. Corwin." When my mother didn't respond, he paused mid-stretch.

"We fell asleep," I explained.

"We?" He finally noticed the wet mark on his chest from my drool, and his eyes went super wide. "Oh. Um. I'm sorry, Mrs. Corwin. I'll head home. Have a good day."

He folded the blanket. At least he had good manners.

"Better use the French doors." Mom pointed behind us. "Wouldn't want to run into Melanie's father on your walk of shame."

"Mom!"

Harris's cheeks flamed. "No. Of course."

"Harris, you don't need to be embarrassed. Mom, last night was completely innocent."

"Still, I'm gonna go." Harris pushed the doors, but they didn't open. He fumbled with the lock because it was that kind of morning and finally got them open when my Dad's voice carried down the hall. From the other side of the glass, he offered a feeble wave.

Elle and Lily peeked through the doorway with wide eyes.

"I didn't think Harris had it in him," Elle said.

To my shock, my mom laughed.

"Mom! Was that whole angry parent thing for show?"

She pointed at me. "No. That was me holding it together when I woke up to find my daughter sleeping on my couch with a boy."

I started to object, but she raised her hands. "Harris or not, he's a boy. That doesn't fly here. You're not kids anymore, sleeping in the tent under the stars. No more. Agreed?"

"Agreed."

She left the room shaking her head, and my sisters took her place.

"Dish," Elle said.

"Nothing to dish," I said. "We fell asleep watching a movie."

"You looked pretty cozy this morning," Lily said. "Did you two finally declare your love?"

"Your love?" Elle asked. "What happened to Square?"

Square? Had I done something unfair to Square? We weren't officially together, and Harris and I were only friends. Snuggling Square on the couch all night would be fireworks right there in the family room. Harris—he was safe. Like home.

"You know what? I have to get ready for practice."

***

IN MY ROOM, I PLUGGED IN MY PHONE TO CHARGE AT least for the few minutes I'd be getting ready and groaned. I'd forgotten about Square's texts in the chaos of the night before with Lily, my mom, and Harris.

Square didn't have phone time until the evening, so I couldn't even apologize for not responding.

Square: If you're feeling up to coming, we have a scrimmage Saturday.

Square: ????

Square: I have to run. Hope to see you there.

Square Weaver had invited me to the football scrimmage. He wanted me to see him play. He wanted to see me.

If I went to his scrimmage, would that mean we were together? Did I need to tell him about last night? I splashed water onto my face.

What if Harris thought the same thing Elle and Lily had thought? I grabbed my phone and texted him.

Me: You get home okay?

Harris: Not exactly. I didn't have my keys since I didn't expect to spend the night. I'm locked out.

Me: Come and grab the extra set we keep here.

Harris: And catch your mom's wrath again? I'll wait.

Out the window, I saw him lounging on his back porch. I waved.

So did he. Normal behavior. That was something.

Me: Funny how our parents didn't realize we weren't in our beds.

Harris: Terrible parenting.

Me: Too trusting.

Harris: Hope that doesn't change. I'm really sorry. You fell asleep, and I didn't want to wake you. I kept watching the movie, but you know how I feel about rom-coms.

Me: They apparently put you to sleep.

Harris: Sorry.

Me: Forget it. I have to go to practice. I'll toss the keys over the fence on my way out.

Harris: Thanks, Mel. You're the best.

Chandra interrupted with a text that read, Soph! her way of announcing she was at the red light two minutes away. I threw a lunch together, tossed the keys over the fence, and hoped practice was as beautiful as the dream I'd had lying in Harris's arms.

***

I SLID INTO THE PASSENGER SEAT OF CHANDRA'S CAR. "No Ashley today?"

"She's driving herself. How's the face?"

"Still there."

"Good," she said. "You focused and ready to rebound today?"

Focused? Me?

"That's a no. Come on, Soph."

"You understand boys, right?"

She studied me with questioning eyes. "As much as anyone could, I guess. Why?"

"If I go to the football scrimmage to see Square play, does that mean he and I are a thing?"

"Only if you say you're a thing."

"And let's say I spent the night—as friends—with another boy."

"This is getting interesting."

"Stop. We were watching a movie—as friends—and we fell asleep."

"Was there cuddling?"

"Um..."

Chandra howled.

"Anyway, is that something I have to tell Square even though it was completely innocent?"

"You and Square aren't official?"

"We haven't even gone on a date."

She turned down the drive that led to our high school. "No. You're good. But if you get serious with Square, you should be careful about doing that kind of thing with a friend. That's where you cross the line."

Made sense.

"You've never dated anyone before?"

"Nope," I said.

"And you start with Square Weaver. That's some good luck, girl." She parked as close to the gym as she could and slapped my knee.

"Ouch."

"Now that you got all that out of the way, you ready to focus?"

"Yes."

"Say it like you mean it. This is a big opportunity. Not only for you. For the rest of us too. If you play varsity, we go into next season with at least one veteran on our team. If Vanessa plays, the entire JV is going to move up together with no experience and no leader. You playing varsity isn't only about this year. It's about next year too."

Way to put the pressure on. Sheesh. I'd never thought about how my playing varsity might actually benefit the other younger players. I only saw it as me taking something away from them, not being able to give something back.

"Do some meditation or some shit and get in the gym ready to go."

"I don't meditate," I said.

"Maybe you should."

We collected our stuff and headed for the gym. The morning was warm and bright with the sun peeking around the rooftop of the school and shining on the morning dew on the grass. The day felt like a fresh opportunity. I'd never dreamed of such a perfect moment as I had the night before. Ally set me. Not Chandra. Ally. That meant I was on the varsity side of the court, not the JV. She gave me a perfect set, which showed she wanted me to do well, and I killed it.

I'd keep that dream in my mind during practice. The reality of that moment was what I was working toward.

CHAPTER EIGHTEEN

LIKE I'D TOLD CHANDRA, I DIDN'T KNOW HOW TO MEDI-
tate, but while we ran laps and stretched, I focused on my breathing
and our counting. Any time a thought of Square, Harris, or my family crept into my mind, I pushed it away. My mental space was for
volleyball. Nothing else.

It might have worked. On our water break after individual drills,
Chandra said, "Soph, I see some of that spark in you."

"I meditated," I joked.

"Whoever you slept with last night might be a good luck charm."

Ashley's eyes widened to the size of volleyballs. "You slept with
someone last night?"

I groaned. "That's how rumors start. I did not. Chandra, stop. My
neighbor was at my house watching a movie, and we fell asleep on
the couch."

Ashley punched Chandra in the shoulder. "Don't play with my
heart like that. You know I love a good hookup story."

Chandra raised an eyebrow at me. Yes, I'd left out some details,
but it didn't matter.

"I'm here to focus on volleyball," I said, taking another swig from
my water. "No more talk of boys, please."

"I can't make any promises," Ashley said. "It is the weekend after all, and I have plans."

Coach blew the whistle, and we hustled to the court for the end-of-practice scrimmage. As usual, I lined up on the JV court in the first server position. I couldn't blame Coach. I'd performed horribly at the scrimmage. I had a lot of making up to do before I stepped onto the varsity court, but I also had time to do it. At the line, I took a deep breath, dribbled the ball, and tossed it high in front of my right shoulder. I popped the ball at the exact moment to send a float serve over the net. It looked out of bounds but floated back in. Ally scrambled for it, and the team couldn't help her enough to put an attack together. They sent a free ball over the net that Taylor passed to Chandra from the middle back position, Chandra set to Ashley in the middle, and Ashley killed around Sam's block.

The JV team celebrated.

Another deep breath, and I served again. This time, another float serve the varsity was ready to pick up. They put together an attack, and we moved into a volley that ended with smiles on the JV court and frustration on the varsity side.

Chandra winked at me.

We were challenging them. And they didn't like it.

The varsity finally ended my serve on the next point with a kill from Sam on a quick set. We moved through the rotation with volleys so intense, I didn't even know—or care about—the score.

I was back, and I wasn't going to lose focus again.

***

LIKE OLD TIMES, I PASSED THE VOLLEYBALL TO MYSELF in the back yard that afternoon. I counted to 212 before Harris called my name over the fence.

"How was practice?"

"Good," I called back, still counting—219.

My phone buzzed, but I ignored it. I'd already texted Square an apology that I couldn't make his scrimmage the next day. It was an hour away. Elle had to miss watching Josh play in the scrimmage because she had a shooting tournament, and I had no other way to get there except maybe Ally, since she'd likely be going to watch her brother, Owen, play. But asking Ally—that wasn't happening.

I also wanted to spend the day resting and getting an extra work-out in. I was refocused Melanie. That meant volleyball was my top priority.

Harris ducked through the broken pickets. His hair didn't hang over his eyes like it once had. It was shorter. Cleaner, yet still with a wave. He looked the same but different.

He looked good.

"You got a haircut," I said.

"Like it?"

"Yeah."

He paused like I might say something else, and he didn't want to interrupt. When I kept quiet, he asked, "Can we talk?"

His voice sounded serious, and I wondered if his parents had given him a hard time about the night before. I caught the ball. "You okay?"

He pointed to the chairs around our firepit. "Wanna sit?"

Worry crept into my stomach. Harris was never this serious. "Are you moving? Did someone die? Are your parents banning us from being friends?"

He grinned. "No. Nothing like that."

"Okay."

He took a deep breath. And said nothing.

"Harris, you're scaring me."

My phone buzzed twice.

"You need to get that?" he asked.

It buzzed again. When Harris finally started talking, I didn't want to be interrupted, so I grabbed my phone. The messages were from Square. He was sorry I couldn't make the scrimmage and asked for me to wish him luck. I did and set the phone down.

"Anything important?"

I shook my head. "Square invited me to the scrimmage tomorrow."

"Oh. Are you going?"

"No. I want to rest and work out a little. Maybe read in the hammock. Do yoga. I need some me time."

"Makes sense," Harris said.

"After tanking the scrimmage yesterday, I decided to refocus, and today was a much better practice."

"You were more focused today at practice? After what happened this morning?"

I shrugged. "Sure. It's no big deal, right?"

Harris looked down at his hands.

"Is that what this is about? Did your parents give you a hard time?"

"Didn't even notice," he said.

"So what's going on? Why are you so heavy?"

The back door slammed, and Elle leaned over the deck. "Hey, Harris." Her voice was suggestive, and it had Harris squirming. "Mel, Mom said dinner in five."

"Thanks," I said and turned my attention back to my best friend. We were on the clock now.

"Elle knows?" he asked.

"She was there," I said. "But seriously, it's not a big deal. You have to stop stressing about it."

"I'm not stressing," he said and directed his intense, scientific gaze on me. "You're completely good with last night. No questions or..."

I got the sense there was something I should've been picking up on but wasn't. What questions should I have had? Was this him opening the door for me to say that our night of snuggling on the couch had been, in fact, something more, like my mother had thought it was? How could I ask without having to answer the question myself?

"Melanie, dinner!" My mom called from the kitchen window.

"I have to go," I managed. "Do you want to join us?"

He stood. "No. Thanks. I don't think today's the day to intrude on your family's dinner."

"Harris, you never intrude. You're my best friend."

He nodded at the comment but didn't make eye contact. "Still. Maybe another time."

"Okay. Science experiment tonight?"

"Nah. Not tonight. Might do some stargazing though."

"Maybe I'll join you."

"Sure," he said. "You're always welcome. You're my best friend."

I wasn't sure if I should've been relieved at his declaration or disappointed. Alarm bells triggered in my head, warning me I teetered on the edge of something. I could lean one way and maybe change things with my best friend forever. Or I could lean the other, which could lead to wondering. Lots of wondering. As he disappeared through the broken pickets of the fence, I realized life might have gotten way more complicated.

***

AFTER DINNER, I CLIMBED UP THE ATTIC STEPS TO THE rooftop balcony to read the book that had been patiently waiting on my nightstand. I read the same sentence four times before closing it again. I swiped my phone to the photos app and scrolled through the folder of "Harris" pics.

I loved his goofy, wobbly grin and admired the intensity in his eyes. He approached everything that mattered in his life with the utmost passion. That was probably why we'd become such good friends. For him, it was science. For me, volleyball. Even though our loves differed, we respected each other enough to not judge. I didn't need him to be a jock, and he certainly knew I wasn't winning any chemistry prizes. We were together in most of the pics. His arm hanging over my shoulder. Us making goofy faces behind a collection of beakers and wired contraptions. Over time in the photos, Harris had grown up. His face had become more defined. His shoulders and arms more muscular. His smile less childish and more attractive.

Attractive.

Harris Fullerton was attractive. How had I never noticed that before?

I guess I'd never thought to.

With charm and swagger, Square was attractive in an obvious, no-way-to-deny-it way. With a smooth demeanor and dynamic personality, he made people want to be around him. Harris's looks could go unnoticed, but scrolling through pages and pages of pictures of him showed there was no denying it.

Wow.

I put down the phone and looked over the fence into his back yard. In the moonlight, I could make out his telescope and his shape.

I shook my head. What was I thinking? So I'd snuggled on the couch with Harris. Like Mom had said, we'd slept in tents together as kids all the time. If she hadn't suggested it could be something more, would I have ever thought it?

And he could have said something earlier about the night before, but he hadn't. If I would have asked if there was anything going on, would he have said, *Yeah, I totally have a crush on you*?

Or did he not have a crush, but the empirical evidence from the night before—snuggling on the couch, sharing a blanket, watching a romantic comedy together, me falling asleep on him—had confused him into thinking that I had a crush on him? Maybe he was relieved that we were still in the friend zone.

I peeked through the curtains in the direction of his house. Only one way to find out.

CHAPTER NINETEEN

I HEADED TO HARRIS'S YARD LOOKING FOR A SIGN, EI-
ther way. The sky was dark. The stars sparkled. We'd be looking
at the universe. The night could be totally romantic, or two friends
hanging out.

I pushed the pickets aside and saw Harris sitting in a chair next
to the telescope. The glow of his phone screen lit his face. He smiled
at whatever he was reading. His thumbs moved over the screen. The
phone buzzed, and he laughed before moving his thumbs again.

My throat caught. Elle had seen me doing the same thing and had
said she'd know that look anywhere. I'd been texting Square.

Flirting with him, more specifically.

Harris was flirting.

The weird vibe from Harris had been him trying to let me down
gently. To make sure I didn't expect anything romantic from him after
my mom's outburst. Because there was someone else.

I'd wanted a sign. Talk about a flashing billboard.

Before he could see me, I slipped back to my side of the fence,
not sure how to feel. Relieved that we were clearly just friends—as
I'd thought? Disappointed we wouldn't be something more when I
wasn't even sure I wanted something more?

I shook my head. No. Friends was good. That meant fewer complications and better focus on the team. That was what I'd wanted.

That was what I'd gotten.

***

THE NEXT MORNING, I STALKED ALL RELEVANT SOCIAL media feeds for news of the football scrimmage. The athletic department. The football team. *The Pittsburgh Herald.* Ally Malone. Not a single post, message, or tweet.

I paced the family room. I rocked in the hammock.

I'd decided not to go to the scrimmage without thinking it would be Julia's first chance to play. I was dying for an update. Had she started? Had she played? How was Square doing? How many tackles and sacks had he racked up?

Finally, I checked the newspaper feed again and found a hint.

> PittHerald: Girl QB Julia Medina on the field for Iron
> Valley. Team scores touchdown on their first drive.

Wow. She'd done it. She'd gotten on the field. And they'd scored a touchdown! A girl I knew, a tough and brave and cool girl had competed against the guys—and her boyfriend, no less. If Julia Medina wanted something, she went for it.

If I wanted her position, I'd have to be tough and brave enough to earn it. Hopefully not cool. I couldn't muster that. I glanced at the clock. Not even noon. The day stretched ahead of me. Normally, I'd go to Harris's to pass the time, but it didn't feel right yet. Besides, he was probably spending the evening with the girl he'd been flirting with by text the night before.

Instead, I opened *Crushing It*, the book on my nightstand and picked up where I'd left off. I couldn't even bring myself to look at the date on the sticky note. It wasn't the quality of the book that had kept me away. It had been me. My life.

In the scene, the main character, Janet, warmed up for the biggest basketball game of the year, challenging herself to bank every layup accurately. Of course she didn't. There'd be no story if she could do it right the first time or every time. Every story had struggle and growth. Like Julia's story.

Like *my* story.

I settled deeper into my pillows and let Janet's story wash over me like a flooding energy. With nowhere to go—finally—I finished the book. When I turned the last page, I held it against my chest and closed my eyes to relish her victory.

And hoped that someday, I'd relish my own.

With *Crushing It* back on the shelf, I picked up the next book in the series and opened to the first page.

***

EVENING SETTLED IN BEFORE I KNEW IT. MOM CALLED us for dinner. For the first time in days, maybe weeks, the five of us crowded around the table. Elle told us about her tournament—she'd won. Dad asked if we were ready to go back to school—the dreaded question. For me, at least. Lily couldn't wait. She talked about her advanced courses and the research projects she'd take on.

Elle giggled at the thought of her senior year, expecting it to be the best.

I wondered where I'd be able to hide in school from the nonstop chatter and bickering of everyone for a few minutes of quiet. In the past, I'd targeted the bathrooms, the back hallway leading to the drama and music rooms, the stacks of the library, and even the empty auditorium.

Going back to school meant less time to practice. Less time with Harris, as long as I could avoid him in the halls.

Was I ready? No, Dad. Definitely not.

When the dishwasher hummed its opening rush of water and the counters had been wiped, I messaged Square an apology for missing the scrimmage and asked how he'd done. My phone rang a minute later, and I couldn't help but smile.

An actual phone call from a guy. Not a text or a DM.

"Hello...?"

His low voice came over the line, making me shiver. "Is this the number for the best volleyball lessons in town?"

My smile widened.

I laid in bed, laughing at his stories about the scrimmage and loving the intensity of competition in his voice. Before I knew it, I looked at the clock, and it was 10:00 p.m.

"You're not going out tonight?" I asked him.

"Nah. My muscles need rest. And your mom isn't the only one who can put on the pressure."

I sighed. "Except for a little yoga earlier today, I've been resting all weekend."

"Yoga, huh?"

"Oh yeah. I love it."

"Can you flip upside down and stuff?"

My body stilled. Was this a...sexual question? Elle's comment about Square not being a virgin and the gorgeous Lacey came flooding my way similarly to how the errant volleyball had smashed my face earlier that week.

"Melanie? You still there?"

"Yeah. Uh-huh. Yep."

"If you tell anyone what I'm about to say, I will deny it forever."

Oh gosh.

"When I was ten," he said slowly, "my aunt taught me yoga."

The revelation was so benign I actually laughed from the release of the tension I'd been holding onto. I'd expected something way more risqué.

"Is that right?" I managed.

"Stop laughing."

I laughed more.

"Stop!" But he laughed too.

"Can you flip upside down and stuff?" I asked him, and we both lost it completely. Until Elle pounded on the wall separating our rooms and yelled for me to keep it down.

"I should go," I said.

"Me too. Mama's giving me the eye. One more thing. When you gonna let me take you out?"

A smile crept across my face. Square felt like a breath of fresh air, not a distraction. And the deeper I got into my hunt for varsity playing time, I needed all the air I could get. "Soon," I said.

"Soon," he repeated.

"Good night, Square."

"Good night, Melanie."

***

SUNDAY MORNING, I THOUGHT OF SQUARE BEFORE I opened my eyes and woke up with a smile. He wanted to take me out. I laid back against my pillow and sighed. A real date.

My phone buzzed with a message from a number I didn't know, interrupting my fantasizing.

Hey, Melanie. It's Julia Medina. Sorry if this is weird, but I wanted to check in on you. I heard you're moving to outside, and I know how intense Ally can be. Anyway, if you wanna chat, I'm here.

I read the message three times before I snapped back to reality and replied.

Me: Hey. Thanks for reaching out. Actually, chatting would be really nice.

Conversation bubbles. More bubbles. Ugh, the bubbles!

Julia: Meet for breakfast at the Diner on Third?

My stomach grumbled at the thought of their delicious breakfast potatoes.

Me: 30 minutes?

Julia: Perfect.

I lowered my phone and stared at myself in the mirror of my closet door. Two weeks ago, I'd been fangirling over Julia. Today I was having breakfast with her. I'd had no intention of being social or, gasp, dating, but somehow, I was on the verge of having a very cute, football-playing senior for a boyfriend. I'd wanted a shot at varsity playing time.

I had that shot.

A lot could change if you let it.

My stomach rumbled again. I bypassed Elle's recent fashion hand-me-downs and opted for athletic gear, pretty sure a girl who played football wouldn't mind.

CHAPTER TWENTY

JULIA SAT AT A CORNER BOOTH WITH A CUP OF COFFEE
and a newspaper. Maybe she and I were kindred spirits with our old
souls. She looked up when the door closed and waved.

"Hey," I said.

"Hey." She moved her newspaper. "Have a seat."

"Thanks."

I settled into the booth across from her and smiled.

"Is this awkward?" she said. "I'm sorry if it's awkward."

"No. It's a nice surprise."

The bell on the diner door chimed again. Julia turned toward
it, and something inside compelled me to do the same. It was Ally
Malone.

What were the chances?

Julia waved her over. Fine. I could say hello. I could be mature.

She made room for Ally to slide into the booth, and suddenly it
felt like I'd be doing more than saying hello. *Not* a nice surprise.

Julia tried to defuse the tension by asking what everyone was
ordering. Ally—a veggie omelet with a side of fruit. Me—the Everything Breakfast with, well, everything.

"You shouldn't eat like that during season."

"Ally," Julia warned. "We're here to mend fences, not plow them over with heavy machinery."

Ally rolled her eyes. "Is that why you asked me here? For some grand apology?"

The waitress interrupted to take our orders, leaving Ally's question hanging in the air.

"Here's how it is," Julia said after we ordered. "Melanie has a shot at being a major contender on the team. As someone who sort of left the team on short notice—"

"High and dry, you mean?"

Julia pressed her lips together and took a deep breath. "Heavy machinery, Al."

"Sorry," she muttered.

"I thought we could help her. If you want it, Melanie."

"Help how?" I asked.

"We could head to my house. Play on the sand court. I could teach you a jump serve."

"You'd do that? Don't you have to practice for football?"

"Yes," Ally interjected. "She does."

"No," Julia said in the same short tone Ally had used. "I don't. I want to help Melanie, and I want you to stop acting like such a..."

Ally raised an eyebrow at Julia, daring her to finish that sentence.

"Al, you're too rough on the team."

"That's the kind of thing a captain would have a say in. Are you our captain?"

I slumped in the seat, wishing the booth had a back door I could disappear through. Watching Ally and Julia battle made me wonder how much Ally actually disliked me and how much of her wrath was fueled by the fact that I wasn't Julia.

"Maybe I should go," I whispered.

Ally smacked her hand on the table. "No. I'll go."

"Don't be like this, Al. Stay. Have breakfast. Help us prep Melanie for the week."

"There are so many things wrong with that sentence. For starters, what makes you think a sophomore who can't jump serve—can barely serve, period—and has only hit outside for one week can replace you? Two, you're not on the team anymore, let alone the captain, so stop interfering. And C, one morning won't be nearly enough to get her"—she swung her arm in my direction and pointed at me as if I were the defendant in a brutal criminal case—"ready."

Ouch.

Ally left without her food or a backward glance.

"That did not go as well as I'd hoped it would," Julia said so seriously I covered my face and groaned.

"You may have underestimated her contempt for me."

She rested her hand on my arm with a kindness I didn't expect from someone I barely knew. "Maybe. But I think it's more about me than you. And her brother and I broke up. The whole thing is a little raw."

"Oh! I didn't realize. I'm sorry."

"Me too."

The waitress delivered our food. Julia asked her to box Ally's to go. "My dad will eat it," she said with a shrug.

We ate in silence for a few minutes, giving me time to think about her offer to help. Vanessa couldn't jump serve. Maybe that would be the thing to make me stand out from her. I could finally earn the starting position once and for all.

"Do you really think I could learn a jump serve in one day?"

"Don't see the harm in trying. Not trying might hurt though. All of the varsity starters can jump serve."

"I missed a serve in the scrimmage. I never miss a serve."

"I get it, but the team is in turmoil." She took a deep breath and steeled herself before continuing. "That's what I'm hearing. Walking into that chaos is hard, even if everyone supports you."

"Did everyone support you when you tried out for quarterback?"

Her eyes widened. "No. A few people did. Square, for one."

Her grin told me she knew we'd been talking, and her declaration was yet another mark for Square as the good guy totally worth my time.

"What did you do about the people who didn't support you?"

She set down her fork and sat back against the booth. "The only thing I could do. Kept digging until I earned their respect."

I'd have to do the same. If Ally gave me a chance to.

"It's random. Don't you think?"

"What?"

"That your mom moved me to outside? We have a senior outside, a junior outside, and two sophomores who've hit outside for years."

"My mom doesn't do random. She moved you to outside because she thinks you can be better than all of them. Her decisions are about what's best for the team."

Maybe Coach thought playing me at outside was best for the team before, but I wasn't sure she still did.

"I'm in," I said between bites of the best bacon anywhere.

"Jump serve?" Julia asked with a grin.

"Jump serve."

"Finish up." She called for the check. "We have work to do."

***

CHANDRA WAS WAITING FOR US ON THE SAND COURT in Julia's back yard.

"Let's do this, bitches," she said, fist-bumping us both.

"Thanks for coming," Julia said.

"Anything for Soph."

Julia walked me through her form when she jump served without actually jumping since she had to rest her ankle from a football injury. Immediately I realized my mistake in the past had been not tossing the ball high enough. A low toss meant I'd hit the ball into the net again and again.

Julia's patience was legendary. She coached me through the motions step by step until I finally landed the serve on the other side of the court.

She high-fived me. "That was awesome!"

"Yes, it was," Coach said from behind us. "Melanie, Chandra, good to see you girls."

"Hey, Coach," we said in unison.

"Your jump serve is looking good, Melanie."

Chandra and Julia grabbed a drink, leaving me to chat with Coach.

"Thanks. I think I figured out what I was doing wrong."

"Good." Coach watched Julia and Chandra for a few minutes with a longing smile. "It's nice to see her out here again."

I didn't know what to say, so I didn't say anything at all.

"I like watching her play football more than I expected, but..." She shrugged, and I got it. Volleyball was something they'd done together. Something they'd lost. Ally had lost it with Julia too.

"I'm sorry. I'm interrupting you. Go. Play. I love seeing that passion again."

"Thanks, Coach."

We had to reapply sunscreen twice, and we cleaned out the Medinas' fridge of Gatorade. But I jump served a lot. More often than not, my serves soared over the net and landed inbounds. Not the powerhouse deliveries Ally's were, but definite progress. Chandra also set me outside with Julia standing at the net correcting my form and movements on every hit. By my second reapplication of sunscreen, I curved my approach at the exact moment to explode into my vertical and hit the ball over the net with precision.

Maybe not precision. But close!

The pool called to us like a cool drink of blue Gatorade.

"We should swim," Julia said.

"We should swim," we repeated.

"I'll round up some swimsuits," she said.

"Did someone say swim?" Jake Medina said from the back porch.

"Hot damn," Chandra muttered. "I will forego swimsuit."

Julia threw the ball at her. "Gross. You will not. Abuelita lives in the garage apartment she affectionately calls a pool house. She's making Sunday dinner, and it will be a little awkward for you if she sees you naked first."

"That all makes sense," I said, "but I'm happy to keep my clothes on even without those reasons."

"You're no fun," Chandra said.

Jake greeted us with nods. He picked up Julia and laid her across his shoulders, heading for the pool. He kicked off his flip-flops along the way.

"No!" Julia screamed. "I will kill you!"

He gripped her tighter, and quite possibly for the first time *ever* in my life, I was grateful to have sisters—not brothers.

"You keep wiggling like that, you could hurt my throwing arm," Jake said. "Or *your* throwing arm."

Close to the pool now, Julia changed her tactic, holding her brother tightly. "If I go in, you go in."

"My phone's in my pocket."

"Not my problem."

"Chandra!" Jake called. "Grab my phone out of my pocket."

She grinned. "With pleasure."

"Traitor!" Julia accused.

Coach stepped out of the house onto the back porch. "Jake! Put your sister down! She's covered in sand." Jake didn't put Julia down. "Jake! Now! The whole pool will need to be vacuumed..."

But Jake and Julia were in the pool, fully clothed, and Chandra was looking satisfied for life.

"Did you see I had to grab his ass to reach into his pocket?" she whispered. "It was gloriously firm."

"Maybe you should put that down somewhere safe," I said. "You wouldn't want to drop it. Jake would be so mad."

Her eyes widened, and she nodded. "You're so smart." She slid the phone on a table under a towel. And I pushed her into the pool.

She screamed the whole way down, leaving me laughing until someone pushed me from behind. The cold water washed the sweat from my skin immediately. After a full day in the sun, I didn't even want to come back to the surface for air, but I did the math in my head. Everyone had been in the pool except for Coach and Abuelita. So who had pushed me in?

I swam to the surface and almost choked on the water. On the deck, wearing that threateningly beautiful smile and a swimsuit that revealed his—phew—torso...was Square Weaver.

CHAPTER TWENTY-ONE

WE ALL HAD DINNER WITH JULIA'S PARENTS AND
Abuelita. She made amazing Puerto Rican food—chuletas, which I
learned were fried pork chops with rice, red beans and fried plantains.
I'd never had plantains before.

I'd missed out.

I came home eager for a few quiet minutes alone before bed.
Being at Julia's hadn't exhausted me like some of the big parties I'd
been to. Maybe days like Sunday at the Medinas were the "happy
medium", as my mom would say, between spending all my time with
books and a volleyball in my back yard or never being home.

Small groups.

Good people.

Chill fun.

That was what I needed. That and a killer jump serve for practice
the next day, especially since Chandra pulled me aside before stretches to tell me Ally had spent Sunday afternoon at the park setting for
Vanessa.

If she could be ruthless, so could I. Julia had told me the night
before how hard it had been to choose herself over Owen when they
were competing against each other.

"It's not a crime to go for what you want, even if someone else wants it too," she'd said.

Vanessa might have wanted the starting spot. Ally might have wanted it for her.

But I wanted it too.

I pushed myself from opening laps. I made sure to be at the head of the pack. I called out every count during stretches. I exploded into every warm-up jump. Every pass, every serve, every hit, I communicated with my teammates, focused my mind, and challenged myself physically.

Every time.

"You're crushing it today, Soph," Chandra said on the water break before team play.

"Thanks." I took a long drink. "Guess we'll find out whether it was enough."

Coach blew her whistle, and we hustled back to the court. She pointed to the middle-back position of the varsity side and called out the positions. "Rachel. Ally. Molly. Sam. Kate. And..."

Melanie. Melanie. Melanie!

"Vanessa," she said.

Chandra squeezed my side. "It's not over until game time."

Coach called my name for the serving position on the JV court, as usual. We had a scrimmage midweek and more time before games began. This wasn't over.

Coach rolled the ball to our side first.

"Let's go, Soph," Chandra called.

Behind the serving line, I took a deep breath and remembered Julia's tips for a jump serve. Ball in front of you. High toss. Take off before the end line. Clean hit at the top of your jump. Land in the court.

Oh, and power. As much power as possible.

Not a lot to think about at all.

I took another deep breath.

"You got this, Soph," Chandra said again.

Coach blew the whistle, and I stepped back from my normal serving spot to give myself room for the approach and jump. Ball in front of me. High toss and go!

At the height of my jump, I feared the ball was low, that I'd hit it into the net. But the white sphere swirled through the air, inches above the tape, difficult to defend. Vanessa and Rachel dove for it.

And missed.

"Ace!" the JV team yelled, and we stomped in unison.

Chandra grabbed my shoulders, and I giggled, releasing weeks' worth of tension. I'd landed a jump serve in practice. An ace!

The varsity rolled the ball under the net to me. At the end line, settled and waiting, I swore I saw a grin on Coach's lips, beneath her whistle.

"Make it two-zero, Soph!"

I nodded to Chandra, and the whistle sounded.

Deep breath. Ball in front. Toss...jump...swing!

The ball soared higher this time, clearing the net by at least a foot. Vanessa got beneath it, but it ricocheted off her arms and hit the far wall of the gym.

"Ace!" *Stomp.*

Ally rushed to Vanessa and whispered in her ear. Chandra retrieved the ball and ran to me. "It ain't over."

I hugged her. "It ain't over."

My team clapped it up until I was back at the end line again. Serve number three. Coach blew the whistle, and I ran through the steps. Deep breaths. Patience. And power.

I served two more aces before Rachel picked up my serve with a wild pass to Ally. Ally set Molly outside, and the volley began. Chandra set the front row equally, spreading the ball around, keeping the defense on their toes. She'd make a killer varsity setter the next year.

"Back row," I yelled when Taylor made a perfect pass to Chandra. She set me nice and high. I approached, making sure to jump before crossing the ten-foot line, and connected with the ball at its peak. I killed the hit into the back corner, making Vanessa scramble for it on a dive.

The JV team erupted into a raucous huddle in the middle of the court. We were winning five to zero.

"JV, get water," Coach called.

We took our celebration to the sideline. Chandra started a chant: "JV! JV! JV!" We took turns drinking, so someone was always chanting.

After an obnoxious minute, we let the chant fade and collapsed onto the floor.

"It feels good to beat them for a change," Nikki said, and everyone nodded.

"Enjoy it now," Chandra said. "Soon enough, Melanie will be on the other side of the net, serving and hitting at us."

My teammates groaned.

Coach blew the whistle, and we hustled back to the court.

"Melanie, Vanessa," Coach called. "Switch sides."

Chandra smacked my ass. "Hell yeah."

Switch.

Sides.

I was going to the varsity court. Wish I could say the experience was like in a movie with some inspiring music and maybe a montage of all the struggles that had paved the path to this moment. Or maybe zooming in on Chandra's look of pride. Or Ally's look of contempt, which I imagined was there.

Instead, I held my head high and ran around the net.

"Serving position," Coach called, and the JV groaned.

Sam greeted me in the back right corner of the court. "Welcome to varsity, Melanie. Play hard."

"Thanks," I mumbled.

Coach rolled the ball to Vanessa in the serving position of the JV side. I might've been on the varsity court, but the spot wasn't mine. Not yet. Vanessa had auditioned trying to return my serve. It was my turn to audition.

Ally hid on the left back, behind Rachel, waiting until Vanessa served. Then she'd run to the setting position in the right front.

"One good pass, girls. Let's go," she called.

Vanessa stepped up to the serving line. She might have worked on hitting the day before with Ally, but by the looks of it, she hadn't mastered a jump serve.

Serve to me. Serve to me. Serve to me.

Squatting, I leaned forward on my toes, arms ready and out in front of me.

Coach blew the whistle. Vanessa took a breath. Tossed. Swung.

The ball sailed high above the net, deep into the back court. It could have been mine or Rachel's ball, but I called it early.

"Mine!"

I moved my feet and pointed my platform toward the setting position. The ball smacked off my arms evenly and sailed to Ally in a perfect pass. Sam called for a quick hit at middle. Ally set her.

The ball smacked against the hardwood on the JV court.

Side-out.

This time, no denying it. Under Coach's whistle was definitely a smile.

***

BREAKING VANESSA'S SERVE RANKED AS THE HIGH point in my varsity debut. Ally refused to set me until Rachel fell down on a pass, and I was the only hitter left in the front row. If she'd had a better pass, Ally probably would have set Sam in the back row to avoid setting me. Instead, she pushed a low ball my way that I had no choice but to tip over the net.

"You have to hit, Soph," she said after Taylor crushed the ball from the JV middle position, and it landed between Sam and Kate on our side of the court. "A tip is like a gift. Might as well give them a point."

"I want to hit. Can you set me a little higher?"

She scoffed. "So my sets are the problem, not your hitting?"

"Enough." Sam rested her hand on Ally's shoulder. "You're the setter. Hitters tell you where they like their sets. You set them there. That's how this game goes. Melanie asked for a higher set. Give her a higher set."

Ally tugged her arm away. "Got it. Higher sets. Sure thing, Soph."

Chandra's term of endearment sounded so far from endearing on Ally's lips.

Chandra stepped back to the serving line and got in position to jump serve.

"How many JV players jump serve now?" Ally grumbled.

I mentally urged Chandra to crush it. She did. Deep into the back court where Molly and Sam rushed for it. Sam called it at the last minute and sent a low pass to Ally, who had to quickly pop it up to the middle position.

Which kind of made sense. Hard to push a high set outside on a bad pass.

But the next pass was perfect, and she still set middle.

The next pass, she set Sam in the back row.

The next pass, she pushed the ball over the net, scoring a point by dropping it into the back corner.

No sets came my way.

None.

Not a high set.

Not a low set.

I basically practiced running up to the net to be prepared to block and releasing when the JV hit. Base. Release. Base. Release.

At least I had that covered.

Practice ended with the varsity barely edging out the JV after their—our—their five-point lead in the first game. In the second game, the one I was on the varsity court for the entire time, we won 25 to 12.

Maybe I'd earned the spot through serving, but I hadn't scored a single kill from the hitting position.

Chandra leaned against me on the bench in the locker room. "Not sure if that was a victory or an omen."

I grunted.

"She set you one time, and it was a crap set."

"Yep."

"Ally?" Coach called from her office and shut the door once Ally was inside. The meeting didn't last long. Neither of them even sat down. Coach said a few words. Ally nodded, and the door was open again. Ally left the office with her eyes on me. Maybe the word *eyes* didn't fit the situation. More like—

"Those are some daggers," Chandra said.

D*aggers* would do.

"I'm familiar with the Ally Malone daggers," I said.

"Not hard to figure out what happened in that office," Chandra said. "Coach told her she better set you tomorrow or else."

"Or else what? You set varsity?"

"Girl, don't wish the daggers on me. Can you imagine what she would say if she heard that rumble? Oh hell no."

Ally reappeared from behind a bank of lockers. "Melanie, Coach wants to see us in her office."

Chandra wished me luck with her wide eyes, or at least that was what I liked to think. I followed Ally to Coach's office.

"Excellent," Coach said. "Come in."

I closed the door and sat next to Ally.

"Great practice today, but we can do better. Ally, did you check your calendar?"

"Yes. I'm good, Coach."

Coach clapped her hands together. "Wonderful. Melanie, are you able to be here an hour early tomorrow?"

"Sure," I said.

"Great. You and Ally are going to practice your timing. I want to make sure she knows exactly where you like the ball set and that she puts it there every time."

So that was what the daggers were about. Ally had tried to ice me out, but Coach wasn't having it.

"Yes, Coach."

"Perfect. Now that Melanie is officially in the varsity spot, I want you two in sync."

Ally's shoulders slumped, but I still needed confirmation from Coach Medina that I had heard what I thought I heard.

"Coach, did you say...?"

She smiled. "Yes, I did. Great work, Melanie. Welcome to varsity!"

CHAPTER TWENTY-TWO

I'D DONE IT. I'D MADE VARSITY.

Those two sentences replayed in my mind while I floated home. They slipped from my lips when I got there, and my sisters screamed. My mom cried. My dad patted my back and grinned.

But they still played over and over. I'd done it. I'd made varsity.

My mom handed me a bath bomb. "Go soak in my tub."

"You never let us soak in your tub."

"I'm sure your muscles need it, and you can consider it a celebration for your big news."

I hugged her. "Thanks, Mom!"

I took the bath bomb and slipped away into the quiet sanctuary of my parents' bathroom. The huge soaker tub called to me with its shelf of books and selection of essential oil–scented bubbles. Definitely what I needed.

I filled the water as high and as hot as I could and disappeared beneath the surface, letting the orange-and-lemon scents wash over me. They reminded me of summer with our grandparents.

Every year, my sisters and I spent one summer day each week with them. If the sun shined, we swam. Gram would cover the umbrella table with pitchers of lemonade and iced tea, sliced oranges, and sandwiches. Grandpa would play in the water with us like we were still children, tossing Lily and challenging us to pool games. Lily always got bored and wanted to read. This year, Elle had wanted to phone flirt with Josh, but I stayed in the water to play volleyball with Grandpa.

I came up for air realizing that was what my life had been for years.

Volleyball in the pool. Extra workouts in the gym. Drills to improve my vertical jump. Passing, setting, and hitting against the side of the house. Any camps or pickup games I could find.

All to play varsity volleyball someday. Today was that day. My chest flittered and fluttered, but part of me feared the reality wouldn't measure up to the anticipation.

Was the pursuit of the goal more exciting than achieving it?

"Why do you look like someone stole your volleyball?"

I opened my eyes to find Elle hovering.

"Maybe someone did."

She pulled my mom's makeup chair from her vanity next to the bath. "Uh-oh. Spill."

"I'm kind of in the bath here. Privacy please?"

"You're completely covered with the full bottle of bubbles you used, and Mom never lets us in her tub. Whatever it is, it's gotta be bad."

"Not bad," I said. "Good. It's a celebration."

Elle's face crinkled like she was working through an advanced math problem. After a few seconds, she shook her head. "I don't follow. If you're celebrating, why do you feel so heavy?"

My sister knew me better than I thought.

"I made varsity, but what if I can't keep the spot?"

Elle sighed and rested her feet on the tub. "I think about this with Josh a lot. Not that I worked as hard as you did in volleyball to date him, but he seems so out of my league. Like one day, he's gonna wake up and realize it."

"Elle, he's not out of your league."

She pressed her hands against her chest. "Did my little sister compliment me?"

"How do you know I wasn't insulting Josh?"

She narrowed her eyes and splashed my face with bubbly water.

I wiped the bubbles away. "Joking! You two are the best together."

She smiled a radiant Elle smile. "Thanks, sis. And you're perfect for varsity. It's not like you're gonna stop working out. It's not like you got there and your work is done. There's always more work to do, and knowing you, you'll enjoy doing it."

True.

"Go to your next practice, and show Ally what you can do, but remember you're on the same level now. None of this *senior versus sophomore* crap. You're on varsity. There are six spots. One is yours. One is hers. You're even."

I flicked bubbles at her. "Aw, Elle. You learned how many players are on a volleyball court."

"Hey, I know some stuff." She smiled, and for the first time in a long time, her beauty felt more friendly to me than intimidating.

"Have you decided on a school for next year?" I asked, secretly hoping it would be close.

"No," she said with a sigh. "It's too big of a decision to make yet."

"Are you and Josh talking about sticking together?"

She checked the hallway. I didn't blame her. If either of my parents heard her say yes to that question, she'd be in trouble. Thankfully, they weren't around.

"We've talked about it, but neither of us knows where we want to go yet. We aren't planning around each other, but we are keeping each other in mind, if that makes sense."

I nodded. "Are you keeping us in mind?"

She tilted her head to the side and puffed out her bottom lip. "Are you admitting you're going to miss me?"

I considered hiding under the bubbles but decided to be honest. "It's been nice talking to you more, and you've been super helpful with all my boy stuff. And Ally."

"It has been nice but look on the bright side: I won't be able to take many clothes to my dorm, so you can wear everything while I'm gone."

"I'd rather have you than the clothes," I said.

"Aw, Mel. You're gonna make me cry."

I rolled my eyes and flicked bubbles at her. "Shut up."

"And the moment has passed." She stood and waved on her way

out the door.

"Wait, Elle," I said, calling her back. "Will you be at my scrimmage this week?"

"Wouldn't miss it. Josh is coming too. You got him loving volleyball now."

Another small victory.

***

AS IF THE WHOLE EXPERIENCE WEREN'T DRAMATIC

enough, Ally arrived in the student parking lot at the same moment my mom dropped me off at the main entrance. The gym was between us. We both walked toward it, facing each other like some kind of old western stare down. If it were Chandra, she'd yell something silly to me. I'd wave to her.

Ally didn't do either of those things.

We met outside the gym doors.

"Hey," she said.

"Hey," I said.

Did I open the door for her? Or was that presumptuous? Should she open the door?

Oh, this was ridiculous. I reached for the handle the same time she did. We both pulled away.

Even more ridiculous.

"Let me get the door for you," I said.

"Thanks."

I followed her to the empty gym.

"Guess you'll need to get the net," she said.

"I can't carry two poles myself."

"Right." She shook her head. "Didn't think about that."

That bordered on an apology. As the starting setter, Ally almost always got a ball after practice. Who knew the last time she helped put the net up?

"Fine." She dropped her backpack onto the bleachers with a thud.

I *'m here to get better. I'm here to secure my varsity spot. I'm here for the team.* I replayed these three sentences in my mind while we set up the net, jogged warm-up laps, and stretched.

"Glad to see you," Coach called from the doorway to the locker room. "While you stretch and warm up your arms, how about some chatter about where you like your sets, Melanie. And anything you'd like to share, Ally. You're teammates now. Get to know each other's preferences."

"Fine. I'll start. I don't want you to play the second ball. Ever," Ally said. "Even if you think I'm far away. Unless I yell, 'Help,' move out of my way. Got it?"

Shocker.

"Anything else?" I asked.

"When I play a ball out of the net, get low and be ready for anything."

Everyone knew that.

"Do you have a preference on sets?" I said. "Do you prefer the quick ones or high?"

"The pass has to be nearly perfect for a quick set, but we have some good passers, so if you want a quick set, call for it, and I'll do my best. Coordinate with the middles on quick sets, so you know who's taking the hit. Once it passes the middle's right arm, it should be yours since both our middles are right-handed hitters."

As a former middle hitter, I knew to let balls past my dominant arm go, but Ally was talking to me without disdain or daggers, so I thought it best to let her continue.

"What about you?" she said. "How do you prefer your sets?"

And this was the question I'd dreaded. I hadn't hit enough outside sets to know where I liked them best, and if I told Ally that, it would only solidify that I was too new to the position to be considered as Julia's replacement. "I have a few I'd like to try to really decide," I said, hoping that was diplomatic enough to satisfy her without picking up her criticism.

If Ally had a reaction, she didn't show it. She stretched her arms across her chest and said, "Let's get this over with."

Coach emerged from the locker room. "You two ready?"

"Yes, Coach," we said, and she rolled the basket of volleyballs to the center of the court and tossed one to Ally. Ally released a high set outside. I rounded my approach and jumped a little late.

"Low?" Coach asked.

152

"No. Let's try that one again," I said, wanting to speed up my approach and see if that worked. It did. I crushed the ball cross court.

"Nice hit, Melanie. Ally, let's give her about five more at that height."

Give Ally credit. She set the same spot five times in a row, which told me two things. First, she rocked at setter. Second, when she pushed bad sets my way, it was because she meant to.

I hit all five.

"Good hits," Ally said.

"Thanks."

"Try some quick sets," Coach said. "Melanie, I want you to start your approach when I release the ball. You should be in the air by the time Ally sets it."

The quick sets were a little trickier, but eventually, we perfected the timing.

"Now, mix it up. Melanie, call for the set you want."

We worked through three different sets like that, mixing things up. Coach threw a few erratic tosses to Ally, and she picked them up. She explained what kinds of passes she preferred for quick sets, so that I could watch for them.

By the time the rest of the team trickled into the gym, I had a smile on my face and hope the upcoming scrimmage would be much better than the last one—although in fairness, I'd set the bar pretty low.

CHAPTER TWENTY-THREE

THE DAY OF THE SCRIMMAGE, I WALKED THROUGH THE
open door to our gym and the sound of volleyballs smacking against
the hardwood. I closed my eyes and let the fuss settle around me.
This was it.

Home.

The day was my shot to show the team and the school I was
varsity material. I nodded to the girls warming up and headed for
the locker room. Quick to position my knee pads and slip into my
shoes, I made my way back to the gym and grabbed a ball to hit off
the wall and warm up my arm. Families and friends trickled in—none
of them mine.

The last few days, I'd spent more time reading and relaxing, so I
hadn't seen Harris. Or maybe he'd been spending time with his new
girlfriend. Warming up to the playlist Ally had put together with picks
from everyone on the team, my heart sank looking at the stands. I
should have told Harris about the scrimmage. He'd want to be here.

Square wandered in with a cluster of football players, including
Julia Medina. She waved to me and headed for our bench. She hugged
her mom and wished us all luck before catching up with her team.
Square gave me the nod, and Chandra catcalled in my ear.

She nodded toward Ally, who was setting to herself in the corner of the gym. "You think she's going to play nice today?"

"I hope so," I said.

"We'll miss you on JV."

"You'll still crush them."

"Hell yeah we will," she said. Coach called her to the setting position to warm up the hitters and came my way. "Melanie, I don't expect you to play JV today, but I'd like you to warm up with the team a little. Get some extra hitting in."

"Sure, Coach."

I jumped into the outside hitting line behind Vanessa.

She high-fived me. "Good luck today."

"Thanks, Vanessa."

"You deserve it, Melanie. Don't get me wrong. I want to play, but as much as I hate to admit it, you're better than me."

My throat became a desert—dry and wordless.

"Good luck, Soph," Nikki said, hopping in line behind me after crushing a high set.

"You too," I managed. "And thank you both."

I wanted to say something more. About how generous or gracious they were. Everything sounded so pretentious in my head. Thank you would have to do.

The first time I had lined up to hit outside, I'd felt so out of place. Today, it felt natural.

Chandra set me high, and I smashed the ball cross court.

A few sets later, I was back up again, hitting deep in the middle. I wanted to hit down the line, but I hadn't mastered that shift of my body yet.

I tried on the next set and hit the ball into the net, but hey, if you couldn't practice something in practice, why practice at all? I tried again. Out of bounds. Again. Net.

"You trying to hit line?" Nikki asked.

"And failing," I said.

"Square your shoulders down the line mid-jump. Like if you're hitting cross court, that's easy because your body is facing that direction on your approach. To hit down the line, you have to either swing your arm across your body, which isn't working for you right now, or turn your shoulders and swing straight."

"Thank you," I said, touched that she took the time to help me. The next set, I shifted my shoulders in midair and the ball landed inbounds. Not exactly down the line, but closer than I'd managed before.

"Keep working on it," Nikki said as Coach called everyone to the bench. She gave a pep talk and sent the JV onto the court. Vanessa had taken my spot. I sat on the bench with the other JV players and the varsity. While they took the court, I scanned the crowd and found both of my parents and sisters—an anomaly, for sure. Dad was almost always working, and Elle usually had shooting practice or a competition. Totally cheesy, but I felt a tickle in my stomach that they were all there.

Wait.

I squinted to be sure, and yes, Harris sat next to Lily. Harris had come. The tickle transformed into an explosion of giddiness, as if Harris had set off one of his signature explosions right there in the gym. Now I could say my whole family was there. With Harris, we were complete.

He waved, and I did the same.

I couldn't wipe the smile off my face until I saw Ally looking at me with her usual judging expression. I remembered what she'd said at the gym about Harris and rolled my eyes. She wasn't going to control me on or off the court, and she'd have to deal with that.

The JV won by impressive margins in both games. I squeezed Chandra into a hug on my way onto the court for varsity warm-ups.

"Nice work," I said. "That was an impressive set from the bleachers."

Late in the first game, she'd played a bad pass by running toward the bleachers. She'd reached as far as she could and popped the ball back onto the court with a forearm pass. And landed in Square's lap.

"I do have moves, you know," she said.

"I don't doubt it. That wasn't a bad landing pad either."

She winked. "It was not. Now, it's your turn to show us your moves, Soph."

My turn.

Phew. Deep breath. The team worked through a passing drill. Every one of my passes went straight to Ally. My serves weren't perfect, but I landed most of them inbounds. On the hitting warm-ups, I rotated hitting cross court and aiming down the line. My cross court hits landed stronger than my line attempts.

Coach called us to the bench. This was it. What I'd worked for. What I'd wanted.

Coach called for us to put our arms in. On the count of three, we cheered and headed to the court. My first varsity start. I bounced on my toes in the left-front position. The refs checked our numbers and positions and took their posts. Back at the serving line, Molly tossed the ball high into the air and jumped.

The game was on.

***

"GOOD GAME," CHANDRA SAID AFTER WE, LIKE THE JV, had won in three games.

I smiled and thanked her, but the victory didn't soar with me like I'd hoped it would. "Is it me, or did Ally only set me when I was out of position and not calling for the ball?"

Chandra squished her face together. "I may have noticed that. You should talk to her."

Ally was on the endline, chatting with her brother Owen and a woman I'd guess was her mother. Someone scooped me up from behind, and I turned to see Harris.

"Hey," I said, giving him and everyone else in my family a huge hug. "Thanks for coming."

"You played amazing," Elle said. "I'm so proud of you."

I hugged her again, words catching in my throat. The last few weeks had been really kind to me and Elle, which got me thinking about her competitions. "When you shoot next, I want to come."

She smiled and nodded. "Sounds great."

"You can ride out with me, superstar," Josh said, looping one arm around me and the other around Elle. "As long as you don't hit any volleyballs at me. That looks a little dangerous."

"I can't make any promises," I said.

Julia joined us, said hello to everyone, and hugged me. "Melanie, your passes and serves were incredible."

I noticed she didn't mention my hits. Couldn't blame her.

My parents headed out with Lily, leaving an opportunity for Square, who had been standing with a few other football players close by a chance to say hello. He hugged me and brushed a kiss on my cheek.

"Impressive," he said.

"Thank you. Still have some work to do, but I appreciate you coming."

He shrugged. "That's what scrimmages are for—figuring out what work you gotta do. And you're welcome."

Glancing at Square's smile, my frustration over Ally's sets—or lack thereof—dissipated. A little.

"Let me take you out to celebrate," he said.

Celebrate a scrimmage? Or maybe it was an excuse for us to finally get together. One-on-one.

Alone.

Breathe, Melanie.

"When?"

"Friday night."

A real date. With a gorgeous, sweet, funny athlete.

I nodded. "Friday night."

He actually pumped his fist.

"That's adorable."

He smiled. "My master plan. Be too adorable to resist."

Coach called us into the locker room.

"Gotta go," I said.

He kissed my cheek again and whispered in my ear, "Friday, Melanie."

When Square pulled away, Harris was at the doorway to the gym. I waved to him, but he left before he saw me. I'd have to catch up with him at home.

Back in the locker room, Chandra swatted my butt and catcalled again. I ignored her and headed to Ally's locker. The days of me sitting back and not speaking my mind were past. Like Elle had said, we were on the same team.

We were equals.

"Ally, can I talk to you for a sec?"

"That's what you're doing, isn't it?"

"Okay. I felt like maybe you weren't setting me a lot today when I called for the ball."

She threw her knee pads into her locker with a thud. "I can't set you every play. There are other people on the team, in case you didn't notice."

"Right," I said, refusing to let this go, despite her attitude. "But you set me when I was out of position and not calling for the ball. A couple of times. It was almost as if you wanted me to look bad."

She slammed her locker. "You think too highly of yourself, Melanie. I set where I can when I can. I thought we talked about that already. And if you want set more, keep working on your hits. I saw you in warmups. It wasn't going well."

Heat pricked at my skin, but I did my best to control my temper. "I was practicing hitting down the line. I was challenging myself to get better, even if that meant making mistakes. Because it was warmups, not the game."

"Well," she said, "you make it look like a challenge."

She left the locker room, and I slumped to the floor with my back against my locker. At our one-on-one practice, I'd sworn Ally had given in to Coach's decision. She'd set me well. We'd planned placement of our sets for the scrimmage.

I didn't get it. What had changed?

CHAPTER TWENTY-FOUR

ALL THE WAY HOME, I COULDN'T STOP TURNING THE situation over in my head. Ally had me burying my face into my pillow when I got home to scream my frustration away. She hadn't set me because I'd been challenging myself to hit down the line? What kind of crap was that?

A tiny part of me did admit that as a setter, she wanted to be confident in her hitters. If she wasn't confident in me, that was something I'd need to change. I knew the person to help. Seeing Harris in the stands at the scrimmage made me realize how much I missed talking to him. Watching his experiments. Listening to his scientific insults. Practicing volleyball with him in the back yard.

So we'd had a weird moment. So he was seeing someone. I was too. It was time to get things back to normal between us.

After I showered, I peeked out the window into his back yard. I couldn't see him, but there were lights everywhere, so I figured he had to be up to something.

Sliding through the broken pickets, I found his yard surprisingly clean. And romantic. Twinkle lights hung in the trees. Candles burned on every flat surface. Afraid I might be interrupting something his parents had planned, I tried to slip back out, but Harris called to me from the porch.

"Mel, I thought you'd be resting tonight."

"Hey. I wanted to talk to you."

"About? You played great today," he said before I could answer. "And on varsity. Everything you've been working toward."

"Thanks for being there. It was a nice surprise."

"Yeah, well—"

"And you're being generous," I said. "I still have some things to work on."

"But you also didn't get smashed in the face with a ball."

"Those are your standards?"

He shrugged, and I smacked his shoulder.

"That actually hurt."

"Liar."

"You're right. I have a few more things to clean up from today's experiment. Mind helping while we talk?"

"Not at all," I said.

I followed him to the picnic tables by the back porch and collected materials to return to the shed. His lab was small compared to the volleyball space. Even though we hadn't seen each other, he hadn't taken down the net. He'd sacrificed his lab for me.

That was why Harris was my best friend.

"You still have the net up."

"Yeah," he said. "You wanna practice this week? Statistically, my tosses are accurate eighty-six percent of the time."

I'd spent the last few days avoiding him, and he'd spent them perfecting his toss to help me? I put away the jars of powder Harris probably used to intensify an explosion and hugged him. Tightly. I didn't know where it came from, but it felt right. He always had my back, and I never even had to ask. Slowly, he wrapped his arms around me too. I settled into their warmth, resting some of my body weight on him and remembered something my mom had said when I was younger. One of the best ways to relieve emotions was a hug, and you should hold the hug as long as you needed to. As a kid, my emotions had usually been anger over a fight with my sisters. Now, my emotions were fear I wouldn't be good enough, frustration with Ally for how cold she'd been on the court, and who-knew-what for Square.

Lots of emotions.

That meant an extra-long hug.

It felt so good, I didn't care. And Harris didn't seem to either. His fingertips ran along the backs of my arms and my neck.

"That feels nice," I whispered.

"You okay?"

I nodded into his shoulder. "Just needed a hug from my best friend."

He squeezed me tighter. "Any time."

I sighed and pressed my face against his neck. He smelled like oranges and peppermint.

Wait. Did I just smell him?

Why?

Aware of his heart rate and mine in this weird rhythm, I slowly pulled away and studied his face. He studied me with intense inquiry in his eyes, like he was watching a chemical reaction in one of his experiments. Maybe he could see the chemical reaction inside my body that freaked me out. Did *he* know I smelled him?

"Your eyes are like basketballs. What's going on, Mel?"

I cleared my throat and stepped back. "Um. Nothing."

"It's not nothing. Talk to me."

"I don't know what to say. I—"

What? I smelled you? I liked this hug? I've had a stressful couple of days, and all I wanted to do was see you. I thought it was because you're my best friend, but now in that moment, I was totally freaked out and had no idea if Harris Fullerton was *only* my best friend.

That I want to simplify my life, not complicate it?

I was going on an official date with Square soon.

None of those things felt like a good call.

"Hello?" someone called from the back yard.

"Who's that?"

Now Harris's eyes were like basketballs.

"I love this net."

Wait. I know that voice. "Is that...?"

I burst through the door of the shed and found Ally Malone in Harris's back yard.

"Ew," she said. "Are you everywhere in my life?"

"I could say the same thing."

Harris ambled out of the shed and toward Ally. In an alternate universe, he bent forward and kissed her cheek.

Kissed her cheek.

Ally Malone.

Harris Fullerton.

Kissed her cheek!

Alternate universe. Alternate universe.

Did alternate universes have oxygen?

"Mel," Harris said. "Funny story."

Ally slipped her arm in his. "We were at the gym together and started talking. You're right. He isn't just a science nerd. And he looks great with a haircut. Who knew?"

Definitely no oxygen in this alternate universe. "Are you two... dating?"

She giggled. I didn't know Ally Malone did that. "Don't be so formal," she said. "We're hanging out. Aren't we, Binky?"

I gave Harris—the guy who perpetually made fun of pet names—a pointed look. "Binky?"

"The candles are so romantic," Ally said. "And the twinkle lights. I've never played volleyball by twinkle light."

"You're playing volleyball? Here? Tonight?"

"Why do you think he set up this net for me?"

And another pointed look to Harris, who had the decency to look embarrassed.

"I'm gonna go," I said.

"You don't have to," Harris said, but Ally's face told me I did. This was their date. Only feet from my house. I'd have to close the windows. And put on headphones. And scrub my memories from my brain.

CHAPTER TWENTY-FIVE

HARRIS IS DATING ALLY MALONE.

My Harris. In his back yard with his science experiments and my volleyball net. Would he let her wear my goggles and show off some explosion? Would they...make out?

My chest squeezed and twisted and lit itself on fire.

What did he see in her?

Where did all the oxygen on this planet go?

"Are you okay?"

Elle's face was inches from mine. Then Lily's appeared.

"She's freaking out. What happened?"

"I don't know."

"I can't breathe," I managed.

"I'll get my inhaler," Lily said.

"Melanie, listen to me," Elle said. "Look at my eyes."

I did.

"Good. Now, take a deep breath in. Hold it there...two...three... four...five. Okay exhale. Good. You're doing great. Another deep breath in. And hold...two...three...four...five. Good."

Elle's voice talked me through another deep breath that chipped away at the boulders weighing down my chest.

"Good. You're doing great, Mel. One more. In...two...three...

four...five. And exhale."

Lily ran back into the room that had come into focus since my last deep breath with Elle.

"Better?" she asked.

"Yeah."

"Wanna talk about it?" Elle asked.

Nothing like that had ever happened to me before. "I felt like I was drowning. But without being in the water. That doesn't make any sense."

"No," Elle said. "It does."

"Stress can do ugly things," Lily said.

Stress? More like Ally Malone. Coach had the right idea forcing us to work together. She'd made it clear to Ally that she'd have to accept we were teammates. And then she kissed Harris.

"It's like she knows when I'm out of position," I blurted.

"What?" Elle said.

"Ally. She sets me when I don't even call for the ball. Maybe I'm not ready. Whatever. She still sets me. But when I call aggressively for the ball, she sends it anywhere else. So yes, she's setting me, which might satisfy Coach. And now, she can't say she's not setting me."

And she kissed Harris.

"This is a little over my head," Lily said. "I'm gonna put my inhaler back."

"Not to mention she's really good. Like, so good. I wouldn't say that if it wasn't true. Because she's so good, she can set the ball wherever she wants. But is that to me?"

"I'm guessing no," Elle said.

"Exactly."

And she kissed Harris!

"Have you tried talking to her, Mel? Like, really talking?"

"I've tried. Ally Malone doesn't talk. She scowls. Judges. Orders people around. Oh, and apparently dates my best friend, but she doesn't do talking."

"Maybe if you—"

"Every moment is an audition, Elle," I said, cutting her off. "It's exhausting. I want to play volleyball. Have fun. Compete. Against the other team! Not my own. I'm starting to wonder if I'll get the chance to do that or if this whole season is going to be lost. It's like every time we get on the court, we're in complete disorder."

Elle climbed onto the couch, pulled me close to her, and wrapped a blanket around us. "Is that Ally next door with Harris?"

I closed my eyes, as if eliminating my vision could make me unsee them together in my memories.

"You and Ally have been at odds for weeks now, Mel. And maybe Lil is right. Maybe the stress from volleyball got to be too much, but I think the near-drowning experience might have been because Ally is with Harris right now."

"Of course, I don't want them to date. He's my best friend. How could he like her? What's to like?"

"Mel..."

I felt the boulders creeping back again. Pressure behind my temples. Finally, the tears came. Along with the permanent images of Ally and Harris together.

"Do you think she's doing this because of you and Josh?"

Elle raised her eyebrows. "Does that comparison suggest there's something romantic between you and Harris?"

"No," I insisted, refusing to think about how he smelled or that I knew how he smelled since I had, in fact, smelled him. "He's my friend. My best friend. Harris is always there for me, but when I needed him tonight, he was with her. Seeing him at the scrimmage today meant everything, but he wasn't even there for me."

"You don't know that. He could have been there for both of you."

"That's the thing. There is no both of us. It's either me or Ally. She made it that way."

Elle sighed. "I don't think this is anything we're going to solve today."

Or ever.

"You should spend some time relaxing. Go read."

The thought of focusing on words—no. "I don't think I can right now."

"Mel, it's going to be okay. It always is."

"Thanks." I rested my head on her shoulder. "This is actually kind of nice. Wanna watch a movie?"

"Sure. Let me message Josh real quick."

"You have plans. Forget it."

"I will not forget it," Elle said. "You're my sister. And we're watching a movie."

She tapped a quick message on her phone and yelled for Lily. Slow, reluctant footsteps found us.

"Yes, princesses?" Lily asked.

Elle pointed two feet away to the table. "We need the remote."

My older sister burst into laughter. I wasn't there yet, but my mouth definitely broke into a smile. I wanted to give in to it. Laughing with my sisters was the best medicine for the tension strangling my body.

"Hilarious," Lily said. "You called me in here to hand you a remote that is two feet away?"

"Not just that," Elle said. "We want you to watch with us."

Lily squinted at us like she didn't fully believe. We'd trained her well over the years.

"And get snacks from the kitchen," I added, and Elle high-fived me.

"You're jerks," Lily said, but she rolled her eyes. "I pick the movie."

"Fine," I said, "But I pick the snacks."

"Fine," she yelled on her way out of the room. "Which ones do you want?"

"All of them!"

***

SPENDING THE EVENING WITH MY SISTERS WAS LIKE Icy Hot for my heart. Lily chose a comedy, and we laughed so hard we spit popcorn everywhere, which Mom totally made us vacuum before bed. But I didn't look over the fence into Harris's yard once, and the tiniest part of me started—only started—to believe Elle might be right.

Maybe Ally and I would figure things out.

Maybe Harris and I would be fine if he dated Ally.

Maybe volleyball would be fun again.

Maybe.

At practice, Ally smiled at me. An actual smile. So of course, I thought she might be plotting to kill me.

"Melanie," she said. "Now that you're a starter, you should join us for V Night."

"V Night?"

"Team night for varsity girls. Super chill. We're hitting a party for an hour or so and sleeping over Sam's. It's gonna be great. I'll message you the details."

Super chill? Sleepover? Great?

Those words did not work together for me.

"Great," I said, hoping she lost my number.

No. You need this, Melanie. You need to bond with this team, and maybe even Ally. Follow Elle's advice. Talk to her.

Only if I could stop talking to myself.

It wasn't until I was on the way home that I remembered on V Night I also had a date with Square.

CHAPTER TWENTY-SIX

WHEN THE WORLD WEIGHED ME DOWN—TESTS,
fights with friends, family demands, sports struggles—I did two
things. Shower and nap. After practice, I showered and closed the
blinds, making sure not to look through the window overlooking
Harris's house. I took the grandmother of all naps.

Until Elle jumped onto my bed and demanded I wake up.

"Your date with Square is in one hour, Melanie."

I pulled the pillow over my head. Somehow the nap hadn't made
my problems disappear.

"I have to go to practice," Elle said. "I only have ten minutes to
prep you. If you want my help, you will get up now!"

I groaned and squinted my eyes open. I could not do this without
my sister. "I'm awake."

"Smile." She clapped her hands. "This is your first date."

A perfect moment for my mom to step into the room and take a
picture.

"Mom!"

"It's a big day!" She took another one.

"Oh my gosh," I said but couldn't help smiling. "Where are the
wardrobe options?"

Elle scooped a pile of clothes I hadn't seen from the floor and fanned them out over my purple bedspread. "Are you thinking shorts or skirt?"

I'd told Square I wanted something low key. He'd asked about outdoors options, and I'd said yes. "Shorts," I told Elle. "I have a feeling we'll be outside. Maybe a hike or something."

"You better take bug spray," Mom said. "And check yourself for ticks."

"Maybe Square could do that," Elle whispered.

Mom glared. "I heard that."

"Joking, Mom!" She looked at me and mouthed, *Not really.*

"Okay, let's get dressed." I did not need to think about Square checking me for ticks.

Elle gave me three crop tops to choose from. "Seriously? What is wrong with a full shirt?"

She sighed and grabbed another pile from under my bed. "I thought you might say that."

I chose a flowing tank with a twisted ruffle that tugged in the waist on one side. The look pulled off the right amount of tight to show my figure but enough material to achieve modesty. I slipped the tank over my head and tugged the mango-colored jean shorts over my hips. "Done."

Elle nodded approval, and we moved on to makeup and hair, which she gave me general instructions on before she had to leave for practice.

"I can't believe I'm going to miss this," she said, squeezing me into an intense hug. "Listen, I know you've been so stressed lately with everything going on with volleyball and Ally and Harris, but dates are supposed to be fun. This is the part of high school and being a teenager where you can get away from all the stress and spend time with someone who's worth it."

"Oh, Elle. How did you get so wise?" I teased.

"Shut up, Mel. We're having a moment here."

I looped my arm in hers and lowered my head to her shoulder. "Sorry. Please continue."

"I see the way you laugh and smile with him, so try to let that other stuff go. Have a good time."

"Thanks, Elle."

"You're welcome. Trust me. All those other problems will be waiting for you when you come back."

"And now you went ahead and blew it," I said.

She hip-checked me. "I did not! I was brilliant. You're lucky to have me."

"I am," I agreed, knowing my hair and makeup would crush if she were sticking around. Without her, I'd do my best. After ten minutes of struggling, I accepted help from Lily.

Embarrassing.

Square texted he was on the way when Lily, my mom, and I stood in front of the full-length mirror in Elle's room. Mom snapped another picture.

"Still think I'm Elle's Barbie doll?" I asked Lil.

"Elle bought that shirt for you today at the mall," she said. "Does that answer your question?"

I scowled at her as theatrically as I could. "Someday you're gonna like a boy, and you'll come to me for help."

She rolled her eyes. "Gross."

"I'll remember," Mom said and hugged us both. "I can't wait to meet him."

"What? No," I said. "I am waiting for him outside. He is not going through the gauntlet."

"What gauntlet?" Mom said.

"Mom! It's our first date. No."

Her shoulders drooped. "Fine. But I'm watching from the window."

I covered my face with both hands. What had I gotten myself into?

***

A TREE SWING IN OUR FRONT YARD GAVE ME THE PER-fect cover to wait for Square. Or so I thought. With my cheek against the rope of the swing, I closed my eyes and thought of what Elle had said. Cute guy plus late summer night plus a hot outfit equaled fun.

Interesting karma in the universe or sense of humor or whatever because the second I embraced Elle's philosophy, Harris snuck up on me from the shadows, making me jump so abruptly I caught my arm on the swing.

"Oh, crap. You okay?" he asked.

"Fine. Thanks," I said, rubbing the rope burn forming on my skin. At least it gave me something legitimate to do besides looking at his face. What if I saw remnants of Ally's lipstick there?

"Can we talk?" he said.

"Sure."

He took a breath but didn't speak.

And then repeat. Repeat. Repeat.

"Harris, do you have something you'd like to say?"

After another breath, words actually formed in his mouth. "I'm sorry you found out that way."

Ally. He wanted to talk about Ally. Like a little kid, he was sorry he'd gotten caught, not that he'd done something he shouldn't have. "Don't you mean you're sorry you're hanging out with her, *Binky*?"

"Okay. I deserve that."

And a lot more. "Seriously," I said, jumping up from the swing. "How could you do this? She has made my life hell these last few weeks."

"Aren't you being a little hard on her?"

Oh. My. Gosh. "Hard on *her*? She's the one being hard on me. Which is great because trying out for varsity when all my friends from the team last year bailed to play a different sport and the one girl I thought I could learn from quit and oh, the coach asked me to try an entirely new position—those things weren't hard for me already at all."

"Melanie, I know it's been rough."

"No," I said. "I thought you knew, but if you knew, you wouldn't have brought her to your house. You wouldn't be with her because you'd know this is hard enough without her giving me crap all the time."

Harris stepped back until he crossed the threshold from my family's property to his, a symbolic retreat for both of us.

Down the street, headlights appeared. I prayed they were from Square, arriving to rescue me from this drama.

"Did you ever think that maybe she's looking out for you?" Harris said softly. "She thinks you can do better."

The tender way he talked about her cut me. "Yeah, I could do better if she actually supported me instead of trying to get in my way all the time."

In a more defensive tone, he said, "Maybe she isn't sure you're ready for varsity."

Square stopped his SUV in front of my house and climbed out. He waved, and I did my best to smile. With a deep breath, I managed to turn to Harris and say, "You are my best friend. You've been telling me for months that if I want this, work for it. You've helped me work hard. Now you're siding with her after you've spent, what, two hours together? Why? Because she stuck her tongue down your throat?"

He glared at me. "That's a shitty thing to say."

"Dating Ally is a shitty thing to do, so I guess we're even."

Leaving Harris on the lawn and refusing to look back at him, I jogged across the lawn to give Square a hug. "Sorry about that. Ready to go?"

"Shouldn't I meet your mom or something? Promise your dad I won't let anything happen to you?"

I wouldn't have guessed it possible after my argument with Harris, but Square actually had me smiling. "My mom is undoubtedly watching from one of the windows." We looked toward the house and saw her silhouette in the dining room. We waved. "And my father isn't home."

He reached for my hand. "Introduce me."

"You don't know what you're getting into."

He showed me his full-wattage smile that would undoubtedly win over my mother in seconds. "My mama taught me right."

I kissed his cheek. "Okay. Let's go."

I led him through the front door and called out to my mom, who had been watching through the dining room window.

"I'm so glad you changed your mind," she said.

"I didn't. Square insisted on meeting you."

As expected, my mother watched Square with acceptance in her dewy eyes. "Is that right?"

"Yes, Mrs. Corwin," he said but didn't stop there. He said all the right things, made my mother laugh, and promised to keep me safe.

"Impressive," I said on the way back to the car. "Is there anyone on the planet you can't charm?"

He bowed his head, humble as ever, opened the passenger door for me, and held my hand while I climbed into the car. I couldn't bear to look at my mom, undoubtedly still watching from the windows. She probably had her hands over her chest and a goofy grin on her face. To my surprise, Harris had been on his porch watching us. I caught a look at his back when he flung open his front door and disappeared inside.

Empirically, he'd say that I wasn't far from him—twenty-five yards at most. In reality, my best friend seemed light-years away.

CHAPTER TWENTY-SEVEN

SQUARE STARTED THE CAR AND PULLED HIS SEAT BELT over his broad shoulders. He nodded toward Harris's house. "You okay? That looked a little intense."

I leaned back against the headrest and sighed. "Just me fighting with my best friend. It's been a rough few weeks."

"You wanna talk about it?"

Elle's words played in my head. Dates were about having fun. "No. Thank you though. I want to talk about you."

A smile crept across his lips as he put the car in Drive. "I appreciate that, but if you change your mind. I'm here."

"Thanks."

He cracked his neck and puffed up his chest. "So. About me, where should we start?"

We both laughed.

"We have about two hours before volleyball team time—again, so sorry about that by the way."

"It's all good."

"Thanks. Maybe you should start with where you're taking your hot date."

"I like that confidence," he said. "And you do look hot."

I'd sort of fished for the compliment, but I still felt my cheeks warming.

"There's this place I like to go. My uncle showed it to me. Good view. I might have a picnic planned."

"You made me a picnic?"

He shrugged. "You know me, the strong, sensitive type."

"That how your opponents on the field would describe you?"

"I hope not."

He chatted about football and what he loved about playing linebacker. He told me about Julia's tryouts and how much he respected her. He asked why I loved volleyball so much, and I told him it was because I'd been really good at the balloon game when I was a kid.

"You aren't gonna let that go, are you?"

"Never!" I insisted.

We talked about our families. He made the cutest face when he told me about his mom. She managed one of the banks in town after working her way up from a teller position all while being a single mom to him and his two little brothers. His pride could have filled the whole car and even spilled out the open windows.

"It took a while, but I finally see how hard she worked for us. She's always been there, you know?"

Guilt scratched at me for sometimes thinking of my mom as single since my dad was almost always working. She still had a partner. Just a relatively absent one.

"I'd like to meet her sometime."

He grinned.

"Sorry. That's really presumptuous. I mean she sounds amazing."

"She is, and you will."

"What are your brothers like?"

He chuckled.

"That bad, huh?"

"They're like Nerf gun battles in the family room, snack hoarders in the kitchen, and back-seat drivers in my car."

"So, little brothers?"

"Basically," he said with a smile.

"They play football?"

"And basketball. And baseball."

"Impressive. How old are they?"

"Ten and eleven."

I wondered if Lily knew them.

The trees thickened as they did in the back roads of Pennsylvania. I wasn't much for camping, unless the camp had a volleyball court, but I appreciated the beauty of the blue-gray twilight sky behind silhouetted treetops.

"Do you come up here a lot?"

"Used to. When I was a kid. Now, life's too busy for the simple things."

With all the demands of the volleyball team so far this season, I understood that to my core.

"My mom's brother used to bring us. He's busy. He coaches football in the city."

"It must be nice to have someone who knows the game in your life." My parents tried, but it didn't come from their core.

"It's nice to have someone who knows life in my life, if you feel me."

I thought about how my older sister had helped me navigate the last few weeks of a world unknown to me. "I'm beginning to."

Square took a sharp turn up a steep hill. A cool breeze creeped in the window, and I shivered.

"I got you." He put up the windows, and the car quieted and warmed immediately.

"I can't believe summer's practically over. Are you looking forward to school starting on Monday?"

"Surprisingly, yeah." He shook his head. "I honestly can't believe I said that."

"Why?"

"I didn't always like school."

"What changed?" I asked.

He took a deep breath but didn't respond right away.

"You don't have to talk about it if you don't want to."

"I want to tell you. That's a little odd for me."

I waited.

"In middle school, I got in some trouble. Nothing major. Messing around at lunch. We poured our drinks onto the floor, being stupid, and a girl slipped."

"Ouch."

"Even worse, she'd broken her arm a couple months before."

I gasped.

"Yep," he said.

"What happened?"

"My mom met me in the principal's office. I'd never seen that look on her face before." He cleared his throat and said quietly. "Like she lost faith in me."

"From everything you've told me about your mom, I can't imagine she could ever lose faith in you."

"No. You're right." He shrugged. "But it felt that way. That day, I promised her I'd never do anything so stupid again—that she'd never get called to the principal's office for me."

"Isn't it a little harsh on you? Part of growing up is doing stupid things."

"Some people don't have that luxury."

The statement teetered on the edge of opening up a can of worms about his life I wasn't sure he was ready to open. I watched the trees roll by outside the window, giving him the chance to keep talking or steer the direction to a different topic. I wanted to give him that choice.

After a minute or so, he scoffed. "Pretty heavy for a first date. I'm sorry."

"Don't be."

"I'm surprised you didn't hear the story before. I thought everyone in school did."

"I wasn't at the middle school then," I reminded him gently.

"Right. You were in elementary school. Man."

"Don't say it like that!"

"It's true! I'm a cradle robber."

"Stop!" But we were both laughing again.

Our laughter settled like a calming breeze after a burst of wind. He glanced sideways at me.

"What?" I said.

He looked back at the road. "I like talking to you."

I turned to the window, afraid to say what I was thinking—that I liked it too. "Have you ever been to the principal's office again?"

"Nope. And I started studying more. I still remember the first A I ever got. It was a math test. I couldn't believe it. But it felt good. Really good. I'd earned it myself, you know?"

"Sounds like you and Lily would get along. She loves getting As."

"I don't know. She sounds a little out of my league. I'm not a straight-A student, but I learned I could do a lot better than I thought. If I tried."

Square's vulnerability was just as adorable as everything else about him. He wove the car through windy roads that climbed slowly into the foothills.

"This feels like the middle of nowhere," I said.

"Just wait." He took another bend, and the trees on the passenger side thinned, offering a stunning view of the valley where we lived below.

"Wow."

"Exactly." He reversed into an overlook parking spot.

"We're gonna die," I said. "How do you know how close you are to the edge?"

"They're called mirrors," he said with a laugh.

"Maybe I should get out of the car and help you."

He covered my hand with his and made some serious eye contact that would have had Chandra fanning herself. "Maybe you should trust."

I tried. Ultimately, I closed my eyes until I heard the keys click and the engine shut down. Then I let out a deep breath.

"Trust issues?" he said.

"Apparently."

"That is a pretty steep cliff." He smacked my leg lightly. "You hungry? Because we're about to eat over it."

My stomach flipped.

Square came around the car and opened my door. He opened the tailgate. "Want to eat in the car or on the ground?"

The back of the SUV looked pretty snug for a guy Square's size and a girl with my height.

"Ground's fine."

He got to work setting up a blanket and laying out food. He actually kicked off his shoes before he sat on the blanket, which twisted up all my insides in a way that made me feel like saying, "Aw," all over again. I removed my shoes and joined him. After carefully sanitizing our hands—his mother's orders apparently—he plated steaming-hot macaroni and cheese and buttermilk biscuits.

"How is this still hot?"

"Mama is magic. Wait until you taste her peach cobbler."

The "aw" came out. "Your mom made us dinner?"

"She likes to see things are done right," he said.

I took a bite of the mac and cheese. Oh. My. Gosh. "We are gonna need a bigger container of this."

He produced two more containers. "There's more. Salmon patties and green beans." He smirked. "Gotta have your veggies."

My stomach grumbled. No shame there. If Square had brought such a feast, he'd like a girl who could eat. A full-time athlete, I had no problem with that. "I've never had a salmon patty."

Square whistled and dropped one onto my plate. Terrified I'd offend him and his mom if I didn't like it, I cut into the crispy edge and brought a small bite to my lips. The outer crunch complemented the flaky salmon. The flavors exploded in my mouth.

"Your mom is divine."

"That's what I've been telling you. Feeding us is one of her many talents."

The stories flowed—so fast, I nearly spit out my food from laughing. But it was too good to waste. The tales about his brothers trumped the others. They got into a lot of mischief and ate everything their mother could manage to cook.

"Sounds like she deserves an award. Or several," I said.

"She does."

"It reminds me a lot of my best friend actually."

"The one from earlier," Square asked.

"Yeah. He does science experiments in his back yard and films them for YouTube. It's part of his college plan. He saves money from monetizing the site, but I think he's also made some really good connections."

"Sounds smart."

"He's brilliant. Although his stepmom doesn't fully appreciate that. In fairness, sometimes he lights things on fire and destroys property—all in the name of science."

Square opened two small containers of peach cobbler. Despite the mountain of mac and cheese I'd eaten, my stomach growled again.

"Is that what you were fighting about?"

"No. He's"—I used air quotes—"'hanging out' with Ally Malone. Who hates me. So that makes being his best friend a little awkward."

"Ally still giving you a hard time?"

"She's made it an actual sport. And you know how competitive she is."

"Owen was pretty rough on Julia. They have that intensity in common."

"I don't get what Harris sees in her."

He scrunched up his face in a way I'd never seen him do before.

"What does that face mean?" I asked.

"Don't take this the wrong way. Ally may be intense, but she's still definitely...um..."

"Yes?"

"You know," he said.

"No. I don't." I crossed my arms.

"She's not for me. Don't mistake it, but she's not terrible to look at."

I scowled at him.

"I tried to do that in the most gracious way possible."

"Didn't fully deliver."

"I felt that," he said.

I took a few bites of the peach cobbler, refusing to let Ally ruin its deliciousness. From a completely objective point of view, Ally might've been pretty. She had a great body from working out all the time, obviously. But. She was Ally.

"She and Harris still don't fit. He's all into science, and she's only into sports."

"Do you know her that well?"

"What's going on here?" I asked.

He raised his hands in surrender. "I'm on your side. One hundred percent."

"Good. Then you get that Ally Malone does not deserve my best friend."

"Mm-hmm." He took a bite of his dessert.

"What does that noise mean?" I asked.

He finished the cobbler and put the lid back on, seemingly working very hard not to make eye contact with me. "Did the two of you ever date?"

This conversation was going so far in the wrong direction. "No. It's not like that. He's my best friend, and she's far from my number-one fan. I couldn't believe when I got this shot to play varsity, and it's like she's tried to sabotage it every step of the way. I guess part of me worries she's going to sabotage my friendship with Harris too."

"If you're really tight, she can't change that. Right?"

"I guess so." I leaned my head on his shoulder. Square was right. Ally Malone could only come between Harris and me if I let her. "Thanks for talking about this."

He slipped his arm around me. "Definitely."

I tilted my face up toward him. The lights from houses and businesses across the river reflected off his dark eyes, which were locked on me. It took a few seconds for my head to tell my heart what was happening. My heart reacted, thumping so hard against my chest, it practically hurt.

"Melanie?" Square whispered.

"Yes?"

"I want to kiss you."

Without meaning to, I licked my lips, and his mouth curled into that gorgeous smile. He raised his eyebrows in a question. My heart thudded in my chest, louder than the sound of a volleyball slapping my forearms in the quiet of my living room. Square wanted to kiss me.

I snuck another look at his lips.

I nodded.

He inched closer until his full lips pressed against mine. They were soft and smooth, like his voice and the way he moved through life. His mouth moved against mine in a sensual rhythm like I'd seen on so many rom-coms, like I'd read in so many books. Square kissed with confidence, nudging my nose with his, teasing my lips and tongue.

The stars, the shining lights, the amazing guy—all should have amounted to the perfect moment. Except there was one problem. In the midst of the kiss, I thought of one thing.

Harris Fullerton's face.

CHAPTER TWENTY-EIGHT

A SMALL VOICE IN MY HEAD WHISPERED THAT I WISHED I was kissing Harris, not Square.

I pulled away and lowered my head, shock rippling through my body so violently I shivered. I couldn't look at Square. I couldn't think of a single thing to say.

I could only wonder if Harris was with Ally, if when he kissed her he thought of me too.

No. He'd defended Ally. Sided with her. The realization sent the toughest hit I'd ever faced crushing into my chest.

"It's about time to get you to that party," Square said, and I nodded.

"You okay?" he asked.

"Yep. I'm good."

He watched me for a few seconds while I cleaned the remnants of our picnic. I couldn't bring myself to make eye contact. He slipped an arm around my waist and lifted me until I was standing and pressed against him. "I'm sorry if I freaked you out."

"No," I said. "You're amazing."

"That I know," he teased.

"I mean it."

"Thank you."

We worked in silence and, when all the mess had been taken care of, climbed into the front seat.

"So where's this volleyball party?" Square asked.

"It's not a volleyball party, but I have the address." I found Ally's message and handed him my phone.

He looked at it and squinted at me. "Are you sure this is the place?"

"Positive. The message is from Ally."

He gave me the phone. "Parties in that neighborhood tend to be bad news. I wouldn't go if I were you."

"Ally wouldn't make us go to a questionable party."

Square rubbed his face with both hands and sighed. "I'm not letting you go alone. I'll walk you in."

***

WE TURNED DOWN THE NEIGHBORHOOD STREETS, which made Square's point strikingly clear. Cars lining both sides and piled into a driveway of a house playing loud music told us we'd hit the jackpot.

If you could call it that.

"You still want to go in?"

"I want to be sitting in the hammock in my back yard, but that wasn't exactly on Ally's list of team-bonding activities."

Square climbed out and opened my door. "Don't leave my side."

I tugged on his arm. "You really don't have to do this."

He squeezed my hand and turned the front door handle. The entry hall was packed with people holding red cups of what I expected was anything but water. A few nodded greetings or high-fived Square.

"Who's your girl?"

"This is Melanie," he said, pulling me closer. I got the sense it was more due to his protective instincts than possessiveness. I appreciated that.

"Hey," I said with a nod, and we were off again, searching through the crowds of people dancing on and around tables. In the den, a group of guys threw a ping-pong ball into cups of beer on a door they'd turned into a table. "What are they doing?"

Square looked where I was pointing and shook his head. "This place would eat you alive. Can you message your friends and see where they are?"

I reached into my back pocket, but my phone was gone. "I must have left it in your car."

"Let's do a loop. If we don't find your friends, we're out of here."

A girl who looked younger than me projectile vomited into a trash can a few feet away. I covered my nose.

"Deal."

Square held my hand down the basement stairs and swore under his breath when we hit the bottom.

"Square! Man!" A short, spritely kid ran at him, grabbed his hand, and bumped his shoulder into Square's. Given the height difference, he didn't actually reach his shoulder. "Don't see you around here much anymore."

"Nope," Square said. "Glad I bumped into you because we're heading out actually."

"So soon? Things are getting interesting down here."

Curious about what was so interesting, I took in the room. Two couches and six random chairs—a beat-up computer swivel chair, two folding chairs, three lawn chairs—surrounded a coffee table littered with phones, cups, and a massive bowl of multicolored...I squinted to see more clearly.

"Are those pills?" I whispered to Square.

He squeezed my hand and stepped in front of me. I interpreted that as a polite request to shut up. So I did.

In time to watch Lacey walk toward Square like a seductress. She caressed his shoulder and tilted forward at an awkward angle that overflowed her neckline. "Yeah, sexy. Stay."

Before I could debate whether I should be jealous, Square pushed me back up the stairs and out the back door.

"What was that?"

"It's called a Skittles party."

"Do they actually take random pills? When they don't know what they are?"

Square nodded.

"Stupid, right?" said a guy I'd never seen before who leaned so close to my face, I thought he might've kept coming and tackled me to the ground. Square pushed him upright.

"Chill, dude," the guy said and wrapped his arm around a girl who had equal difficulty standing. How long had these people been drinking? It was only eight-thirty. "I don't mess with pills, man."

"Probably a good idea," Square said in his deadpan voice that always made me laugh.

"Yeah," the girl said. "You never know what you'll get. I brought some of my mom's stool softeners."

Her apparent boyfriend threw back his head in laughter. His momentum kept taking him in that direction, but the side of the house broke his fall. He righted himself and said, "Classic. I threw in a few prenatal vitamins."

"Those might actually come in handy," Square said.

The guy high-fived him. "I know, right!"

"Please get me out of here," I mumbled.

"With pleasure."

Square led me around the house back to the street.

"What was Ally thinking?"

"I have no idea, but none of your teammates were there. Would she have set you up like that?"

I closed my eyes and took a deep breath, but it did nothing to calm me. Ally set me up.

Ally sent me to the party from hell.

Deep breath.

I'd had enough of her. I found my phone between the seats and messaged Sam. She responded immediately to say the team was at her house.

Not at a party.

"You need a ride somewhere? It's really no trouble."

Ally's wrath for arriving with Square would be nothing compared to the anger festering in me right now. What if Square hadn't been with me? What if Lacey and her friends had come at me like they had at the last party Ally had insisted the team go to?

"If you really don't mind, that would be great," I said.

Square turned toward the north end of town. In less than ten minutes, he parked on Sam's street, and fortunately because of the number of cars, a few houses away. He turned off the ignition and sat back against the seat. "Tonight was not exactly the kind of date I expected."

I scoffed. "No."

"You're clearly not into the party scene, so what kinds of things do you like to do?"

Everything I thought of sounded lame—swinging in the hammock, watching Harris explode things, practicing volleyball in my back yard. "I'm more low key."

He nodded.

"Which is not the popular answer, I know. Everyone is so worried about how many people they see on a Friday night and who has more followers on this social network or that one."

"Who got more likes on the photo they posted online."

"Exactly!" I said. "I'd much rather leave my cell phone in the house and go outside where it's quiet than always be connected and bothered. Which makes me totally weird."

"That's not weird. It's refreshing."

"Thanks." I looked down at my lap. Square was a total surprise. Liked by everyone but still able to be true to himself. Well known, yet a loner. I watched him as he looked straight ahead at the road. His shaved head was about a centimeter short from grazing the roof of the car, and he filled in the seat with ease. I didn't play football, but I knew that if he was coming at me full speed, I'd definitely run in the other direction. He turned to me and smiled.

"What?" My cheeks warmed.

"Were you checking me out?"

I burst into laughter.

"You were!" He grinned in that smoldering way of his. "I don't mind." He tugged up the short sleeves of his shirt. "I'll even flex for you."

"Stop," I said, crying from the hilarity. And embarrassment.

He wrapped an arm around my shoulders and pulled me close. "You make me laugh, Melanie. I like that."

"Me too."

There was one problem. When he'd planted those perfect lips on my mouth, it had been Harris's face I'd seen. Square was funny, adorable, and thoughtful. He worked hard at football and life. A week earlier, thoughts of his smile and flirty messages had sent giddy flutters through me. He deserved a girl to feel that way about him.

But something had changed. I didn't know exactly when or how or why, but even if I wanted to, I couldn't take it back.

How did I tell Square that? Before I could figure it out, someone pounded on the window.

CHAPTER TWENTY-NINE

I TURNED TO SEE ALLY'S ANGRY FACE AND THE REST OF the varsity team—including Sam—behind her.

"I'm sorry," I muttered.

"That girl and her brother are two peas in a pod."

Literally, since she and Owen were twins.

"Thanks for the ride." I pecked Square on his cheek and hopped out of the car. The tough conversation would have to wait.

Square waved as he drove away.

"I can't believe you showed up late because you were hooking up with a guy that the captain of your team likes," Ally shouted.

"Wait a second," Sam said. "I can speak for myself. I told Melanie to go out with Square. He's a great guy."

Ally turned around and headed for Sam's house, making us all follow to continue the conversation. "Which you know because you've been infatuated with him for the last two years."

"Ally, you're way out of line," Sam said.

"Yes, she is," I piped in. "And I wasn't late because of Square. I was late because you sent me to that awful party."

A few of the girls gasped, including Ally. "You went to that?"

I held up my phone with the message from her. "You told me to! You insisted it was team-bonding time. Thankfully, Square came with me. When we didn't see you, we were in and out in ten minutes."

Sam crossed her arms and glared at Ally. "You messaged us this afternoon that there was a change of plans. Why would Melanie think we were still going?"

I tightened my grip on my phone. "This afternoon?"

In Sam's back yard around the firepit, Ally's eyes widened like some endangered animal. Like she was wounded, and I was the one inflicting the pain.

I didn't buy a second of it.

"I may have accidentally sent the second message to the group I had for the starters at the beginning of the season, not the updated one."

Sam pulled out her phone, scrolled, and rolled her eyes. "Melanie, I'm so sorry. When we heard about what was going down at the party, we changed our plans. We'd never expect you to do something so dangerous. Ally, do you have any idea what could have happened to Melanie at that party if she'd been alone?"

"I screwed up!" Ally scooped some dip onto a chip and tossed it into her mouth as if the conversation was over. As if she hadn't plowed into the net on the play, causing the team to lose a point—hell, the game point.

"So that's it?" I said.

She shrugged. "What? You're fine. It was an honest mistake. I'll be more careful next time. Good enough?"

I wanted to say no. I wanted to tell Ally Malone that she was too pushy, and that she needed to lay off people. But she'd sort of taken accountability and in front of the whole team. I couldn't do anything but accept, or I'd look like the jerk.

"Fine."

Sam exhaled. "Let's forget about this mess and have some fun. That's what we're here for, right?"

Everyone dug into the snacks. We ate and painted our nails. I chose black polish and staked my claim on a spot by the firepit while they dried. Ally sat on the opposite side of the flames. A memory of Harris leaning toward her and planting a kiss on her cheek had me smashing my pop can and giving an edgier look to my already edgy polish.

"You okay over there?" Chandra asked. Although she wasn't a starter, as the backup setter, I guessed she qualified for bonding events.

"I'm good."

"I can't tell if it's the reflection of the flames on your face or if you have some wicked-anger thing going on."

"Both. Maybe."

She sat in the chair next to me and roasted a marshmallow. "But at least you got to go out with Square."

I rested my head in my hands. Two weeks ago, I would have gushed about it—at least to Chandra. The winds of high school romance apparently shifted quickly.

"Did you kiss him?" she asked.

"Yes," I said, not seeing the point in lying and really wanting to talk to someone about it.

"How was it?"

I paused searching for the right word. "Nice."

"Just nice?" Chandra said. "I would have expected more from Square."

"It's not about him. He's amazing, but..." But it was like going to a restaurant knowing the salad was good for you but only wanting a hamburger, fries, and milkshake. I shook my head. I was not comparing Square and Harris to food.

"Oooh," Chandra interrupted my thoughts. "There's someone else, isn't there?"

I sucked in a breath. How obvious was I?

"Who is it? Better not be Jake Medina."

"It's not Jake." That ring was way too crowded for me to throw my hat in. Not to mention, he sort of felt like an annoying older brother.

"Good. Don't hold out on me, Soph."

"I'm not. He's seeing someone else, so it's hard to talk about."

Chandra gasped. "It's your sister's boyfriend!"

"No!"

"Too bad," she said. "That'd be some good drama."

"I don't want any more drama," I said with more whine in my voice than my mother would have liked. "I want to play volleyball."

"And hook a hottie."

I slumped in my camping chair. Yeah. Maybe that. Just not the hottie I'd thought.

The team cozied up around the fire. With each story they told, I settled into my chair deeper. I took in their faces, one by one. The yellow-and-orange flames from the fire battled with the shadows, but I recognized each of them to a depth of detail I hadn't during our summer workouts. Back then, I'd gone to the gym, pushed myself in every drill without talking much to anyone, and gone home to practice more.

Now, I knew that Sam Strutters competed with intensity but also had a quiet grace about her. She'd encouraged me to go out with Square when she liked him. She kept Ally in line as much as anyone could.

I knew Chandra Jackson loved intrigue, as long as it wasn't about her, but when she decided to be someone's friend, she did it with the utmost loyalty. I knew Molly Mattola lived a boy-crazy life, but she also carried a novel from the English department reading list everywhere and snuck reading time every chance she could. I knew Abby Turner could pass and dig better than anyone I'd ever seen, and she had a photographic memory for every play in every game. Her stories bested everyone else's.

Ela Gupta loved to cook traditional Indian food and brought some to every team night. Rachel Baxter blocked even better than Sam and showed videos of her three-year-old brother reenacting *Thomas & Friends* episodes and her seven-year-old sister tumbling like the proud big sister she was. My teammates were more than people to pass or set to. They were more than opportunities to reach my athletic goals.

They were friends.

That shocked me more than anything.

Around the fire with them, I felt safe—the complete opposite of the party where my classmates had been doing drugs, puking, and doing who knew what else. Some of them had been there by choice, but what about the others? What about the people who, like me, had been made to go, but unlike me, they didn't get to leave?

"We should take turns choosing what we do for team time," I blurted, and the team quieted.

"Excuse me?" Ally said.

"I didn't want to go to that party tonight—"

"I thought we were past this."

"It'll keep happening," I said. "The team should get to choose our team activities, and if someone is adamantly against doing something, we should respect that. It shouldn't always have to be about parties and s'mores either. Maybe we could help Chandra with one of her domestic violence shelter collections. Or a different community service project. I don't even know what kind of community service everyone does."

"I play games with the sweet people who live in my grandmother's nursing home," Rachel said.

"I tutor at the library on weekends," Sam said. "They could always use more help."

"See," I said. "That would be great! Besides, how else are we going to build rapport as a team? If we force each other into things, we'll all end up resentful."

Sam nodded. "Melanie's right. From now on, we'll vote on our team time...if that's what everyone wants to do. Can we take a vote right now? There are two options. Option one is that the captains select the team activities. Option two is that we take turns making suggestions, and everyone must be comfortable with the plan for it to happen. All those in favor of option one?"

Ally raised her hand.

"All those in favor of option two?"

Every other hand, including Sam's, went up.

"Fine." Ally sighed. "I change my vote to option two."

Sam clapped. "It's unanimous. For our next team time activity, the plan will come from Melanie."

Me and my big mouth.

CHAPTER THIRTY

I WOKE UP EARLY—WAY TOO EARLY—SATURDAY
morning. I dressed in jean shorts and the T-shirt my mom had made
for us. It had our last name on the back and Elle's team logo on the
front.

When I'd said I couldn't sleep over Sam's because of Elle's competition, everyone else had bailed too.

Ally had bailed to Harris's back yard. I groaned at the memory
of trying to fall asleep and hearing her voice carry from his property
to ours. I'd slammed the window shut, put the pillow over my head
for extra protection, and finally fallen asleep.

Not that I slept well. By the time we got to the range, I'd perked
up and—honestly, dork mode—swelled with pride at my big sister.
I'd teasingly called her Katniss Everdeen since she'd gotten serious
about archery a few years earlier. The comparison held up. Indoors.
Outdoors. Targets at several distances. Even moving targets. She hit
them every time.

By lunch, she'd collected her first-place medal, and our family
drove to a nearby diner she loved to visit during tournaments. My
parents gushed about her performance over burgers and fries, and for
the first time in I don't even know how long, I did too.

Eye roll, but I guess I'd grown up enough to realize just because my parents adored Elle didn't mean they didn't adore me. Not that I was ready to apply that logic to Harris's relationships with me and Ally. Totally different. My sisters and I loved each other.

Ally and me? Not so much.

And school started this week. I'd have to be around people all day. No quiet time in the hammock. Evenings under the stars replaced by late night homework assignments and much-needed sleep.

Square would be there.

Harris would be there.

Ally would be there.

I was starting to depress myself, so I refocused on relaxation for the weekend, reading two good books and sleeping as much as I could until that dreaded Monday morning.

Old friends greeted me in the hall. Chandra hugged me and introduced me to a few of her friends. I thought the day was going okay.

I thought wrong. After lunch, Elle found me in the hallway to drop a bomb. Lacey had ended up in the hospital after the party Friday night.

"I'm so glad you left," Elle said.

"Me too. Is Lacey going to be okay?"

"I think so. I wouldn't worry about Square running back to her or anything."

"No. I wasn't worried about that. I mean, she's clearly not my biggest fan, but I don't want her to be hospitalized."

"Yeah," Elle said. "Promise me when I go to school next year, you'll stay away from all that."

I held up my pinky, and she took it with hers. "Promise."

After hearing the news, my ears tapped into the huddled conversations in the hallways. Everyone was talking about the girl who'd almost died at a party over the weekend. I wanted to check on Square, but I didn't know his schedule. I opened our messages but couldn't decide what to say. Every option I thought of seemed to imply he cared more about Lacey than he probably did. Or maybe that he cared less than he did. I didn't want to make any assumptions about how he was feeling, so I tucked my phone back into my bag and went to chemistry.

"Sorry for the interruption, class," my chemistry teacher said when we were supposed to be reading the textbook. "Melanie, it seems they need you in the office."

Me?

The obligatory "ooh" and "busted" comments bid me farewell from my afternoon class.

What could I have possibly done in the first few hours of school to get me called to the office? Doomsday scenarios pummeled my brain. The secretary asked me to sit and wait.

And wait.

And wait.

"Excuse me," I said finally. "If this isn't so urgent, maybe I could be in class until you need me."

"Miss Corwin," Principal Welch called from his office. "Come in, please."

I sat in the cushy chair opposite him and noticed the books on his shelf were all formal and boring. The wall decor—his college degrees. Absolutely zero personality in the whole space. He sat on his side of the desk. Quiet. Staring. Trying to make me uncomfortable. Putting me on edge. Which was a total waste of time since I'd been on edge since I'd been summoned here.

"So, Principal Welch, what can I do for you?"

He took a folder from a pile and held it in front of him.

"Miss Corwin, you're aware of the Student Athlete Code of Conduct at this school?"

Coach Steve had had us read the code during volleyball camp. It talked about behavior at away games, how to represent the school in an "appropriate manner," and stuff like that. "Yes, sir."

He nodded. "So you realize you're in violation of that policy?"

No.

"Mr. Welch, the team hasn't even traveled anywhere for me to represent the team in a poor way."

"I never said a trip with the team, Miss Corwin. One of our students was recently hospitalized after a party."

Lacey. But what did that have to do with me?

He sat back in his chair and watched me with those teacher eyes that thought they knew when they didn't. "Do you know anything about that?"

"I heard about it today."

"Today, huh?" He opened the folder and slid it across his desk. "Then why does she have pictures of you on her phone at the same party where she got sick?"

It took me a minute to recognize where they'd been taken. In the basement. Square's back was to the camera, and we were far enough away that he wasn't clear in the shot. In the foreground was a huge bowl of multicolored pills.

Mr. Welch slapped a piece of paper on the desk in front of me. The title read *Possession by Association*. My heart froze like the images on the photo. This wasn't about representation of the team and school. This was about being present in places where drugs and alcohol were being consumed.

This...was a lot worse.

"Miss Corwin?"

I ignored the hot fear and anger swirling through me and raised my gaze to make eye contact. "Yes?"

"Why does she have pictures of you on her phone?"

I set them back on the desk and closed the folder. "I don't know."

"Who went to the party with you?"

I was not bringing Square into this. And technically, he hadn't come to the party with me. He'd been dropping me off. I hoped I could get away with that technicality. "Nobody."

He dropped his pencil. "You mean to tell me you went to a party where you knew nobody, and you were all alone?"

"Yes, sir."

"Not exactly the smartest thing to do."

C*learly*, I wanted to blurt. But I wasn't sure attitude would get me anywhere better than the trouble piled around me at that moment. "No, sir."

"Why?"

"Excuse me?"

"Why did you go to the party?"

I weighed my words carefully. "It was a misunderstanding. I thought I was supposed to meet some friends there—"

"What friends?"

"The volleyball team."

"The whole team was at this party?"

Fireworks exploded in my head. "No. Just me. The team realized the party was bad news and changed their plans. I had only joined varsity, so I was accidentally left off the contact list. I didn't get the message until I was already at the party. I was there for ten minutes and left."

His squinting, judgmental eyes told me he didn't believe me.

"Ask any of the girls on the team. I was with them the rest of that night at Sam Strutters's house."

"I will do that, Miss Corwin. But for now, why don't you go collect your things from your locker while I call your parents."

My parents? Oh no.

CHAPTER THIRTY-ONE

MY HEAD FELT MORE CHAOTIC THAN THE BUSTLING IN
the halls. The principal had proof I'd violated a school policy. Would
I be suspended? Kicked off the team I'd worked so hard to make?

What would happen if they found out Square had been the one
standing next to me? I leaned against the cold, tile wall and waited
for my body temperature to drop to something resembling normal.

Ally Malone. This was all her fault.

The bell rang again. School was over. Ally would be in the locker
room. I'd had enough of her. Beyond enough.

I knocked over two people on my way to the locker room, but
what did it matter? The consequences from that paled in comparison
to the principal thinking I had done drugs alongside Lacey. That I
might have had something to do with her ending up in the hospital.

The locker room doors crashed into the wall, startling my teammates.

"Melanie, are you okay?" Sam asked, but I didn't answer her. I
set my eyes on Ally and dove across the bench knocking her onto
the floor.

"What the hell?"

"I know you did it on purpose." I smacked her face, and she
tugged at my hair.

"Get off me!"

Hands grabbed at us, but I swatted her however I could. Her face. Her arms. I might have even gotten a kick in before the team dragged me away.

"Melanie, chill!" Chandra screamed in my ear. "Chill."

"What is this?" Coach's voice was like a cold shower. I dropped my head into my hands and prayed I was dreaming. Or maybe reading a book back in the comfort of my bed and this was the character's dark moment when everything seemed lost.

Kind of like me.

"My office. Now."

Chandra helped me up, and Sam walked between Ally and me.

"You can go," Coach told Sam. "Neither of them would dare have the audacity to put hands on the other in my office. Isn't that right, girls?"

I nodded.

"Girls?"

"Yes, Coach," we both said.

Sam closed the door, and through the glass window, I watched the rest of the team head to the gym with our assistant coach. Coach Medina didn't say anything. She sat at her desk with her hands crossed over the blotter from two years ago. I avoided her gaze by studying the newspaper articles on the wall behind her. All the championships. All the accolades. And this year, the team wouldn't achieve anything.

Because Ally and I couldn't get along.

"In all my years of coaching, I've never had two players fighting in the locker room."

I lowered my eyes.

"I don't know what it is with you two, but if we've learned anything this season, it's that anyone can be replaced."

"Or maybe that sometimes people can't be," Ally said.

Coach glared at her. "When I want your opinion, Ally, I'll ask for it. You are stripped of your assistant captain title."

"What? She attacked me!"

"Is that so, Melanie?"

"Principal Welch thinks I violated the Possession by Association policy."

Coach's eyes widened. "That's serious."

"I know. Ally made us do all this team bonding, and one of the activities was a Skittles party."

"We knew that party was bad news," Ally said.

"Except you didn't tell me. You told the rest of the team, so I ended up there by myself. Someone has a picture with me in the background from the ten minutes I was there looking for the team."

"Did you take drugs at the party?"

"No," I said, finally looking Coach in the eye.

"Is this the party where the student became seriously ill and hospitalized?"

"Yes."

Coach sighed.

Sam knocked on the door, and Coach waved her in.

"Melanie's dad is here."

"My dad? Are you sure?" My dad was nowhere but work at this time of day.

"Yeah," Sam said. "He's in the gym with Principal Welch. He said he needs to see you right away."

"Ally, go to practice," Coach said. "Melanie, come with me."

The adults mumbled—or it sounded like mumbling—about me and my behavior and the "very serious" situation. I wondered why Lacey had taken a picture of me with Square. Was she really that jealous?

Or vindictive?

Had she given the photos to the principal to purposely get us in trouble? My head hurt from the possibilities. I never wanted to be social again.

"Melanie!"

My dad shook my shoulders until I made eye contact with him. We were in a conference room alone. I hugged him.

"Oh, Melanie," he said, hugging me back. "What have you gotten yourself into?"

"A ridiculous amount of trouble for a person who didn't do anything wrong."

He squeezed me tighter. "You know I've heard the whole 'I'm innocent' routine before."

"Don't defense lawyer me, Dad."

"Okay. Sit. Tell me what happened."

I didn't sit. Instead, I paced, but I did tell him everything about Friday night.

"Why were you with this Square?" Dad asked.

"We were on a date."

"You're dating? Does your mother know this?"

Patience with my father's lack of presence in our family—not happening right now. "Can we stay focused?"

"Fine. But we talk about the boy stuff later."

Right. When you're home, I thought to myself.

"The bottom line is we did nothing wrong. In the photo, there is no proof we violated the policy. We were there when other people were *about* to violate the policy. People hadn't even started taking the pills when we were there."

"But they were drinking," Dad said.

"If the principal wanted to punish every student who has ever had a drink at a party, he'd be out of a job. And shouldn't he be pursuing all other summer parties with the same fervor or whatever? Why this party? How is this fair?"

Dad smiled. "You make good points."

"Points you can use to get me out of this mess?"

"Definitely."

"Good. Here's one more. If the picture is time-stamped and the volleyball team can corroborate when I arrived at Sam's house, it would be clear we weren't there that long."

"I can use that. You're a good little lawyer."

Or good at getting myself out of trouble. Myself and Square. "Thanks, Dad."

Dad pulled up the policy on his phone, read it closely, and made some notes before we left the conference room to find Square and a woman I assumed to be his mother in the waiting area of the principal's office. Square looked scared. I'd never seen that particular expression on his face. His mother looked scared too. And angry.

I remembered his promise to her to never be brought into the principal's office again. He'd broken that promise. Because of me.

I tugged on my dad's sleeve. "You have to help Square, Dad."

"That him?"

"Yes."

Dad squeezed my hand and marched toward Square and his mom. "I'm Melanie's father, John Corwin. It's nice to meet you."

"I'm Victoria Weaver. This is my son." Mrs. Weaver shook his hand but didn't look particularly happy to.

"I'm a lawyer," Dad said, and Square perked up.

"A lawyer?" Mrs. Weaver said. "So you're here to defend your daughter, so she doesn't get into any trouble while my son takes the blame?"

"Mom," Square pleaded.

"Hush."

"Not at all, Mrs. Weaver. I've been talking with Melanie, and I think I have a defense that will protect both our children from any punishment."

Mrs. Weaver looked skeptical.

"I've reviewed the policy in detail, and I don't believe they've violated it." Dad went on to explain our strategy.

Square stood and hugged me. "Thank you, Melanie."

I hugged him back. He held me so tightly I felt bad for the opponents he'd be tackling Friday night. But the good news was if my dad's plan worked, Square would be on the field, tackling them, not suspended and watching the livestream from home instead.

"Mrs. Weaver," I said, "I want you to know that the only reason Square went to that party was to make sure I was safe. He stayed by my side the whole time we were there, which was at best ten minutes. Neither of us drank or took any drugs. In fact, almost everyone we saw there said they were surprised to see him."

At least a head shorter than Square, Mrs. Weaver looped her arm through her son's and reached up to kiss his cheek. "I'd expect nothing less from him."

"You raised a really special person. I'm so grateful to be his friend."

She smiled cautiously. "Thank you, Melanie. And thank you, Mr. Corwin. Let's discuss our strategy, then. I don't want either of our children disciplined for something they didn't do. My son has football practice to get to and homework after that." She gave him a pointed glance. "I don't want any of that interrupted."

Once our defense was solid, Square and I drifted away from our parents and pretended to be enthralled with the awards hanging on the walls.

"Sorry about all this," I finally said.

"This is all Lacey."

Or at least ninety-eight percent of it. Ally had to take at least two percent of the blame.

"Have you heard how she's doing?"

"She'll be okay," he said.

"Good."

He shook his head. "Not sure why she would do this. She knows how I feel about my mama. No way she'll ever let me near the girl again."

"Maybe she realized it was really over but wanted to take you down in any way she could."

"She tried to take football away from me. And you."

Something had already shifted between us, at least on my end, so I didn't really feel like Lacey had done that herself. But the principal's office didn't seem like the best place to bring that up.

"You coming to the game Friday?" he asked.

The principal called Mrs. Weaver and Square into his office. My throat went dry.

"Mr. Corwin, Melanie, I'll be with you in a few minutes."

"Actually, Principal Welch, we'd like to talk with you together," Mrs. Weaver said.

"That's not usually—"

"It affects both of our children the same," she persisted.

"I agree with Mrs. Weaver," my father said.

Talked into a corner, the principal nodded and pointed to his office.

Square took my hand and squeezed. "We got this," he whispered.

"Thanks," I said. "And, Square?"

"Yeah?"

"No way would I miss your game."

CHAPTER THIRTY-TWO

MY DAD AND MRS. WEAVER BLEW THROUGH PRINCI-pal Welch's arguments like a hurricane. They left nothing standing. By the end, Mr. Welch apologized to us.

With the mess finally settled, Square and I headed for the gym. When I'd told him I needed to grab my things from the locker room, he'd offered to walk with me. The halls were dark and quiet except for the cleaning staff passing with brooms or mops. The elation from winning our battle with the school policy settled into dread with each step.

I had to end things with Square.

No way around it.

"Your mom's great," I said to break the tension. And she was. Her passion for Square in that office had put off enough energy to power the lights over the football field.

"She is. Thanks. Your dad's great too. It's funny to me how grown-ups always crumble under legal talk, you know?"

"My dad certainly makes people crumble."

Square laughed. "I get that. Good thing he wasn't there before our date."

"There? He didn't even know we'd gone out. He works a lot."

"That's rough."

"Yeah. I wonder if all lawyers work every second of the day."

He shrugged.

"I want a job that gives me time to chill at home. With my family. With my books."

"Sounds right for you."

"What about you?" I asked. "What do you want to be?"

He opened a door for me, and I thanked him, careful to keep my hands clasped in front of me, hoping he didn't reach for them.

"I don't know. Right now, I want to be good at football. And school. And life, I guess."

"Makes sense," I said.

Outside the gym, the late afternoon light shone sideways through the windows, reflecting off the metal in the trophy case. Life was literally shining a light on me and Square. One thought of Harris, and I knew exactly what the spotlight was for.

"Square, we need to talk."

His reaction far from what I expected, he burst into laughter.

"Okay..." I said.

"I'm sorry, but I think I know where this is going?"

"And that's funny?"

He reclaimed his most serious expression. "I agree, is all."

"You do?" Did he really know what I was going to say?

"You're really amazing," he said. "Beautiful and fun and talented."

Oh, thank goodness! He did know. "Exactly. Same to you," I said. "Except for the beautiful part."

"Hey!"

"No. I mean you're attractive. Kind of sexy."

"You think I'm sexy?"

Suddenly, it didn't feel like we were ending. "Stay on task."

He sobered. "Right. We just...you and me, we..."

"Aren't a good fit," I offered.

"Exactly."

"Exactly," I agreed.

"You're into someone else."

I groaned. "Is it that obvious?"

"Yeah," he said slowly.

"I'm sorry. I wasn't when we first started talking. Or at least I didn't know I was."

"It's cool. I get it."

After a few moments of silence, I exhaled a puff of relief. "That went so much better than I expected. I've never broken up with anyone before. Not that you were my boyfriend." Kill me now.

"Nah." He smiled. "I knew you'd be cool."

"So, friends?"

He hugged me. "Definitely."

"Even though this went really well, I'm kind of sad. I like hanging out with you."

"Friends hang out. They don't think each other are sexy, but..."

"Right. Okay. You know you think I'm sexy. Do I have to put on that jean skirt and crop top again?"

"Yes, please," he said, deadpan, and I knew we'd stay friends. "It's cool. I'm glad we got to know each other. I like making new friends."

"Me too," I said and thought of someone who might have better timing than me. "Square, as your friend, can I give you some advice?"

"Hit me with it."

"Ask out Sam Strutters."

His eyes widened like the thought had never crossed his mind, which meant he had no idea she'd been crushing on him for years.

"No matter what she says, I see the way she looks at you. And she's an awesome person. You two would be perfect together."

He fist-bumped me. "I'm the kind of guy who respects his friends' opinions, so I will seriously consider it. Good enough?"

"Good enough."

The gym doors flew open, and a very angry Ally—saying a lot considering Ally was Ally—stepped into the hallway. Maybe it was the bruising on her cheek or the scratches on her neck that made her seem angrier.

"Figures. I'm sitting in the locker room waiting for you, and you're out here flirting."

"What happened to your face?" Square said.

Ally pointed at me. "She happened."

"Props," he whispered, and I stifled a giggle. Launching myself at her in the locker room had felt really good at the time.

Now, not so much.

"Ally, nice to see you too," Square said. "Thanks for apologizing for sending us to that party and almost getting me suspended from football."

"Sorry," she said, and I could hear my mom's voice in my head saying, *Like you mean it!*

Ally didn't mean it.

"Sometimes, she reminds me of rainbows and bunnies," I said.

"Maybe cute little kittens," Square suggested.

"I'm standing right here," Ally said.

"We know," he said. "See you at the game Friday, Melanie."

"See ya."

Ally held the gymnasium door open wide. "Coach wants to see us."

My shoes caught on the waxed floor and screeched. The sound echoed in the silent gym. Ally sat on the bleachers close to the locker room. I gave her some distance and took a seat farther away.

Coach emerged a few seconds later. "How did it go?"

"Good. Principal Welch agreed Square and I had done nothing wrong."

"No suspension?"

"No, Coach."

She smiled, but I didn't really feel like this was a smiling conversation, so I held out feeling any relief. "Glad to hear it. Now let's talk about what happened in the locker room today."

Ally's body stilled.

"Fighting in the locker room—among your teammates—will not be tolerated. You will both be suspended from the first two games."

"Coach!" Ally objected.

Coach shook her head. "This isn't a discussion. Ally, we've talked about this. Julia isn't playing. If I can get over that as her mother, so can you. You've done nothing to welcome Melanie to the roster. Nothing. Melanie, I see your frustration. Maybe I should have stepped in more and insisted you two work it out before it got this far. But it's never acceptable to put your hands on someone, especially in anger. There will be no fighting in my locker room. Ever again. Is two games enough to ensure that?"

"Yes, Coach," we both said.

"Excellent. I suggest you spend this time working out your differences. Don't bother coming to practice either."

Ally huffed. I might have puffed. Or vice versa. No practice. No volleyball. I couldn't play in the yard with Harris, not with Ally over there. What was I going to do for a week with no volleyball?

"Come on," Coach said. "Get your stuff."

Ally and I didn't look or talk to each other. She scooped up her bags from the locker room since they were already packed and left. I didn't have the strength. The weight of the day pushed me down on the bench. I stared at the empty, dull, gray metal locker. Full of potential. I could put pictures of me and Chandra inside. Or the team competing. Or candid shots of me hitting. Something inspirational.

"Melanie?" Coach said, locking up her office. "I didn't realize you were still here."

"I meant to go."

She sat next to me and put her hand on my shoulder. "Varsity not as glamorous as you expected?"

"Guess not."

"The season hasn't gone how I expected either."

I leaned my head against the wall. "You miss her a lot."

"Yeah." The word came out as a whisper, like Coach couldn't give anything else to the question. After a few seconds, she took a deep breath and said, "Maybe I haven't been the best coach to you. I asked a lot—switching positions, stepping into a beloved player's shoes."

"I wanted the opportunity," I said.

She nodded. "I suggested you switch to outside because I knew you could contribute to this team. I still know it. But I've coached a lot of years, and I've learned that it's almost always the heart of the team, the love the players have for each other, that determines how far they will go. The starting six played together for years. Their dynamic was flawless. Asking you to step into that dynamic as if nothing had changed..." She squeezed my hand and looked me in the eye. "I should have realized how much pressure that would be for you. I'm sorry I didn't."

It was my turn to whisper. "Thanks, Coach." I wanted to apologize that I couldn't make it work, but I didn't think the wall I'd built up around my emotions could hold them back if I spoke another word.

"Grab your stuff when you're ready. I'll be outside."

I nodded.

"And, Melanie?"

"Yes?"

"The dynamic may not be there yet, but I have no doubt it will be someday."

I hoped she was right. And that by the time we figured it out, it wouldn't be too late.

CHAPTER THIRTY-THREE

"YOU'RE NOT GOING," MY MOM INSISTED FRIDAY AFTER dinner when I told her about the home opener football game. I'd even volunteered to wash the dishes and clean up in the hopes that would soften her to the idea of me watching Julia be the first girl to start in the varsity quarterback position at our high school.

"Mom, it's the first football game."

She folded the kitchen towel and hung it from the oven handle. "You were suspended from the team this week for fighting, Melanie. Even if that weren't reason enough to keep you home, how can I trust you won't get suspended from school for fighting with this girl again tonight?"

I closed the dishwasher—lightly. I didn't slam it, I swear. After years of spending every weekend in my room reading or in the back yard practicing, I didn't have much experience breaking the rules and talking my way out of trouble.

"Mom, let her go."

Fortunately, Elle had experience.

"Elle, not now."

"Yes now," Elle said, pushing my mom to wide eyes and crossed arms. "Listen, Melanie is doing exactly what you asked her to do."

"Fight? In school?"

"Don't be so literal, Mom." She moved around the kitchen preparing a dessert—bananas with Nutella—as if this were the most casual conversation in the world. "You asked her to get to know people, to get out there and learn about life. She's learning that not everyone can be trusted."

I sat on a stool at our island and let the pro do her work.

"Yes, she got angry, but she's paying the price for that with the loss of two volleyball games. For Melanie, what could be a bigger punishment?"

My mom tilted her head to the side as if considering the accuracy of that argument. I could see her warming up to Elle's point of view.

"Tonight, she wants to watch her mentor make sports history as the first female quarterback at our school. As a feminist, you can appreciate that."

Oh. She was good.

"Yes, but still," Mom said, doing her best to hold out.

Elle raised her hands in surrender. "I get it, Mom. I really do. But I will be with Mel the whole time and take responsibility for her. No way will she put her hands on Ally again. She's learned her lesson, right, Mel?"

"Absolutely. One hundred percent."

My mom didn't look fully convinced, so I dared to jump into the battle. "Mom, I know what I did was wrong. I was angry. And that's no excuse. Nobody has ever done anything so deceitful to me. Not to mention what it could have done to Square, who's a really nice guy I never would have met if I didn't follow your advice and get out more."

Her sigh told me I was on track.

"I'm gonna make mistakes—hopefully not as big as I made this week. Sometimes bigger. Trust me. I've learned my lesson with this one."

She squinted her eyes, but I held firm. Straight face. Chin up. Unbreakable eye contact.

"No more fighting?"

"Promise," I said.

"Elle, you'll stay with her the whole time?"

"Promise."

We had her.

***

I HUGGED MY SISTER THE SECOND SHE CLOSED THE door of her bedroom with us inside. "I can't believe that worked. You are a pro."

"I've had some experience, sadly. Glad it could pay off for you. Remember to pay it forward to Lily when I'm away at college."

I pancaked on her bed and closed my eyes. "First of all, no way Lily ever needs me for that."

"I would have said the same about you a year ago. Who knew you'd go wild and attack one of your teammates on school property?"

"Funny," I said.

"What's the second thing?" Elle asked.

I picked at a string on her stuffed bunny. "Something else I never thought I'd do."

"Fall for Harris?"

"Okay, a third thing."

She laughed so hard she fell on the bed next to me. "At least you admit it. What's the third thing?"

"Miss you."

"Aw. Mel." She pulled me close, and we snuggled like we were little kids with little worlds and little problems. I didn't know how long later her phone buzzed, waking us.

Elle stretched. "We have to get going, or we're going to be late."

She touched up her makeup and braided her hair into something—as usual—adorable. Also as usual, something I could totally not pull off. She changed into a pair of purple-and-black tie-dyed booty shorts and a white tank top that was, wow, bling.

"Your shirt is intense," I said.

She spun, showing off Josh's name and number on the back and the Iron Valley Viking mascot logo on the front. The letters, numbers, and outline for the logo dazzled.

"Amazing, right!" She grinned and handed me a folded white shirt. "I actually got you one too."

No, she didn't. My goal for the evening was to blend in, not stop the nighttime traffic. "Um...thanks. But Square and I aren't really..." Not sure what we were to begin with, I didn't know how to finish the sentence. Square was the kind of guy I'd wear a shirt for as a friend but wearing a guy's number on your shirt—especially a sparkly one people could see from across the field—it meant something. The kind of something I didn't want Harris to see and think I meant. Even though Harris had never gone to a high school football game in his life. He could see me on the way or a pic on social or hear about it some other way. Whether he was with—groan—Ally Malone or whatever, I didn't want him to think anything about me and Square.

I buried my head into Elle's pillow. The only guy's name I'd want on a shirt was Harris's. Not that people wore personalized, blinged-out shirts for science competitions.

"Look at the back, dork," Elle said.

I held the shirt up, the bottom falling loose, and spun it around. The back read, *MEDINA* with the number *12* on it.

"Julia?"

"I know you've always admired her."

"It's gorgeous!" I hugged Elle and held on extra for all the times I should have hugged her but hadn't.

"Good. Go change." She tapped her watch and tossed me a pair of tie-dyed booty shorts identical to hers. "Pregame is calling."

I swapped outfits in her room while she fussed with the perfect makeup colors for my complexion.

"You know, Mel. I couldn't make you a Square Weaver shirt. I knew you were into Harris before you did."

I checked out my butt in the shorts. Cheeks were safely tucked inside. "Did you also know he was into Ally?"

She scrunched her face into a *something stinks* expression. "I'm not convinced he is."

"I blame Mom."

Elle pulled me into her vanity chair, kneeled, and dabbed my face with powder. "Why Mom?"

"She made a big deal about Harris falling asleep on the couch."

"You mean you and Harris *sleeping together* and *snuggling* on the couch?"

I threw a dirty shirt from the floor at her. "Whose side are you on?"

She smelled the shirt and tossed it into her closet. "Continue."

"It was a seed that grew into a weed that wreaked havoc on my life."

"Speak in non-metaphors, please."

"The thought of Harris being an actual boy and maybe liking me made me wonder if I liked him. It put ideas in my head. And those ideas started sounding good."

"And turned you off Square," Elle suggested.

"Who is super nice."

"And hot."

"That too," I said.

"Do you regret ending things with Square?"

No.

The answer had come so naturally I knew it was true. "Even if I can't be with Harris, that doesn't mean I should be with Square. It should be real. Like you and Josh."

Elle smiled, then her eyes widened. "Yes. Josh! We have to go. Grab your purse."

"I don't have a purse."

"Take one of mine. Let's go!"

CHAPTER THIRTY-FOUR

MY FIRST YEAR AT IRON VALLEY HIGH SCHOOL, I'D GONE to two home football games with my volleyball friends—who didn't even play on the team anymore. Harris never wanted to come. He spent Friday nights filming science experiments in his back yard for his channel. He'd wrangle me to help him so I didn't play volleyball in my back yard—or in other words, make noise in the background of his recording.

The evenings would go something like this:

I'd pass the volleyball to myself, counting into the hundreds.

He'd yell, "Mel, that noise is messing up my audio. Can you please stop?"

"No can do," I'd yell back. "I beat my record. Two-twelve. Two-thirteen."

"When you drop the ball, can you please stop?"

"Two-twenty. Only if you don't make me drop it. Two-twenty-two."

"How would I do that?" he'd say.

"Pick your explosion," I'd answer. "Two-twenty-nine. And don't think that keeping me talking will mess me up. Two-thirty-three."

He'd pretend to wait patiently but really groan and moan every few seconds.

"Mel!"

"Two-fifty. Fine." I'd catch the ball. "You're lucky I love you."

"Can I be lucky with you on this side of the fence, please? I need your help."

And I'd assist him in whatever scientific adventure he had planned for his twenty-three-thousand viewers.

Those two Friday nights I'd gone to the football games, I'd missed Harris. Now, walking into the football stadium, with the band playing and fans munching on snacks from the concession stand and catching up with friends after summer, I wondered what Harris had planned that night to make his stepmother roll her eyes.

"Melanie?" Elle snapped her fingers in my face. "You with me?"

My chest tightened. "Maybe I shouldn't have come."

She looped her arm in mine and squeezed my hand. "Yes. You should. Let's get a spot by the fence, so we can see Josh and Julia when they come out of the locker room."

I took a deep breath and thought about how tough Julia'd been to defy her parents and follow her heart. She'd chosen herself over a boy—a really cute one she had history with. If she'd had the strength to do that, I could find the strength to be here for her.

People packed the fence line. Between the clusters of them, the faces of seniors smiled and smirked from the banners honoring their last year playing the sport. Square's huge grin brought a smile to my own lips. Josh had tried a mean sports face in his picture, but I knew him well enough. Josh didn't do "mean".

And then there was Julia. Tall. Tough. Strong. A little girl holding a football stood in front of Julia's banner, posing for a picture. I snapped a pic on the sly to show Julia later.

We squeezed through the crowd to where Elle's best friend, Isla, held a spot right in front.

"This place is intense tonight," Isla said.

Elle hugged her. "Thanks for saving us a spot."

"Sure thing. Hey, Melanie. Congrats on making varsity."

"Thanks." I glanced at Elle, who shook her head the slightest bit. She hadn't told Isla about my suspension.

"They should be out soon," Isla said. She wore the same shirt and shorts as Elle and me, but the back of her shirt sparkled with smaller numbers. Josh's and Julia's along with every other senior on the team. Across the top, it read, *SENIORS*.

"I like your shirt," I said.

"Thanks," Isla said. "I'm not really a long-term relationship girl. Too risky putting one number on a shirt at the beginning of the season."

At least she knew herself.

"Here they come," Elle said.

Down the tunnel, at the entrance of the locker room, the football team huddled in a massive clump of jumping black-and-purple jerseys. One player led, shouting, "Offense like..." and the rest of the team hooted. "Defense like..." and they hooted again. "It's time like..." and the fans around us joined in.

"And making their way to the field for their first game of the season is the home team. Here are your Iron Valley Vikings!" the announcer screamed into the microphone.

The team exploded through the tunnel. Everyone around us cheered so loudly, I felt like I was in the middle of a scream. Josh blew a kiss at Elle, and she put her hands over her heart. My big sister. The total romantic. I hoped someday I'd have a swoon-worthy romance. For now, I tried to remind myself that playing varsity had been the goal.

Coach's suggestion that Ally and I use the next week to work out our differences seemed like a good idea in my head, but every time I remembered her playing volleyball with Harris in his back yard... let's just say making up wasn't my next thought.

If it was even possible, the crowd cheered louder when number twelve emerged from the tunnel. Julia's long ponytail hung down her back, reminding everyone that a girl led this team now.

A girl. Led the football team.

I'd never imagined it. As a kid, I'd never thought to play football. Maybe because I hadn't been interested. Or maybe because I hadn't thought I could. In the stands, girls Lily's age and younger stood and clapped, calling Julia's name, reminding me of the little girl taking a picture next to Julia's banner. Maybe they wouldn't play football, but at least they knew they could, if they wanted to.

Julia had shown them that.

"Let's go, Julia!" I yelled, but my voice faded into the chorus of fans around me.

Someone covered my eyes from behind, and I stilled. I grabbed the hands and spun to face Jake Medina.

He hugged me. "Hey, Melanie."

"Jake! Hey!"

"I hear you over here shouting Little J's name. I respect that, but you know, I wore that jersey better."

I crossed my arms. "Not so sure about that. She looks pretty good out there."

He tilted his head to the side as if considering it. "She does. You win."

Isla elbowed me in the ribs.

"Jake, I think you know my sister, Elle."

He gave her a nod. "Elle, yeah. How's it going? I see you have Brighton's name on your shirt. Good choice. Although your sister is wearing *my* number."

I punched his shoulder. "In your dreams. This is *Julia's* number."

He rubbed his shoulder. "I'm injured."

"Maybe your pride," I said.

"You two bicker like brother and sister," Elle said. "I'd be jealous except she saves enough of her sass for me. How's college, Jake?"

"So far, so good. Haven't had much opportunity to get into trouble yet."

Elle draped her arm around my shoulders. "Some people don't take long."

I rolled my eyes at her.

"Seems like there's a story here," Jake said.

"Not at all. Do you know Isla?"

Before he could answer, Isla hugged him and whispered something in his ear that actually made him blush. I had to bite my lip to keep from laughing.

Jake composed himself. "Nice to meet you, Isla. Elle and Melanie, good to see you. Come by the house for the after-party later." His eyes flickered to Isla, and I was pretty sure she planned to accept that invitation.

Jake disappeared into the thick crowd.

"Isla, what did you say to him?" my sister asked.

"A lady never tells."

"Good thing you didn't commit to one number on that shirt," I teased.

"See!" Isla said. "I told you that wasn't my style."

"But Jake Medina is?" I asked.

"Jake Medina *so* is."

Elle looped her arms in mine on one side and her best friend's on the other. "Let's go get some seats."

CHAPTER THIRTY-FIVE

THE STUDENT SECTION WAS THICK WITH TIE-DYED gear, the student-proclaimed theme for the game. Rompers, dresses, crop tops, muscle tees, tennis shoes—you name it, and someone in my school had tie-dyed it.

Wearing a tie-dyed sports bra and lounge pants with her hair slicked back in a braided ponytail, Chandra found us and squeezed me in a hug.

"You look amazing," I said.

"You too," she said. "This your sis?"

"Elle," my sister said.

Chandra introduced herself and the rest of the JV team. Elle complimented each of my teammates on their outfits while Chandra whispered to me, "Did you see Jake?"

"I did."

"Are you going to the after-party at his house?"

"Not sure. He invited us."

"You have to! Although I might be too busy to hang out with you, if you know what I mean."

I remembered Jake's encounter with Isla when we'd arrived at the game. "I do." I also knew that Jake had spoken too soon when he'd said it was early in the school year to get into trouble. If Chandra and

Isla had anything to say about it, trouble would find him within hours.

The rest of the volleyball team joined the student section soon after, but Ally wasn't with them. Which had me sighing in relief. I didn't plan to fight her again or anything, but not seeing her sounded a lot easier to handle than standing next to her all night. Maybe she would sit with her family since her brother played.

Square, Julia, Josh, and Owen linked arms and walked out to center field, and I couldn't stop the smile on my face. Julia had gone from captain of the volleyball team to captain of the football team. I wished I had half of her badassery.

The other team won the toss and deferred. That meant Julia would be on the field right away. I stomped my feet on the bleachers with the rest of the school during kickoff. I didn't know everyone on the team, so I couldn't say who returned the ball, but it was a good effort. He brought it back to our forty-yard line.

Julia listened to something her coach said and ran onto the field. I scanned the crowd to find Coach Medina. She was as far from everyone as she could be with praying hands covering her mouth. My stomach flipped more than gymnasts at the Olympics, so I couldn't imagine how she felt.

The Iron Valley players on the sidelines urged the crowd to quiet down. Julia leaned into the huddle, and the team approached the line of scrimmage.

Elle squeezed my hand. I squeezed back.

The entire volleyball team held hands too. Nobody said anything, but we could feel the magnitude of the moment, our entwined fingers communicated the message like a ripple through us.

You got this, Julia.

The center snapped the ball, and Julia dropped back to pass. She threw to Josh, and he caught it for a first down.

Elle jumped so high, she knocked me down. "Sorry! Oh. I'm sorry."

I wrapped my arms around her—if nothing else to protect myself from future outbursts. The team set for the second play. This time, a run for twelve yards.

"Who's the running back?" I asked Elle.

"D. He's really good. Josh says he's a great blocker for Julia."

That was good news.

Two plays. Two first downs. Not bad at all.

The next play, the defense blitzed and got through the line. Julia had to throw it away to avoid a sack.

Coach hid her face behind her praying hands. Jitters rippled through the crowd. The people who didn't believe in Julia chirped about how another quarterback would have made the play. The way I saw it, another quarterback might not have avoided the sack.

Back to the line, Julia called the play, snapped the ball, and dropped back. D picked up a blitz to give her more time.

"Owen's open!" I yelled, as if Julia were listening to my commentary instead of seeing everything for herself.

She zipped the ball into Owen's arms. He pulled it in at the ten-yard line and ran untouched into the end zone.

My world was a tornado of cheering, jumping, and hugging.

Julia Medina had thrown her first touchdown pass in an official game on her first drive. To Owen. Her ex-boyfriend, who she'd beaten out for the position.

Julia sprinted down the field to Owen. He ran to her too. They celebrated with a hug that held on a little long. They pressed their face masks against each other's, and Owen tapped her on her helmet.

It was one of the sweetest things I had ever seen in my life.

With Elle and Josh around all the time, that was saying something.

"Are they back together?" Elle asked.

"Maybe," I said. "I don't know."

They ran off the field side by side and accepted congratulations from their coaches and teammates. Square picked up Julia and swung her around.

Elle glanced at me.

"I know. He's a good guy."

Just not *my* guy.

Owen ran by the sideline fence and high-fived someone in tie-dyed shorts, a tank top, and a headband. The crowd settled in for the next play, but the girl at the fence kept screaming.

For her brother.

Ally Malone.

"That's kind of sweet," Elle said. "Nice to see she has a sweet side, right? Maybe there's hope for you two after all."

Maybe. If we could get along, we could build that dynamic Coach had talked to me about. The kind of dynamic that could lead us to a winning season and maybe even playoff victories.

Elle grabbed my arm.

"What?" I followed her sightline to the fence to see Ally's arms around a boy.

My boy.

Elle groaned.

Harris had come to a football game. With Ally. He wasn't at home filming a science experiment in his back yard. He wasn't missing me.

He was...with her.

Ally pulled him closer, tilted her head, and... No...

She kissed him. Ally kissed Harris. At the football game. In front of our entire world.

"Who's that Ally's kissing?" Chandra said.

"I don't know, but he's cute," Ashley added.

The crowd noise faded into the distance. I was alone in the stands with my pounding heart and chest being ripped open.

"Melanie, are you okay?"

No.

"Melanie, breathe. Like we talked about. Deep breath in. Hold. Two...three...four...five. Good. One more. In. Two...three...four...five. Exhale. Good. Look at me, Mel."

Elle's face came into focus slowly. "Oh, Melanie."

"I can't do this."

"It's okay." She hugged me, but I barely felt it.

"I have to go."

"Where?"

"I don't know."

"Wait. I'll come with you."

"No. I need to be alone. I'll text you."

I pushed through the crowd, urging the weight of my tears to hold. I could see the long bathroom line from the bleachers. I couldn't go there. The year before when Harris and I had wanted fresh air in the middle of the school day, we'd eat our lunches on a bench behind the football equipment shed.

To get there, I'd have to pass Ally and Harris. I didn't care. I inched through the crowd near the fence, keeping my face turned away from them. The doors to the shed were open, but nobody was inside. Around the back, I fell onto the bench and leaned forward, hanging over my knees. The tears came. Hard. Fast.

Uncontrollable.

"Melanie, are you okay?"

I turned my back to the voice and wiped my face. "I'm fine."

"Can I sit with you?"

I recognized it then. Jake Medina. My breathing hadn't normalized enough to answer without some ugly sob sneaking out.

"I'm sorry. I was catching up with some friends down at the fence, and I saw you run by."

Inhale...two...three...four...five. Exhale.

I turned to face Jake's concerned eyes. "You're going to miss Julia's game."

"Defense is on the field."

The home crowd erupted.

"But the offense might be heading back out," he said.

So strange. A few weeks ago, Harris Fullerton had been my science nerd—I meant that in the best possible way—best friend next door. Julia Medina—the soon-to-be captain of the volleyball team. Jake Medina, a stranger. My sister had been more annoying than worthy of adoration. And I'd been hoping for a shot at varsity time.

A lot had changed. Maybe too much.

"Melanie, are you back here?"

I recognized that voice immediately. Harris. He came around the corner of the shed to find me standing a foot away from Jake. Harris looked at Jake and me and back at Jake.

"Are you crying? What did you do to her?"

Harris rushed at Jake, their faces only inches apart. I stepped between them and pushed Harris back. "Stop. Jake didn't do anything to me."

"Then why were you crying?"

B*ecause of you.*

"Melanie, do you want me to go? Or stay?" Jake asked. "Or you can come back out there and sit with me and my family?"

His kindness felt like a warm hug. Unlike Chandra or Isla, I had no misconceptions about my relationship with Jake. He saw me like a little sister, and having a big brother felt good.

"I'm okay. This is Harris. He's my best friend."

"Oh." Jake smiled. "I get it now. Harris," he reached out his hand, "nice to meet you, man. I'm Jake Medina. Melanie's friends with my little sister."

Harris nodded and shook his hand. "Sorry about earlier."

"No sweat. You good, Mel?"

"Yes. Thanks. See you later maybe."

He waved and was gone.

Harris glared at me.

"What?"

"What?" he repeated. "Jake Medina? Seriously? What about Square?"

"You heard him. We're friends. He's like a big brother to me."

Harris rolled his eyes. "Why are you lying to me?"

"Me? Why am I lying? You came here with *her*."

He stepped back as if I'd pushed him. "Ally? Is this about how you two don't get along or whatever? I think if you gave her a chance—"

"I gave her a chance! I followed all her stupid team rules, and she sent me to a sketchy party that got me and Square in serious trouble with the principal."

"What kind of trouble? What are you talking about?"

"Of course she didn't tell you. Did she tell you we got into a fight in the locker room and were suspended from volleyball for a week?"

"Like, a physical altercation?"

"Yes, Harris. A physical altercation! The kind that left marks on her face."

"You can't play volleyball?"

"We're missing the first two games."

"I had no idea."

He was quiet for a minute, but the wide-eyed surprise on his face transformed into squinted, angry eyes. "Why didn't *you* tell me?"

"When was I going to tell you? Maybe you should ask why she didn't tell you. Maybe you should ask why she's even dating you."

"What does that mean? That I'm so nerdy that nobody could like me?"

I closed my eyes and felt the weight of tears pressing against me again. "That is not what I meant."

"Or is the problem that I'm making new friends too? All summer, it was you and me, but then volleyball starts, and you're out with the team all the time. Or with Square. And now you and Jake Medina are hiding behind a shed at a football game together."

"I told you it wasn't like that."

"You left me behind, Melanie. Any way you look at it. And when I found someone else to spend time with, you ignored me. Did you ever think it's not your place to decide who I date?"

"Did you ever think that a girl should have more than one friend?"

He nodded slowly. "Yeah. I do. Definitely someone other than me."

Harris left me in the shadow of the shed with my breath caught in my throat. Had he broken up with me? Could you break up with your best friend?

The black hole in my chest, slowly sucking all of the energy and strength from the rest of my body into its void told me, *Yes. You can.*

CHAPTER THIRTY-SIX

THE NEXT DAY I HID IN MY ROOM, THE ONLY SAFE PLACE on the planet.

Our backyard swing called my name, but the last thing I wanted to do was see Harris. How would that work now? Did we both avoid our back yards? For a few days? For forever? I laid in bed and stared at the ceiling. Harris's red, angry face took shape. I heard his voice yelling at me all over in my head. With the crowd cheering for the team in the background, he and I had aired everything.

Well, not everything.

How many romance novels had I read over the years where in a moment of passion the main characters embraced and locked lips while disagreeing? How many books played out the best-friends-to-lovers trope? Or, better yet, the next-door-neighbor hookup?

None of those would be my reality.

I streamed old TV shows all morning. Anything to keep from looking out the window. I couldn't bear to see Ally there.

How would I ever make peace with her now?

I'd lose my sport, my best friend, everything.

By noon, I didn't have the strength to continue the day. I nibbled the sandwich my mom brought up for lunch and fell asleep in the comfort of my pillow and blankets.

Until...

"Wake up!"

I shot upright to find Chandra hovering over me. "What the hell, Chandra?"

"It's team time. Get dressed."

I growled at her and pulled the pillow over my head. Sleep was my refuge. She'd taken away my refuge.

Then she took away my pillow. "Not taking no for an answer, Soph."

"I'm suspended."

"Still on the team."

"I quit," I said.

"Shut up. Elle picked this out for you." She tossed me something pink. "Get dressed."

"Not going."

"You have five minutes, or I'm sending in your mom and sister."

She'd mastered the Corwin family dynamic fast. I couldn't deal with any more of my mom's hovering, and Elle was a master manipulator.

"Is it just the team? Or are people bringing dates?"

"Team only," she called on the way down the stairs.

Good. Harris wouldn't be there. I rolled out of bed and fell to the floor. Elle had picked out a hot-pink dress for me. It had a sweetheart neckline and spaghetti straps.

I tossed it onto my dresser and wore a T-shirt and shorts instead. Chandra sighed and rolled her eyes when I came down the stairs, but she must have decided the battle wasn't worth fighting.

"What's with the box?" she asked, pointing to the package I carried in my arms.

"Socks for the shelter. I spent my allowance this month on the softest socks I could find."

She reached inside, pulled out a plaid blue-and-purple pair, and brushed them against her cheek. "These are amazing. Thank you for doing that."

I tried to ignore the swelling in my chest. I'd bought the socks because I wanted to, not for any recognition, but the whole thing had made me feel really good about myself and my friendship with Chandra. "You've been really good to me. I appreciate it, and I wanted to show you that I'm here for you too."

She blew me a kiss.

"Lip balm in winter, right?"

"Right," she answered.

"Count me in."

"You're all right, Soph."

"Yes, she is," my mom said, brushing my hair out of my face. "Have a good time with the team. Make friends."

"You mean one particular friend?" I asked.

"It couldn't hurt, honey."

Thinking of Ally with Harris hurt a lot actually.

Chandra patted my shoulder and told my mom goodbye. We climbed into her car, and she told me to buckle up. "This is gonna be a ride."

To say the least. Team time. Ally would be there. My heart wasn't ready for that.

Chandra pulled out of the driveway. "Team time was my call this week."

"I thought I got to pick the next time."

"Nope. Not when you're suspended from the team for smashing our setter's face in."

"Whose side are you on?"

"Yours. Always. It was fun to watch, but consequences are consequences."

"I'm learning that," I said. "Thanks."

Chandra picked up Ashley. After a few minutes along the route, I realized we were in the Medinas' neighborhood. Sure enough, she parked in Julia's driveway.

"Julia is hosting team night?"

Chandra waggled her eyebrows. "Not just Julia."

Jake.

"I thought you said no dates!"

"He lives here. That doesn't count."

"How did last night go?" Thinking about the night before twisted my chest.

She closed her eyes and sighed. "Lovely."

Grateful to be thinking about someone's drama besides my own, I wondered how Isla felt about that.

Chandra added, "I told you. His—"

"Ass. I know."

She shrugged. "When you find a good thing..."

A good thing. Like volleyball. Harris. My friendships with the girls on the team? All things I'd messed up.

Julia greeted us in the back yard, where a few of the girls were already playing a pickup game on the sand court. I wrapped her in a hug, a spark of happiness igniting so brightly my pain faded. "Julia! Congratulations!"

Elle had updated me on the football game when she'd gotten home the night before. Iron Valley had won their first game of the season 21–7. Square had three sacks, and Julia had thrown two touchdowns. One to Josh. One to Owen.

"Thank you. We missed you last night. I met Harris. Jake said he's your best friend."

My throat closed. Entirely. I managed a nod.

"You okay?"

"Uh-huh."

Apparently not convinced, she looped her arm in mine. "Come with me."

Past the pool, we slipped into Abuelita's apartment in the detached garage, and Julia pulled the sliding glass door behind us. She closed the blinds on the door, and I heard something click outside.

"What was that?"

"I didn't hear anything." She led me to the couch. "How are you holding up?"

"You heard about Ally?"

"And the suspension."

I slumped into Abuelita's couch, which was perfectly worn in. "I fought all summer and through camp to start varsity, and when I earned the spot, I got suspended from the team. I don't know how to make this work."

Maybe I'd snuggle on the couch the entire night. Avoid Ally completely. A peek at Abuelita's bookshelf told me I'd have any number of options to keep me company.

The bathroom door opened, and who else but Ally Malone walked into the living room.

"You've got to be kidding me," she said.

All I could see was her arms around Harris, her lips on his. "I was thinking the same thing."

"Stop," Julia said. "You two have to work together. You are a setter and a hitter. You literally depend on each other. There's no getting around that. You've both done some messed up stuff to each other, but I know you. You're both kind, funny, and super intense competitors. If you can get over this, you two will be unstoppable on the court. You'll crush every team you play."

Ally crossed her arms and transformed her eyes into daggers again.

"Al, I know I hurt you the way I quit. I should have told you before I did it. I should have asked for your advice and support. I was a mess. So scared, even though I didn't realize it at the time. I felt like life was suffocating me. I missed Jake so bad it clawed at my insides. Don't tell him that." She glanced at the door as if he might've been right outside listening. "I was a mess, and when people are a mess, they usually do stupid things."

"Is this you apologizing, or you telling me I'm doing stupid things because I'm a mess?" Ally asked.

"Both."

"This is ridiculous."

"Ally, how can you not see that how you've treated Melanie is awful? How can you not see that she needed someone on the team to support her, and you plotted against her every chance you got?"

"Vanessa was better," Ally said. "Why was I the only one who saw that?"

"And now?" Julia challenged. "Is Vanessa still better?"

Ally's eyes flickered to me, and my stomach dropped to the shag carpet. Did she admit, even telepathically, that I deserved the spot over Vanessa?

"Not gonna work, Al," Julia said. "We're locked in here with the team and my brother's friends patrolling the outside of the garage. Nobody gets out until I say so."

So the clicking sound had been Jake locking us in here. Great.

232

"You're not serious," Ally said.

Fine by me. I wanted to stay there all night reading anyway. Although I wouldn't have minded if Ally left.

"Beyond serious. I felt guilty leaving the team, but I did it to follow my passion. I may have hurt the team's chances at the perfect season or whatever, but Ally, what you're doing is worse. So much worse."

"You don't know what you're talking about," she countered.

"You're purposely sabotaging everyone. And Melanie, maybe you weren't at first, but enough bad blood has boiled between you two that I think you might be doing it now too."

"Me? I've tried everything I could to break through Ally's steel curtain."

"Oh, yeah, right," Ally said.

"I have. I went on all your stupid team bonding events when I wanted to be home resting from practice. Or working on getting better. I loved hitting middle, but I switched from middle to outside because Coach said the team needed me to. I practiced my approach bouncing the ball off my roof so much that my sister was ready to kick me out of my house. I worked with Julia to learn a jump serve. I have been busting my ass for this team. And for you. Meanwhile, you start dating my best friend, who I know you don't actually like, and I didn't even claw out your eyes for it." At some point I'd stood and directed my finger in Ally's face.

"Sharing is good," Julia said, "but maybe we rein in it a little."

"Fine. You worked hard. But don't pretend you try on team nights."

"I do try. And Chandra has become one of my best friends because of it. Sam and I are a lot closer. I'm not a people person. I don't have lots of friends. I like to be in my house, in my room. I like to read and hear the quiet. I'm not a party girl every weekend. I don't like a full schedule, but did you give any consideration for that? No. You expect me to give all of my time to you and this team, and you treat me like crap for it."

Ally curled up on the couch and said something that made my breath stick in my chest. "I'm sorry."

CHAPTER THIRTY-SEVEN

JULIA AND I BOTH FROZE.

"You heard me." Ally rolled her eyes. "I'm not saying it again. My little brother doesn't like to be around people. Sometimes he hides in the bathroom at school to get away for a few minutes."

I'd actually done that a lot in elementary school. I still did.

"Jules," Ally said, "can you give us a minute?"

A smug grin on her face, Julia nodded and tapped an elaborate combination of sounds on the sliding door. Something clinked outside, and the door opened.

"Should we get the Jell-O pool ready for some wrestling?" Jake asked.

"Shut up," Julia said, and the door closed again.

She hadn't lied. We were locked into this garage apartment until we ended this. My mom letting me come made a lot more sense now.

Ally paced around the room for a few minutes that felt like hours. "I have control issues."

"You think?" The words flew from my lips before I could scold myself for saying them out loud.

"I'm trying to be the bigger person here and actually admit I'm wrong. Maybe you can do me the courtesy of being quiet and listening?"

"Sure. Sorry."

Ally took another deep breath. "I'm not going to get into the psychology of my life story or anything, but I like being in control. It's why I'm the setter. I get to touch the ball every time it comes over the net, and I also get to pick who hits it."

I didn't say anything because I didn't know what to say. I waited quietly until she told me it was time to speak or said something else, which was obviously giving her control yet again.

"Volleyball has always been something I can control. When Julia quit, it sort of felt like everything crumbled."

I nodded. I'd felt that too, so I couldn't imagine the depths Julia's best friend and longtime teammate had felt it.

"I shouldn't have taken it out on you."

"Thanks," I said.

We let the silence settle.

"I should have told you that I needed more time to myself," I said.

"Why didn't you?"

"You didn't make it easy to contradict you."

"Yeah," she said. "I get that."

"And I was afraid that if I spoke up and said I didn't want to be with the team all the time, everyone would see that as, I don't know, me not liking you all. It's not like that. I need time to myself."

"I get it. Like I said, my brother's the same way. Your idea for us to rotate who picks team activities was actually pretty great."

"I think that's the first compliment you've ever paid me."

"Don't get used to it," she said, and we both smiled.

If Ally could make a big gesture with a sincere apology, I could take a turn too. "Do you want to get together this week and practice?"

"Just the two of us?"

I nodded, and she considered for a minute. Or two. Or ten.

"Yeah. Okay."

I exhaled in relief. "Look at us. After all these team nights of fighting, and we're actually bonding...I think."

"We are. Which is why I should tell you I'm not dating Harris."

I sat upright and instantly regretted my clearly uncool response.

"I knew it!" she said. "You are so into him."

"Am not."

"Look. He's nice and cuter than I realized, but I have the feeling he has a thing for you too."

My beaten and bruised heart sat upright too. "He told you that?"

She shook her head. "Last night, you two had a fight, right?"

"Yeah."

"He told me he couldn't date anyone who didn't get along with his best friend."

Oh, Harris.

"Thanks, but I think I have to accept nothing's happening with us. We're friends."

"It's more than that," Ally said.

I couldn't believe that. My heart had been through too much to let it hope. "If there was something between him and me, why would he date you?"

"I was his experiment."

"What?"

"Apparently, he's been hitting the gym, cut his hair, and generally reinvented himself as part of an experiment to see how an unknown can get the attention of a popular girl. I found his notebooks last night."

That sounded so Harris, and it made sense why he'd been weird about bumping into me at the gym. But it wasn't like him to experiment on human subjects. That violated his code of ethics. "I'm sorry you got caught up in that."

She waved away my apology. "We hung out for, like, two minutes. I'm not devastated. And the thing is, I'm pretty sure you're the girl he was trying to attract. If I learned anything from the whole thing with Josh and your sister, it's that I don't want to get in the way when two people are clearly meant for each other," Ally said, standing.

"We made up!" she yelled to no one. "Let us out." She removed her phone and keys from her pocket and set them on Abuelita's counter.

"You can't know that," I said getting back to the topic of Harris.

"He built a volleyball court for you in his back yard."

Yeah, but that was just the way he was. He'd dated Ally. He'd ignored me. He'd fought with me. Sadly, any romantic feelings in the relationship were one-sided.

My-sided.

The sliding door opened, and Chandra poked her head around the curtain. "Are we over this once and for all?"

"Yes," Ally and I agreed.

"Are we ready for the perfect season?"

"Yes," we replied again, but this time with a little more enthusiasm.

"Let's go."

Ally grabbed my arm before I stepped through the doorway. "You should leave your phone and anything you don't want wet in here."

I emptied my pockets and dropped Elle's cross-body purse onto the counter. "You think they're going to throw us into the pool."

"It's the Medina house," she said. "Everyone gets thrown into the pool."

I didn't make it two steps out the door before Square scooped me up and flipped me over his shoulder. "Hey, Soph. Ready for a swim?"

"Can I convince you to let me change into a swimsuit first?"

"Not a chance."

"Then cannonball it is!"

Beside me, Jake carried Ally. He and Square counted to three, and we soared into the water.

Together.

CHAPTER THIRTY-EIGHT

CHANDRA'S PLAN FOR TEAM TIME WAS SWIMMING and playing a two-on-two sand volleyball tournament. Ally was my assigned teammate. Surprisingly, it was a blast. She never gave up on a ball, had a killer serve, and set to me no matter where I was on the court. Julia had been right. Both Ally and I were competitors. Now that we'd worked out our differences, I couldn't wait to get on the court with her as my teammate, not my nemesis, especially against Pacific, which would be our first game back after suspension.

We won the tournament against Chandra and Sam. Ally tackled me to the ground, sweat picking up every possible granule of sand.

Coach congratulated us. "I'm proud of you both. Thank you for working out your differences and dedicating yourselves to the team. I can't wait to see you on the court together."

"Are you so proud that you'll let us play this week?" Ally asked.

Hope soared through me, but Coach squashed it.

"Sorry. A consequence is a consequence. Hopefully this one is big enough that you carry this new sense of camaraderie throughout the season."

"And the playoffs," I said.

Ally high-fived me, giving me hope that we could actually get along and make it to the playoffs. Our friendship felt new and vulnerable, but for my team, I'd try. Like, really try.

"Yes," Coach said with a grin. "And the playoffs."

***

WITH NO ALTERNATIVE, ALLY HAD CALLED HARRIS AND asked if we could practice there after school that week. I still hadn't talked to Harris since Friday night behind the football shed.

Me: I'm not going there. We can go to the park.

Ally: The park doesn't have a regulation height net. If I can ask a favor from the kid that dumped me, you can walk across your yard.

I couldn't.

Ally's last message read: Be there, Soph.

After avoiding Harris any chance I could in school, I sat on my bed, looking out the window into his back yard. No sight of him. The clock ticked forward, closer to the 3:30 time Ally and I had agreed—*agree* was probably not the right word—on to meet at Harris's.

"Go talk to him," Elle said from my doorway.

"And say what?"

"Sorry you fought. That he's your best friend and too important to you to fight like this."

Nothing about how I felt about him.

"You think we should stay friends?"

"I think he feels like you traded up when you had the chance. You and I both know you didn't do that, but he doesn't. If you want something more with him, take it slow. Spend time together."

"And what? It'll happen?"

"Exactly."

I doubted it. It hadn't in all the years we'd spent every day together.

Harris's back door slammed, and I saw him on the porch. He looked down at his watch and then up at my bedroom.

"Go," Elle said.

I took a deep breath and trudged down the stairs. When the pickets slammed behind me, Harris stood up from the back porch swing and waved.

I waved back.

"Hey," he said.

"Hi."

Silence.

"Thanks for letting us come here to practice."

"You know you're always welcome."

I raised an eyebrow at him.

"Okay, last time we talked, I didn't give that impression. I know."

"Talked?" I said. "Don't you mean *got into a verbal altercation?*"

He cringed. "I'm sorry."

"Me too."

I allowed myself to look at him then. His hair, although shorter, still hung across his forehead. He tilted his head to the side, so it fell away from his eyes. His dark, gorgeous eyes. His lips curled into a tentative smile. Ally had kissed those lips. I never would.

I looked away.

"Mel, please forgive me. I was a crappy friend. I said things..."

"I'm sorry I stopped spending time with you. I didn't mean to. Ally's team activities, and Square..." Now my voice trailed off.

"So you and Jake really aren't together?"

"No. I'm not with Square either."

"Oh," Harris said. "Ally and I are over too."

"I heard. Sorry, I think."

He crossed his arms. "You're not, but that's okay."

I smiled at that intensity in his gaze that reminded me every second he was an observer. All the books I'd ever read had taught me this was the moment everything changed. If it was going to. Him looking at me. Me looking at him. He would tuck a strand of my hair behind my ear or brush his fingers against my cheek. Maybe touch my lips with his fingertips and put his mouth on mine.

He didn't do any of those things.

"I'm glad we made up," he said.

"Same."

"So you and Ally are really friends now?"

"Working on it."

"Speak of the angel," Ally said from the porch. "Your stepmom let me in. She's so lovely."

"Not the word that comes to mind," Harris said. "I'll let you two get to work."

He went inside, and Ally raised an eyebrow at me.

"Don't," I warned.

"Fine. Let's get started." She poured a mesh bag of volleyballs into the yard. "I can't believe you slapped me in the face and now we can't play in the first two games of the year."

"I also knocked you off the bench and maybe even pulled your hair," I said.

She threw a ball at me. "I'm serious! I'm a senior. This is my last first game of the season. Besides, I think I bit you."

I threw the ball back. "No. It's not. And you didn't. Next week will be your last first game of the season, and we're going to crush them."

"If you can manage to hit the ball inbounds."

"If you can manage to set it above the net."

"Is this you two getting along?" Harris interrupted. I didn't even hear him come back outside.

We both threw a ball at him.

He covered his face. "Hey! You know I'm not athletically inclined."

"I *never* knew that," Ally said.

"It's dangerous out here," Harris said. "I'm going in the shed to organize my beakers."

Ally's eyes widened, and she did her best to hold in laughter, at least until Harris disappeared into the shed. "Organize his beakers? So hot," she whispered.

"Shut up," I whispered back.

"When are you gonna make a move?"

I glanced at the shed, terrified Harris would be standing there. He wasn't. I thought back to a few minutes earlier, when we could

247

have had a moment.

But we hadn't.

"I'm not," I said. "We're best friends. He's not into me, and it would be too weird to cross that line."

Ally rolled her eyes and shook her head. "Whatever. I have an idea for a game."

"I'm afraid to ask."

"You said you like to challenge yourself. When I set the ball, I'm going to call out a code. *L* for line. *C* for center court. *X* for cross court."

"Highly classified code."

"I wasn't finished. I'll add numbers after each one."

"What do the numbers mean?"

"Nothing. That's the thing. My brother told me that in football, they add a bunch of stuff that makes no sense when the quarterback calls out the play. But it's all to confuse the defense. Only the offense knows what to pay attention to and what's gibberish."

"So we're confusing the defense?" I asked pointing to the grass on the other side of the net.

"Can we just play?"

"Fine. We will let you *control* where I hit the ball by calling out coded letters and random numbers."

Ally scrunched up her face in an expression I could only hope signaled a revelation of some sort. "Huh. Yeah. I see that now. Let's play anyway."

So we did. I tossed to Ally and alternated calling for the ball high outside, quick outside, and short outside, which was somewhere in between the quick and the high sets. As promised, Ally shouted letters and random numbers. Within minutes, our rhythm clicked. Unlike our practice in the gym the week before, we celebrated with each other. We even—gasp—laughed.

"Okay, this is you getting along," Harris said from the shadows after we'd gone through ten or so rounds of hitting. "Impressive."

"Thanks, Harris," I said, feeling a blush on my cheeks. No. I needed a drink. That was all. I was playing too hard. I was not blushing in front of Harris. "Water break, Ally?"

"Sure!"

Harris pointed to his lab table by the back porch. "I boiled and filtered the impurities from the water. It's also infused with fruit. That was my stepmom's doing."

"You did not boil our water," Ally said.

"Oh, he did," I said. "That's Harris."

"Cute and useful. I can see what Melanie sees in you."

My heart stopped. So much for all that training. I went into cardiac arrest and died right there in the grass.

"As her best friend," Ally clarified.

Harris smiled at me, missing the innuendo completely. Thank the universe. "I'll go get more ice."

"You are evil," I whispered after he'd gone inside.

Ally cackled.

Harris brought an ice bucket, and we dumped its contents into our water bottles, followed by a long pour from the boiled, filtered, chilled, fruit-infused water.

"He's like a teenage-scientist Martha Stewart."

"Yeah," I said. "Exactly like that."

"Harris?" Ally said. "I have an important question for you."

I closed my eyes and hoped that she was not going to ask anything else remotely suggestive about me.

"What else are you good at? Livestreaming, perhaps?"

"I livestream my science experiments all the time."

Ally smiled at me. "Excellent. Think you could livestream the volleyball games this week, so Mel and I can watch?"

That was a brilliant idea, and Harris was the perfect person to do it.

"Sure," he said as if no big deal. "But I'm going to need a different channel. I don't think my followers are gonna wanna watch that. No offense."

I hugged him and jumped up and down at the same time. "I thought I was gonna have to piece together the games from social media, but this is so much better. Thank you, Harris."

After the initial excitement over being able to watch the games had fizzled, every part of my body that touched Harris's sparked instead. Best friends hugged. But how did they hug? Should I have let go already? Did I let go and turn away? Or was that obvious? Did I avoid his eyes or look in his eyes, just not too long? Oh gosh. Why had I hugged him?

"You okay, Mel?" Harris asked.

"Yeah, Mel? You okay?" Ally asked with humor in her voice.

"I'm good. Just excited." I went with no eye contact and slowly turning away to grab my water bottle and take a drink. Totally natural. Totally cool.

Probably not cool at all.

"C'mon, Soph." Ally blew me a kiss. "Let's pepper and work off some of that excitement."

The fence pickets slammed, drawing our attention. Our teammates, sweaty from practice, waved.

"What are you doing here?" Ally said.

"We have Pacific next week," Sam said and gave me a pointed look. "We need to practice as a team."

My fluttering heart tripped over itself as awkwardly as I'd tripped in Elle's shoes. The team wasn't complete. Not without me.

"Didn't you just finish practice?" I said, trying to calm the flutters.

"Yep," Sam said, "but I heard we have a place to play here."

"No diving," Ally said. "Not in the grass. We'll be injured for sure."

Sam grinned. "No diving. But we can hit, right?"

I tossed her a ball. "Oh yeah. We can definitely hit."

CHAPTER THIRTY-NINE

AFTER SCHOOL EVERY DAY THAT WEEK, ALLY AND I practiced in Harris's back yard while he prepared a science experiment for Friday night. I'd occasionally stare at him. Ally would roll her eyes. That was how it went.

Monday and Wednesday, the rest of the varsity team had pushed through the pickets to practice hitting and blocking together. Tuesday and Thursday evenings, Harris packed up his camera equipment and livestreamed the volleyball games for us. We watched in my basement. Ally moved around the room like she was on a court.

"Chandra's doing great. Come sit down."

"I can't," she said, bouncing on her toes. "Crush that, Sam!"

Sam did.

The Tuesday opponent was a warm-up. We won easily in three games: 25–12, 25–16, and 25–10.

"Thursday will be tougher," Ally predicted, and she was right. Not only didn't she sit down, but she didn't stop bouncing.

"You're making me nauseous."

"Coach was right," she said. "This is so painful. I will never get in trouble again."

I felt the same way. And worried that someone on the team would step up and take the starting position I'd worked so hard to earn. I'd never put it in jeopardy again.

Thursday was a section matchup. We won in five games by three points. Way too close.

"It won't be like that the next time we play them," Ally said to the television. "Let's go hit some more."

"We hit for two hours today. My arm is going to fall off."

She finally sat down. "This is because you don't want to see Harris."

"He asked me to come watch his experiment Friday night."

"And miss the football game."

"They're away this week, and it's a drive."

"And you want to be with Harris."

I shrugged. "I always help him with his experiments. If that's what a best friend does, I should do it." *Since I'm his friend.*

"The friend zone. It kills dreams."

"Yep."

"Melanie," my mom called down the basement stairs, "time for dinner. Is Ally staying?"

That would make three times this week. The first night, when Elle had come in from shooting practice, there had been an awkward old western stare down, but after dinner, they'd whispered in the pantry, and since then all was well. I glanced at Ally, waiting for her to answer, and she rolled her eyes.

"It smells amazing, so definitely. But do you ever wonder if we're too bestie lately?"

"As in you never leave my house?"

"No, you're right. You'd miss me."

What shocked me most was that she might have been right about that. I followed her up the stairs amazed at how far we'd come.

***

FRIDAY NIGHT CAME QUICKLY. I MESSAGED JULIA GOOD luck and stood in front of my closet way too long. For the first time in my life, I *wanted* to look good. Elle had left for the game an hour earlier since it was away, so I didn't have her help. I aimed for that easy-going, flawless look she'd mastered. This was a backyard science experiment. A dress was trying too hard. Athletic clothes painted me as the unchanged, next-door neighbor. I wanted Harris to see me as a girl, if that was possible.

I went with jean shorts and a casual tank top. I played with Elle's curling iron, and my hair draped down my back in soft curls.

"Where are you off to?" Harris asked when I pushed through the pickets.

"Here," I said. "For your experiment."

He observed my clothes. "A little overdressed, aren't you?"

I steeled myself. He *so* did not see me as a girl.

Harris prepared his experiment the same way he had for years. He weighed the beakers to ensure absolute accuracy. He triple-checked his list and lined up his materials so he could access them at crucial moments in the experiment. His simple movements that had been so natural and casual to me my whole life stirred this inexplicable need to reach out and touch him. To tug him toward me, press my lips against his, and bury my fingers into his hair that looked so good now that he'd finally trimmed away the excess.

"...so I had no idea what caused the reaction when I saw it. Was it chemical or physical? I had to test it for myself."

I nodded and hoped Harris didn't pick up on me not actually paying attention.

"You weren't listening to anything I said, were you?"

Crap. I couldn't exactly reveal my reason.

He looked at the ground. "Sorry this stuff bores you so much lately."

I grabbed his arm. "No. It doesn't."

In an alternate universe that slowed time, Harris and I stared into the depths of each other's eyes. In his back yard. With his impending experiment surrounding us and his dark eyes and dark hair. The intensity in his gaze. What if I did it? What if I kissed him? I could have the moment I'd daydreamed about lately through every class, every practice, and every time the two of us were so close to each other that I tricked my mind into believing it might actually work.

What if he pushed me away? I'd have to hide in my house every day. I'd have to find a new lab partner.

A new best friend.

Maybe even move!

"Mel, are you okay?"

I choked on a breath. "Fine. Let's get this experiment started."

"You sure you don't have a party to get to?"

A memory of Square and me in the principal's office flashed in my mind. "I am never going to a party again."

Harris smirked. "My birthday's coming up."

"I'll mail you a present."

He laughed. I wanted to grab the sound out of the air and hold onto it forever.

Harris advised me where to stand as he rambled about how this could possibly make the research project for competitions this year. I watched his beautiful lips move and felt totally pathetic.

"When this is ready, I need you to stand back, okay?"

"Sure," I said, familiar with Harris's warnings.

"I mean it. This could splatter, and I don't want you to get burned."

"Promise."

He examined the kosher salt he was melting, and that irresistible wobbly grin appeared. "Almost ready."

A fish tank full of water rested on a table a few feet from him.

"What's the fish tank for?"

He shook his head. "Where's your head been?"

"I was totally paying attention!"

And lying.

"I'm going to pour the melted salt into the water, which should set off a minor explosion and potentially some splattering. To analyze the reaction, I'd need a high-speed camera, which I can get from the school. However, I have to write an analysis report first to request the camera. Thus, the reason for this first attempt at the experiment. If we get a good reaction, I'll definitely score the camera."

"Great!"

"I think we're ready. Stand back!"

I retreated and leaned against the fence. Using a pole, he held the molten salt as far from his body as he could and poured it into the fish tank. Immediately, the glass walls of the tank popped and shattered, sending glass and liquid in every direction.

Including mine.

I shielded my face and felt something hit my forearm.

"Melanie!"

My heartbeat pulsed through the burning cut on my arm. I leaned against the fence, assessing the damage. A small piece of glass had hit me. Thankfully, nothing else. Harris's face appeared inches from mine.

"I'm fine." I reached for him. "Are you okay?"

"Let me see." He ran his fingers along my skin, searching for the glass and mixing pleasure with my pain without realizing it. "I'm so sorry. I didn't think it would splash that far. Oh, Mel."

"Harris..." My voice was low. A rasp against the evening wind.

"There's a small cut, but no glass," he said. "Thank God."

My fingers found their way to his hair. It was thick. Soft. And perfectly tangled in my hands.

"I think I have bandages in the emergency kit." He stepped backward, but I went with him, refusing to remove my hands from his hair.

"Harris," I whispered again.

As if realizing for the first time our intimate position, he made eye contact, his gaze questioning. I feared my heart was pounding wildly enough to set off another explosion. He'd trained himself to observe and record details. Had he collected enough empirical data—the minimal space between us, my hands intwined in his hair, the suggestive (if I was doing it right) look in my eyes—to know that his next-door neighbor and lab partner had fallen so hopelessly in love she couldn't see the world beyond him?

In case he needed more evidence, I leaned closer. So close that if I puckered my lips, they would touch his. And with the discipline I'd refined over years of athletic training, I looked into his dark eyes, then back at his beautiful mouth, and waited.

I couldn't do this alone. I needed him to want it as much as I did.

Time stilled long enough for me to suspect he didn't want me, for rejection to sting my insides more intensely than a million shards of glass could sting my skin. And to debate if he'd let me get away with pleading utter confusion over being impaled by something so infinitesimal. When my heart rate approached a dangerous pace and my stomach squeezed in the most hurtful disappointment, Harris's lips curled into that wobbly smile of his.

He closed the practically nonexistent distance between us and pressed his lips against mine so softly I wondered if it was real.

A true scientist, he explored my mouth like he was recording data to support the perfect hypothesis. Was our kiss an experiment for him? Would he decide kissing was a stupid mistake for two best friends? Or would his hypothesis lean another way? I wavered between wanting to enjoy the moment and fearing he'd pull away, leaving me embarrassed and lost.

When his fingertips gripped my shirt and he pulled me closer, I smiled against his kiss. His hypothesis had turned out in my favor. I let my soul fall into him, letting go of the fears, the risks, and even my heart.

Anyone could come into the backyard to reprimand Harris for the explosion. But I had waited. I had fantasized. I had tempted and scolded myself for thinking of Harris as more than a friend. Now that his perfect mouth was on mine and his hands moved from my neck to my hair to my face and back again, I would have chased the whole neighborhood away before I'd let them stop us.

The most beautiful moment of all? When I realized Harris had absolutely no interest in backing away from me either.

"Harris!" his stepmom screeched from the back porch. "What was that noise?"

We stopped kissing but didn't move away from each other.

Harris leaned his forehead against mine. "She has the absolute worst timing."

"What in the world—Oh, Melanie, dear. I didn't realize." She squinted as if her view of us wrapped in each other's arms was somehow flawed. "Okay, well..." She shook her head and went back inside.

"She seemed confused," I whispered.

"Can't blame her." He brushed his lips against my cheek, and I leaned into him. "How many times has she come out here to yell at me, and she's never once seen this?"

"Never," I agreed.

Harris tilted my head back and pulled my bottom lip into his mouth for one more soft, delicious kiss. "You know what I think, Mel?"

"What?"

"It's about time."

CHAPTER FORTY

I HAD KISSED HARRIS FULLERTON. I HAD A BANDAGE ON my arm from his experiment, but without that glass, who knows if his lips would have found mine. And what a loss that would have been. It took hours to fall asleep that night. I laid in bed wondering if he was stargazing in his yard. And if he was, what would happen if I climbed out of bed and joined him. And what would happen when we saw each other at school.

I found out when he appeared next to my locker before first period. He approached slowly. Tentatively. Not at all the blazing entrance followed by the romantic embrace I'd envisioned all night.

"Is everything okay?"

He shrugged.

"Harris...?"

He tapped his fingers against my locker, careful not to make eye contact. "I guess I'm not really sure how to act around you."

I moved close to him and whispered, "Because we made out last night?"

A smile tugged at his lips. "That would be an accurate assessment."

Suddenly self-conscious, I asked, "How do you want to act around me?"

His dark eyes found mine. "I want to reenact last night every time I look at you."

Oh, thank Einstein. I wrapped my arms around his neck and kissed him right there in the hallway with friends and strangers rushing around us. Like the night before, my chest simultaneously twisted and expanded while bells and Harris-quality explosions went off in my mind.

"Get a room," someone yelled.

Someone else bumped Harris, pushing him into me. I fell against my locker and felt the strength of his arm behind my back, holding me upright.

"Even though this is my first experience kissing in the hallway," he said, "empirical data has proven it to be dangerous."

Despite the amazingness of the kiss and the feeling of his fingertips tickling the skin above the waistline of my pants, I couldn't shake the self-consciousness that had started our conversation. "Harris, why did you not know how to act around me?"

"Mel, you're the stunningly beautiful, up-and-coming volleyball star. I'm a science nerd."

I kissed him again. "You're *my* science nerd."

His lips curved into the slightest smile. "I did hear you defend me when you were with your team at the gym. You called me a genius."

"I'm sure I didn't go that far."

He laughed and pulled me into a hug. The bell rang.

"Although I can say with certainty, I won't be able to pay attention in any of my classes, I better go." He kissed my cheek and wobbly grinned before rushing down the hall.

Harris Fullerton not able to pay attention in class? Be still, my socially awkward heart. Trying not to be late, I grabbed my morning notebook and the few books I needed and hustled in the opposite direction. Right into Ally.

"Finally made a move, huh?" She squeezed my arm and had the sincerest smile on her face. Wow. The nice side of Ally Malone. Never thought I'd see the day.

"There was an explosion. Seemed like the moment."

"Sounds about right," she said. "He better be at my last first game."

"You mean my first first game?"

"That's what I said, right?" She blew me a kiss and merged into the hallway traffic.

***

ALLY'S LAST FIRST GAME. MY FIRST FIRST GAME.

The pasta and chicken I'd eaten for dinner churned in my stomach. Outside the gym doors, Harris hugged me, doing his best to squeeze away my anxiety. Ally grabbed my arm and tugged me into the gym.

"Get focused," she said.

I nodded, wondering if I had any hope of it. Fans wearing brown and gold piled through the doors at the other side of the gym to support Pacific. Our JV had won in a close battle, but the varsity matchup was the one to watch—a preview of the regional championship, if chatter around sports circles could be believed.

The thing about sports chatter was that something could always go wrong.

If you let it.

Harris sat in the bleachers with my parents, sisters, and Josh. Square and Julia were there with six rows of football players. In the pregame huddle, we could barely hear Coach over the fans. The home stands shook from everyone stomping the beat of "We Will Rock You". The Pacific fans stomped and screamed.

"This is like a playoff game, not a first first or a last first game," Ally shouted in my ear.

I nodded.

We broke the huddle, and I took Julia's—no, *my* position in the left front. We turned our backs to the down ref, so she could check our numbers against the lineup Coach had submitted. I bounced on my toes and closed my eyes.

This was it.

Varsity.

The biggest regular-season matchup of the year.

The refs rolled the ball to Pacific's first server, and we dropped back to serve receive. Ally hid behind me, waiting for the serve to run to her home position in the right front of the court.

"You got this, Melanie," she said. "Give me a good pass."

"Give me a good set," I answered, and she laughed.

"Deal."

But I didn't give her a good pass. Pacific served the ball to the back row, and Molly passed it to Ally instead.

"Outside!" I yelled over the fan noise.

Ally set her feet and pushed the ball high and outside to me. I watched the arc, curving my approach and timing my jump to meet the ball at its peak. We weren't a gym with fans, expectations, and stakes.

We were two girls who loved volleyball, practicing in my boyfriend's back yard. Nothing different. No one else. Me, my setter, and the ball.

I jumped and piked my body, swatting the ball with an open hand, strong wrist, and full weight of my body's momentum. It slipped right around the middle hitter's block and landed in the center of the court.

My first kill.

Our fans erupted. My teammates squeezed me into a hug.

"Nice hit," Ally said.

"Nice set," I answered.

The bench chanted, "Soph! Soph! Soph!"

The scoreboard read 1 to 0.

A Pacific player rolled the ball under the net to Kate, who jump served an ace, but that was where Pacific's zero score ended. They returned the next serve and out volleyed us to score their first point. The game went on like that—our fans cheering, their fans cheering, and ours again—until the score was us leading 24–22.

Game point, and I was heading back to the service line with a knot in my stomach the actual size of a volleyball.

Coach called a time-out.

"We fought hard for these twenty-four points, girls. Let's put them away now and take this victory. Push yourself on this point. No mistakes." She nodded at me. "Melanie, put this serve in play."

Ally patted my back. Sam squeezed my shoulder. The team came together in the huddle. Sam counted to three, and we cheered, "Iron Valley!" I couldn't look at the stands. Or the other team. I inhaled, held the breath, and walked onto the court. The line judge tossed me the ball. *Exhale.* The ref climbed the small ladder to the platform above the net. *Inhale.* She checked that the players on both sides were in position, held her arm out to me, and lifted it at the same moment she blew her whistle. *Exhale.* I could barely hear the whistle over the screaming in the gym, but I saw her cheeks puff and her arm rise, so I knew.

It was time.

CHAPTER FORTY-ONE

INHALE. I STEPPED BACK FROM THE LINE, MENTALLY measuring the distance I'd need for my jump without foot faulting. *Exhale.*

I tossed. Approached. Jumped.

The ball soared over the net. Into play. Deep on their side of the court. So deep—oh no. No, no, no! The Pacific players stepped away from the ball, holding their arms in the air, shouting, "Out!"

The ball came down hard. On. The. Line.

The ref pointed her hand down and blew her whistle. My teammates tackled me.

"It was in," I said, my chest numb from the moment.

"You bet your ass it was," Ally said. As her smile widened, the feeling came back to my core, and then my arms and legs. I had served an ace.

We won. We won!

The score of the first game was 25–22. The Pacific players lowered their heads.

"It's not over," Sam said.

She was right. We had two more games to win if we wanted to take the best-of-five match.

The second game started with a missed serve by us and then Pacific's strongest server. She sent three deep balls right near the end line. Molly shanked one into the stands. The other two fell untouched inbounds. Coach stood and shouted to us, but I couldn't hear the words over the cheering Pacific fans behind her.

We all got the message.

No more serves would drop inbounds. Abby played the next one, and we sent a free ball back at Pacific that they crushed at us. Before we knew it, the score was five to nothing, the high from our victory in the last game fizzled, and Coach called a time-out.

"Take a breath, girls."

We did.

"Good," Coach said. "Now, take another one."

We did.

"Okay. She's a strong server, but you know you can't let one server beat you. One good pass. One good set. One good hit. Then we side-out. Got it?"

"Yes, Coach."

"Another breath."

The ref blew the whistle.

"Get out there. You got this, girls."

We hustled to our positions on the court. I begged the ball to come to me, but being in the front row, I probably wouldn't have the chance to pick up the forceful jump serve. Molly did. She set her feet, turned her platform toward Ally, and let the ball slowly pop off her arms in a perfect pass. I called for a quick outside set. Sam called for a quick middle. The blocker opposite me cheated to the middle. Ally sent the set to me, and I had a wide-open hit that I crushed down the line for a side-out.

We came together in the center of the court and celebrated.

"One point at a time," Sam said. "We got this."

But we didn't. For every point we scored, Pacific picked up two—at least. At the end of the game, we were the ones hanging our head with a loss of 25–16.

At the bench, Coach assigned us more breathing. "This match is best of five. Let that be our game of mistakes. The score is zero to zero. They serve first. I want you to get this into your head—they get one serve. Every time they go to the line. One serve. That's it."

"Yes, Coach," we said.

"Ally, they're digging their heels in for strong hits. Keep them on their toes."

Ally nodded, a grin curling at the corner of her lip.

"*Iron Valley* on three. One. Two. Three."

"Iron Valley!"

We hit the court determined to take the game and a two-to-one lead in the match. I glanced at the stands. My sisters cheered louder and waved. Harris pressed his fingertips to his lips and kissed them. I wanted to play hard for them and for my team. Months earlier, I'd been a quiet girl playing volleyball alone in her yard. Maybe I was still a little quiet, but I had friends to push me and support me. And a boyfriend. I shook my head at that.

But most of all, I wanted to play hard for me. I wanted to show myself that I wasn't the intimidated girl from the first day of volley-ball camp—not sure how to talk to the strongest hitter.

I'd be the intimidating one, or at least I'd try.

In position for the serve, I slapped Ally's hand. "We got this."

"Yep," she said, no doubt in her voice.

The Pacific player jump served, and the ball caught the edge of the net. The ball trickled over, falling fast to the hardwood. I dove and caught it right before it hit the floor. Ally made a play on the rough pass with a high set to the back row. Molly jumped and attacked the ball. Pacific's middle hitter blocked it, and I hit the floor again, this time, digging the ball just in time. Abby picked it up in the back row and set Sam, who crushed the ball deep. Thankfully, it hit the floor.

"Good defense, Melanie!" Coach called.

I nodded to her and got into position at the net, waiting for Kate's serve. The whistle blew. She jump served, and the volley began. They passed, set, and hit. We blocked. They passed, set, and hit. We did the same. A kill by them. A kill by us. A well-placed tip by Ally. Or two. Or five.

We worked for every point, a certain beauty in the level of com-petition between us. The crowd appreciated the beauty—cheering and gasping in awe at the right moments. Adrenaline coursed through every inch of me, even when we lost a point. I'd mentally applaud them for the work they'd done to earn their point and move on, ready to earn one right back.

Pacific called a time-out when we led 24–19.

Coach clapped hard and loud as we approached the bench. "Girls! I love it. I'm so jealous. I want to be out there playing with you. This is what this sport is all about. These volleys are amazing. I'm so proud of you."

We laughed at her gushing. She gave compliments, but never to that level of excitement.

She took a deep breath. "I need to take my own advice and breathe here. Change nothing. It's their serve, so a side-out wins us this game and puts us one step closer to the match. One good pass. One good set. One good hit. Arms in."

I pressed my hand over Ally's. Under Sam's. With the rest of my team's hands on top. All of us invested in this moment, in this win.

"*Iron Valley* on three. One! Two! Three!"

"Iron Valley!"

Our teams moved into position, staring each other down through the checkered net that separated us.

Sam looked at Kate and me, all of us in the back row on the rotation. "Call this ball. Nothing hits the floor without one of us hitting next to it."

Kate and I nodded and got low and into position. The ref blew the whistle and raised her arm. I took a deep breath and mentally urged the server to send the ball to me.

She bounced the ball. Once. Twice. Three times. Tossed. Approached. Jumped. Crack!

The ball soared over the net toward my corner of the court. It was deep and close to the line. I could let it go, but my instincts told me it was in. No way would I let game point fall to the floor without being played.

As the ball got closer, I moved with it, getting low to send a perfect pass to Ally.

B*ut it could be out,* I thought. If it was, and I let it go, we'd win.

"In! In!" Ally called. "Play it."

Exhaling a whoosh of relief, with confidence I waited for the ball to contact my arms. When it did, I pulled them backward, toward my body to take off some of the momentum from the forceful serve. The ball wasn't perfect, but it soared in Ally's direction, high enough for her to set. Rachel called for the ball at middle. Ally raised her arms.

P*lease, please, please,* I urged.

"Middle," Ally called, and I blinked. She never called out the play, but sure enough, Pacific moved into position to block a middle hit. Ally tipped the ball to the front corner, and nobody was there to pick it up.

I squeezed her so hard, I thought she might split in half. "You sneaky thing!"

"I have some tricks up my sleeve," she said and accepted congratulations from the rest of the team. "In fact, I have an idea for the next game."

CHAPTER FORTY-TWO

"NO," I SAID. "IT'S A RIDICULOUS PLAN."

"I think it's brilliant," Ally said.

The "trick" was for us to use our backyard code. Since we'd established the code could be discovered by a toddler, we would hit early in the game with the code. Ally would call out *L*, and I'd hit line. She'd call *C* for center court and *X* for cross court. I'd hit to wherever she said. When Pacific picked up on it and started cheating to those spots, we'd switch it on them.

"Don't you think this might be a little distracting?" I asked.

"Only if we hadn't practiced it for a full week. They're playing right with us every step of the way. I want to win in four games, and this could be the edge we need to pick up a few extra points and walk away with this thing."

It made sense, but would it work?

I guess only one way to find out.

The first set of the game, Ally pushed my way and called out our code, "*L* slash!"

The "slash" meant nothing, but the *L* told me I should hit down the line. I did. The Pacific defender dove for it and hit the ball into the stands.

"She's been cheating center court every game," Ally said, high fiving me. "I'm calling *line* again. Be ready."

The next set went to Sam in the middle. She was blocked, but our back row picked up the pass, and Ally pushed the set to me. "*L* slash!"

Again, I hit down the line. This time, the defender played the ball better, but the pass wasn't on target. We ended up with a free ball. Ally called "*L* slash" again, and the middle hitter cheated to my side, blocking my hit. Luckily, Sam picked it up, and the volley continued. After several trips back and forth over the net, the ball came to Ally. She called "*L* slash" again. Pacific's middle cheated my way again, and I got ready for my approach, thinking my only option would be to tip the ball over the block. Instead, sneaky Ally set Sam in the middle, and Sam killed the ball without a block to stop her.

Ally jumped onto Sam, who shook her head.

"You are devious," I said, and hugged her.

Pacific called a time-out. We hustled off the court smiling, until we saw Coach's face. "What are you doing out there?"

Ally grinned and said, "Having fun."

Coach rubbed her chin and glanced at the scoreboard. We were up 3–0. "It's a good start, but the second you're more focused on the codes Ally's calling than the game, we stop this. Understood."

We all nodded, and Coach grinned. "Go have some more fun."

Back on the court, Molly served again. On the volley, we scored another point on a tip from Ally before Pacific sided-out, bringing the score to 4–1. On the rotation, Pacific subbed in a particularly tall girl I didn't remember playing in the first three games. Actually, I thought she might have been the JV middle hitter. When the ball went into play, she ran to their right side and lined up across from me. Ally set me calling for a cross court hit, and the Pacific player blocked me. Sam picked it up, and Ally set the back row. But every set she brought my way after that, the Pacific player either blocked or got a hand on.

Slowly our lead dwindled, and with a few volleys and two side-outs, we were suddenly behind, 8–7. Coach called a time-out.

"That blocker is all over you," Ally said.

I grunted an unfortunate agreement.

"Girls, we got this," Coach said, clapping. "Their strong blocker will rotate out of the lineup this next side-out. Rachel, I want you to come around Ally for a quick back set. Ally, you also have three hitters in the back row. Use them. Everyone be ready to pick up these blocks. Nothing hits the floor. Got it?"

"Yes, Coach."

"*Iron Valley* on three. One. Two. Three."

"Iron Valley!"

It was my serve. Waiting for the up ref to climb the platform to her position, I eyed Pacific's new blocker, dropped back to serve receive in the right front. I swore she smiled at me.

Oh, hell no.

The ref blew the whistle. I shifted my position to the left slightly and began my jump-serve approach. When I hit the ball, I took some of the power off it. It was a risk, but the fire in my core convinced me the risk was worth it.

The ball looked short. Maybe too short. Crap. At the last second, it clipped the top of the net and fell onto Pacific's side, in front of their star blocker. She dove late, and the ball hit the ground. She bounced it back under the net with a huff.

Now it was my turn to smile.

Ally scooped up the ball and ran it back to me. "Did you do that on purpose?"

My smile widened.

"Okay, Soph. Bet you can't do it again."

I raised an eyebrow at her. The ref whistled, and again, I dropped the serve in the right front. This time, the Pacific player reached low for it and the ball flew into the net before landing on their side.

We had the lead again.

Pacific's team cheated toward the net, expecting the short serve. Instead, I crushed the ball, launching it deep, so they had to backpedal to make a play. The pass landed in the bleachers. They picked up my next serve, and the volley began again. Rachel attacking from Ally's back side and our back-row hits had Pacific moving around and unsettled. Molly finally killed the ball on a quick set outside when their blockers fell out of position.

On the next play, Pacific's setter caught us out of position and dropped a tip on the second hit into the middle front. Our two-point lead faded. We played catch-up before taking the lead again. Our lead faded. Back and forth. Back and forth. Time-outs. Deep breaths. Trick codes. Blocks. Net plays. Missed serves. Aces.

We were down, 24–23. Pacific's serve. If they scored on this point, we'd have to go to five games. I didn't know if I had it in me. The server tossed the ball for their first game point. Sam passed it, and Ally dumped the ball into the center of their court, catching them on their heels. Three players dove for it, but the ball hit the floor, bringing us to a 24–24 tie.

My teammates and I rushed to each other, celebrating.

"Two more points," Sam said. "Let's end this now."

We cheered, and the stands thumped to the tune of "We Will Rock You" again.

Ally jogged back to the service line. My heart fluttered. I never knew Ally to miss a serve, but she could. No. She wouldn't. I looked at the scoreboard like it had somehow changed.

The ref signaled for Ally to serve. She launched a jump serve to the back row. Pacific played it in three hits, and Sam got hands on their attack. The ball came off her block high and wild toward the stands.

"Mine!" I shouted and ran for it, prepared to land on a fan in the front row. I reached for the ball, not sure how close I was to the bleachers and popped it with my forearms back to the center of the court. I tripped over the edge of the bleacher and fell into the crowd. Someone caught me and pushed me upright and onto the court where Ally was playing the second ball in a gorgeous back set across the court to Molly outside. Pacific doubled the block, so she pushed a tip deep into the corner. It hit the floor inbounds.

We charged at each other, screaming. The score—25–24, us. We had to win by two. Ally was about to serve our first match point.

"You got this, Ally!" I shouted.

She nodded. The ref blew the whistle, and Ally moved into her serving rhythm the same as she always did.

Inbounds. Inbounds. Inbounds, I mentally urged.

Steady as ever, Ally placed the ball into the center of Pacific's court. The crowd noise and even my teammates faded. The white ball, spinning through the air, took my entire focus. Pacific passed it. The setter pushed it high and outside. Kate and Rachel moved to the right side to block. I positioned myself in the open lane beside their block. Kate got a piece of the ball, and it popped up. I moved my feet and easily passed it to Ally. Molly swung. Pacific picked it up and volleyed it back. Sam passed. Ally set a quick ball to Rachel in the middle. A strong block pushed the ball back at us. Kate dove to play it. Ally called for help.

"Mine," I called, moving into position to set. "Sam!"

I set Sam in the back row. She approached. Jumped and crushed the ball over the net deep into Pacific's half of the court. Someone dove for it.

The white ball spun up, up, up.

Into the stands.

The whistle blew.

The gym erupted.

My teammates pushed into a huddle that stumbled to the ground. We fell into each other's arms, screaming and laughing. The rest of the team joined us from the bench, peeling us off the hardwood. Chandra and Ashley sandwiched me, shouting praises for a game well played.

Ally had been right. If this had been my first first game, what would the playoff games be like?

We shook hands with Pacific's players and coaches. A few of them mentioned they'd see us again. They would. Later in the season, we'd play them on their home court and probably again in the playoffs who knew where, but we'd worry about that then. Tonight was for celebrations.

Tonight was for my team.

CHAPTER FORTY-THREE

AFTER OUR TEAM TALK, ELLE AND LILY GREETED ME
first.

"You played amazing!" Elle said. "I've never seen you like that."

"Yeah," Lily said, "I might concede volleyball is more complicated than I gave it credit for. Maybe."

I rolled my eyes at her almost compliment. "Thanks for being
here."

My parents hugged me next. Then Julia and Square. When the
celebrations faded, I grabbed Elle's arm. "Where's Harris?"

"Sorry. I forgot to tell you. He said he had to take care of something, but he'd see you back at home."

I forced a smile to hide the sting of her words. Harris couldn't wait
a few minutes to congratulate me? That wasn't like him.

"Oh my gosh," Elle said.

"What?"

"Is Square talking to Lacey Nash?"

I followed her line of sight to find Lacey leaning close to Square,
whispering into his ear. My body filled with equal parts concern for
my friend and relief I didn't have to deal with Lacey's wrath anymore.

"Yep," I said.

Square hugged her, and they separated.

"Wonder what that's about," Elle said, and when Lacey made eye
contact with me and walked in our direction, my sister added, "Looks

like we might find out."

"Crap," I muttered.

Lacey stopped a couple feet from us and took a deep breath. "Hi, Melanie."

"Lacey," I said.

She nodded at Elle like she wanted her to walk away, but my sister crossed her arms and didn't leave my side.

"I owe you an apology," Lacey said.

Elle grunted, but I was too surprised to say anything.

"I shouldn't have given Mr. Welch those photos."

"No," I mustered.

"I told him you and Square were only at the party for a few minutes and didn't touch any drugs or alcohol," she said.

"Thanks, but we're good on that."

"I heard, but still," she said. "I wasn't in a good place. It's not an excuse. It's the truth. It wasn't about you, and I never should have made it about you."

"Thanks," I said cautiously.

"You won't get any more trouble from me."

I was skeptical, but she'd apologized. I gave her points for that. "Are you doing okay now?"

"Yeah. Thanks for asking. More embarrassed than anything. I could have lost my spot on the cross-country team. Stupid."

I nodded, trying to let go of the anger that she could have lost me my spot on the volleyball team.

"Anyway, congrats on the win. See you around." She walked away with a wave.

Elle wrapped her arms around my shoulders. "Wow. Never thought I'd see the day Ally Malone and Lacey Nash would apologize. You're, like, a miracle worker."

Something like that.

"Let's go home."

***

I CLOSED MY EYES IN THE SHOWER, LETTING THE HOT water roll over my body. The moments from the game replayed in my mind. I loved a good dig—the other team prematurely celebrating earning the point, and you ripped the victory away from them at the last second. I'd made every serve, some of them impressively. A few line shots had earned us aces. I'd also had fifteen kills. Not bad for my first varsity start.

Most importantly, we'd played with the kind of dynamic we needed to win. The kind of dynamic that gave us a chance at making a run this season. One game at a time.

I turned off the water, hoping I'd never forget what it felt like to be on that court, soaring through the air, crushing the ball, celebrating with my team.

The rush.

I never wanted it to end. Although I'd learned about a different kind of rush lately. Outside my window, Harris's back yard was dark and quiet. He hadn't messaged or called. I dressed and dried my hair before climbing the steps to the attic to get a better look at his yard.

Instead, I found Harris and his telescope. Waiting for me. This was what he'd had to take care of?

"Hey, Mel."

I pressed myself into his arms and kissed him. The rush of the volleyball court came from quick movements and fast decisions, but the rush with Harris resulted from slow sweetness.

"Good game today."

"Thanks for being there."

"You were amazing."

"I worked so hard all summer but wondered if it would be enough when it came down to it, you know? What if I went out there and realized that all that time was wasted? That I didn't have what it took to compete at the varsity level?"

"I believed in you."

I squeezed him. "It might be cheesy, but I appreciate it."

He nodded toward the telescope. "It's a clear night. Want to look at the stars with me?"

"How romantic!" I nudged him with my hip. "Can we see Saturn?"

"Some things change," he said and kissed me, "but other things don't. Saturn, huh?" He looked through the lens and twisted the knobs. "Got it right here."

I slipped between him and the telescope and pressed my face to the eyepiece. My heart rate slowed at the sight of the brilliant oval shape and the ring surrounding it. I'd watched that little ringed oval so often, seeing it felt like coming home. The planet moved across the night sky and out of view. I pulled back.

"It's gone," I said.

Harris leaned over my shoulder to refocus the knobs. A memory of him doing that a few weeks earlier and feeling awkward about his arms around me made me giggle. Nothing about the moment felt awkward now. If anything, I wanted to lean into his touch.

"What?" he asked.

I kissed his cheek. "Nothing."

"It's ready."

I reclaimed my spot and watched Saturn again, so far away but seemingly right in the palm of my hand. Kind of like everything in life. Scary and impossible, yet attainable. Harris kissed my neck, and I gasped. He kissed his way to my ear and whispered. "Melanie?"

"Yeah?"

"I'm in love with you."

My breath caught. "What?"

I spun to see him running his hands over his face and pressing them against his cheeks. "You're gonna make me say it again?"

"You're in love with me?" My voice had a bit of a squeal.

"Maybe this is bad timing. We've been together for, what, four days?"

"Are we together?" I teased. I saw him as my boyfriend already, but we hadn't had the boyfriend-girlfriend talk.

Harris groaned and covered his face entirely.

"No," I said, peeling his hands back. "I'm sorry. I was teasing. It's...*nice* that you're in love with me."

His eyes widened. "Nice?"

"Really nice."

"I honestly can't tell if you're messing with me right now," he said.

I wrapped my arms around his neck and kissed him in a way that I hoped showed him I wasn't messing around. "Want to know something else really nice?"

He gave the slightest nod.

"I have this science-nerd, next-door-neighbor best friend that I fell obnoxiously in love with when I wasn't looking."

His lips wobbled into that Harris smile I loved so much. "That sounds intense."

"It was. But also..."

We said "really nice" in unison and laughed.

He tucked a stray strand of hair from my ponytail behind my ear and ran his fingertips along my cheek. "I love you, Melanie."

The romance reader in my heart giggled with swoon-worthy satisfaction. "I love you, Harris."

He kissed the tip of my nose. "Now, would you like to see more stars?"

I ran my lips along the curve of his chin. "Will they still be there tomorrow?"

"Yes," he whispered. "And so will I."

In the same way Saturn moved across our view in the telescope, everything in life was fleeting. But for now, at this moment in time, the world was perfectly in order.

I had every intention of enjoying it.

ACKNOWLEDGEMENTS

Writing the Iron Valley Vikings series has reminded me in the most beautiful ways of the positive influence sports have on my life. Reliving the moments I shared with friends on and off the court motivated me through the struggles of bringing this book to fruition.

That said, I want to thank my people.

Thank you to my elementary gym teacher and volleyball coaches over the years who taught me the sport and made playing it fun–Michael Stitt, Carol Perroz, Diane Swigart, Beth Ryce. Thank you to the many friends and parents who looked out for me, giving me rides to practices and games, so I could play the sports I loved. Thank you to my volleyball teammates at Valley High School! You all were the best!

I could not write books without my critique partners and beta readers. Thank you to everyone who graciously reviewed early drafts of this book and gave their honest feedback: Allie Blumhorst, Tara Creel, Kathleen Heidecker, Dana Kramaroff, Elyse Kramer, Caitlin Lennon, Deborah Maroulis, Tracie Martin. Special thanks to Abigail G. Scheg who read this book TWICE!

Authenticity is crucial. I can't thank my authenticity readers enough for their work on this story–Beth Ryce, Valerie Gray, and Crystal Rupert. Thank you to the friends who guided me on authentic details for the characters including Lise-Michelle and Lise-Pauline Barnett and Christine and Jordan Hutchinson.

Thank you to my writing friends who take my calls and texts all hours of the day, across time zones. Your support means everything–Chelsea Bobulski, Tara Creel, Annette Dashofy, Kimberly Gabriel, Tracy Gold, Molly E. Lee, and Nova McBee. Thank you also to the writing organizations that have supported, educated, and encouraged me: Sisters in Crime, PennWriters, and Pitch Wars. Thank you, also, to my clutch band of work colleagues; you are a blessing in my life!

To my babysitters, I literally could not do this without you–Olivia Awes, Grace Love, and Jessica Stawinski. Special thanks to Grace Love who has also assisted me with so many marketing tasks for these books! Thank you to my crew of besties – the beautiful, intelligent, fierce women who make me laugh and inspire me: Rachida Essadiq, Alicia Giordano, Janet Menhart, Abigail G. Scheg, and Heidi Waugaman.

Thank you to the amazing team at Wise Wolf Books. Your belief in me is everything, yet you surpassed that by making magic with my books–twice! Thank you for bringing Melanie's story to readers.

To my family–you are the absolute best. Thank you to my relatives who support and encourage me including my in-laws, Barbara and Frank Girardi; my siblings in blood and in marriage: Roxanne, Wes, Scott, George, Michael, Colleen, David, and Kristen; my cousins in Pennsylvania, New York, Arizona, and elsewhere around the world; and my aunts and uncles who looked out for me and watched me play sports way back when, especially my Uncle Bob who took time out of his weekends to get me in the gym. To the family I've lost, especially my parents, ChrisAnne and Gregory Simpson, and my grandparents, Anne and Clarence Farneth–thanks for believing in me!

To my children Frank, Clara, Gabriella, and Domenick–how exciting that our days are filled with watching you compete in the sports and activities you love! Dom, glad to be cheering for them by your side in the stands. The evenings are busy, and so are the Saturdays, but the blessings are many, too.

I want to also send a general thank you to everyone reading this who has ever volunteered their time to coach a youth sport. You make the experiences, emotions, and lessons in sports possible. Never underestimate your value in a child's life.

Sports empower you. They humble you. They inspire you. Nobody wins every game, and nobody gets to the top without sacrifice and dedication. Melanie and her teammates learn amazing life lessons in this book. To the teen athletes out there, I hope you're taking in all the lessons sports have to offer! Feel the rush of those incomparable highs, and embrace the depth of emotion from the devastating lows; both will fuel your future.

Since this is my second book, and I legitimately have readers now, I can honestly say: thank you to my readers! After so many years of writing and my manuscripts only seeing the inside of my computer's hard drive, words can't describe the honor it is that you're reading them. Thank you for sharing the book on social media, reviewing it online, and requesting it at your public libraries. Your support astounds me! I hope you enjoy Melanie's story. Please feel free to reach out through my website or on social media. I'd love to hear from you!

A LOOK AT BOOK THREE: ULTIMATE TAKEDOWN

Fiery competition and unexpected romance will melt your heart in book three of Tamara Girardi's swoon-worthy, young-adult contemporary series.

Iron Valley High School senior, Annalise Fiori is the only girl on her school's wrestling team. With daily early morning lifting sessions and extra evening, she's earned her place on the high school team and respect from her male teammates. Her goals for the season are to earn a wrestling scholarship to a college with an amazing art program and interact with her middle school wrestling rival, Sebastian Love, as little as possible.

When Sebastian's school doesn't have enough wrestlers to field a team, her coaches welcome the Forest Run High School wrestlers to co-op with Iron Valley's team. Now, Annalise will have to face Sebastian every day at practice and maybe even compete against him to hold on to her weight class and prove herself to college coaches. Will the secret Annalise has been holding on to put everything she's worked so hard for at risk?

AVAILABLE SEPTEMBER 2022

ABOUT THE AUTHOR

Tamara Girardi grew up playing sports with the neighborhood kids. Often the only girl, she loved nothing more than smashing a home run at the opportune moment or stealing the basketball from one of the guys and scoring two on a breakaway. In high school, she fell in love with the quarterback and played football in the back yard with him and his two quarterback brothers. Watching them play, she wondered, "What would it be like if they'd had a baby sister? Would she play quarterback, too?" And just like that, the idea for Gridiron Girl was born.

Also an academic, Tamara is an Associate Professor of English at HACC, Central Pennsylvania's Community College where she teaches creative writing, technical writing, composition, and literature online. She has a PhD in English from Indiana University of Pennsylvania and studied fiction at the University of St. Andrews in Scotland. Tamara also writes picture books.

She lives in a suburb of Pittsburgh, Pennsylvania with her husband and four adorably rambunctious children.